Caught In The Crossfire

REBECCA DEEL

Copyright © 2019 Rebecca Deel

All rights reserved.

ISBN-13: 9781709183584

DEDICATION

To my amazing husband, my knight in shining armor.

ACKNOWLEDGMENTS

Cover design by Melody Simmons.

CHAPTER ONE

Nicole Copeland glanced at the clock and frowned. Riva was late. Cosmo, her beautiful Doberman-Great Dane mix, had been shampooed, pampered, and buffed, and was more than ready to go home.

She turned back to her computer, glared at the two unopened emails. Why did Ivan contact her after two years? She thought she'd made herself perfectly clear at their last encounter that she never wanted to see or hear from him again.

Ignoring the uneasiness caused by the emails she now deleted, Nicole refocused on the matter at hand. If Riva didn't arrive in the next few minutes, she would have to call her. Pet Palace didn't board pets although she was considering adding it to her growing list of services.

Boarding pets, however, required additional workers to staff the grooming salon overnight. Maybe Dawn, her employee and friend, would know a few students from the community college suitable for the position.

Nicole glanced at the clock again. She didn't want to leave late tonight. Mason was picking her up for their dinner date soon. Nicole smiled as she thought of Mason Kincaid, the dark-haired, broad-shouldered construction worker with a heart of gold and kisses powerful enough to weaken her knees. The best day of her life was the day she arrived in Otter Creek, Tennessee, and met Mason. The day he asked her to marry him ranked a close second.

A car door slammed nearby, and Cosmo barked. Who needed an alarm with him around? Maybe Riva was here.

A moment later, the front door opened, and Dawn Metcalf, her co-worker, rushed in with her arms full of grooming supplies. "Sorry I'm late. I know you need to leave soon, but Colleen wanted to talk."

Nicole smiled. "No problem. We'll whip this place into shape for business tomorrow morning in no time. We have a full groom with Tank first thing tomorrow." The chocolate Lab was a sweetheart.

"Aww! I love Tank. Hopefully, our order will go into the mail tomorrow morning so we won't have to return to Cherry Hill for more supplies."

"Tristan assured me our supplies will be here by the end of the week."

Cosmo barked again.

Dawn frowned and peered into the holding room. "Cosmo is still here?"

"Riva will be here soon." She hoped. What was keeping her? Nicole stepped around the counter. "I'll start cleaning while you take the supplies to the storeroom. If Riva doesn't arrive in the next few minutes, I'll call her." Good thing she and Mason chose to watch a movie at his house rather than go to a theater.

"Don't you have a date with Mason?"

"Dinner and a movie at his place. He'll understand if I'm delayed."

"You've been here late every night this week. Go home. I'll stay tonight." Dawn's voice sounded muffled as she walked toward the supply room. "It's not like I have a hot date to worry about." She returned a moment later.

"I don't want either of us staying late," Nicole said. "Tank will arrive at 7:00 a.m. along with three of his buddies. With both of us cleaning, we'll finish fast and figure out what to do about Cosmo if Riva still hasn't shown up."

"If we offered boarding, we'd have a worker to handle late customers as well as care for pets staying overnight." Dawn smiled.

Nicole held up a hand. "I know. I'm thinking about it. If you know of two people interested in overnight work, tell me their names. No promises, but we'll see."

After working fast for thirty minutes, Nicole dumped the last of the dog hair in the trash and tugged the bag from the can. "Go home, Dawn. I'll find out what's keeping Riva. Maybe I can drop off Cosmo for her. With her real estate job, she's all over the county. Perhaps a client delayed her."

Skepticism gleamed in Dawn's eyes. "Almost two hours late? No matter how amazing a house is, nobody has that many questions. Call her again. This isn't like her."

Nicole grabbed her cell phone and called Riva Kemper for the fourth time in two hours. After five rings, Riva's voicemail message kicked in again. Great. Looked like she would have to text Mason to let him know she'd be late. Again. Good thing the man she adored was understanding.

At the prompt to leave a message, Nicole spoke. "Riva, it's Nicole at Pet Palace. Cosmo looks amazing and is ready to show off his buffed nails. Since your house is near mine, I'll swing by your place with Cosmo. If you're not home, I'll take him to my house. Call me, okay? I'm starting to worry."

She ended the call.

"Still not answering?"

Nicole shook her head. "Riva knows Cosmo hates to be in a crate and she adores him. This doesn't make sense."

"Maybe you should wait for Mason before going to Riva's. If something is wrong, you shouldn't be alone."

"He's picking me up at home and Riva's place is only four blocks from mine." She grabbed Cosmo's spiffy red leash and opened the crate. "Come on, buddy. Let's get you home."

Cosmo barked and dashed from the crate.

"Sit."

The dog plopped onto his butt, dark eyes bright and alert.

"Good boy." After attaching the leash to his collar, Nicole walked with him to the front door. "Do you mind locking up, Dawn?"

"Wait for me. You're not going to Riva's alone."

"I'll be fine."

"Going to Riva's with you will only take a few minutes, and I'll feel better knowing you aren't alone."

She rolled her eyes. This was Otter Creek, an idyllic small town. What could possibly happen in this sleepy little burg? She also had Cosmo. Big dog plus big bark meant almost no chance of someone attacking her. "Let's go. Cosmo is ready to see his human mom."

Nicole unlocked her vehicle, opened the back door, and signaled Cosmo to hop in. When the 80-pound dog leaped into the back, she secured the dog with the seatbelt adapter she routinely carried and circled to the driver's door.

Fifteen minutes later, Nicole and Dawn parked their vehicles on the street in front of Riva's bungalow.

Nicole frowned. Riva's red SUV sat in the driveway. Had she just arrived? Uneasiness crawled up her spine. Perhaps she should have asked Mason to meet her here. This was weird and, frankly, a little creepy. Too late now. She was already here. Riva would probably offer a sincere apology along with a story about an impossible potential client.

She partially lowered a window for Cosmo and exited her SUV. Although Riva's vehicle sat in the driveway, the house had no lights on. Goosebumps prickled her skin.

Cosmo voiced his opinion about being left in the vehicle. She winced, glad she wasn't inside with him. That boy had a loud, piercing bark.

"Better find Riva before Cosmo eats your upholstery," Dawn said.

That thought brought a scowl to her face. "He better not. My brother-in-law will have a fit if he does."

Her friend grinned. "It's not a good idea to tick off a PSI instructor."

Nicole walked to the porch and reached for the doorbell when she noticed the front door standing ajar.

"What's wrong?"

"Door's open." Man, what she wouldn't give to have Mason at her back. "Something's wrong."

"Let's go back to the vehicles and call the police."

"Riva might need help. She could be hurt."

Dawn didn't look convinced.

"I don't want to call the police for a wellness check when Riva might not realize the door didn't close properly. She might be in the shower or something."

"At 7:00 in the evening?"

Yeah, it was lame, but Nicole's gut was screaming at her to check on the bright, vivacious real estate agent. "I want to check first. If we think something is off, we'll scoot out and contact the police."

"No way, Nicole," Dawn said softly, her gaze fixed on the door. "I'm calling the police. Riva wouldn't leave her door ajar. What if someone hurt her and they're still inside? Come on." Dawn gripped Nicole's hand and tugged her toward the street.

She turned to accompany her friend when a moan sounded inside the house. She yanked her hand free. "Call for help. I'm checking on Riva."

When Dawn grabbed her cell phone, Nicole used her elbow to nudge the door open wider and peered inside. "Riva?"

Another moan. Nicole dashed inside and climbed the stairs. She called out again and followed the weak response to a large bedroom.

Her breath caught. Blood splattered the walls and Riva lay on her side near the bed, her clothes torn and bloody. "Riva." Nicole rushed to the woman's side and dropped to her knees. "Hold on. Help's coming."

Riva's eyelids fluttered. She whispered something.

Nicole leaned closer. "What?"

"Run."

A footstep sounded behind her. Starting to turn, she caught a glimpse of someone dressed in dark clothes with an arm raised. A second later, pain exploded in her head and darkness swallowed her.

CHAPTER TWO

Mason Kincaid scooted out from under the kitchen sink with its dripping pipe and wiped his face free of the moisture with the towel provided by Lincoln Creed.

"What's the verdict?" Linc asked.

"Rusty drain pipe. If I don't replace it, you'll have a puddle under your sink every day."

The Personal Security International instructor flinched. "How soon can you do the job? Won't take much water to create expensive problems with these hardwood floors."

Mason laid the towel on the counter. "I'll complete the repair in 30 minutes or less, barring complications."

Relief filled Linc's eyes. "You're a lifesaver, Mase. I know my way around weapons, but I'm all thumbs with home repairs."

He chuckled. "You and your friends from PSI keep me busy. I might I have the pipe I need in the truck. If not, I'll have to go to the hardware store." That would necessitate a call to Nicole to delay their date. Good thing his future wife was an understanding woman.

"Duct tape won't work for this, huh?"

He grinned. "My cousin swears duct tape fixes everything in a pinch. I wouldn't recommend that solution for your problem, though. As amazing as duct tape is, water will seep around the edges and drip."

Mason's cousin, Rio, worked for Fortress Security and trained bodyguards for them at PSI. As a medic, Rio learned to be creative in treating wounds on the battlefield. Duct tape was a standard part of the supplies in his mike bag.

Linc held up his hands in mock surrender. "I'll bow to your expertise. I worked with trainees all day at the gun range, and my clothes smell like cordite. Need anything from me before I go clean up?"

Mason shook his head. "If you're not out of the shower by the time I finish, I'll leave the bill on your counter. We'll settle up later."

Outside, Mason unlocked his vehicle and sorted through the various pipes stored in a box behind the driver's seat. He located the right pipe along with his hacksaw and returned to the kitchen where he crawled back under the sink.

Moving his toolbox so it was more accessible, he crawled back under the sink. Mason dug in his toolbox for his favorite pipe wrench but couldn't find it.

Frowning, he searched a different section of his toolbox. Still nothing. Weird. He'd used the wrench earlier in the day at the Oakdale site. He must have left the wrench in one of the buildings. Good thing he returned to the same site tomorrow. Hopefully, his equipment would still be there. Several of his tools had gone missing the last few days.

Mason grabbed his backup wrench and loosened the nuts on the pipe, removed the rusted section, and used it as a template to cut the new pipe to the correct length. Within minutes, the new pipe was in place. He tightened the nuts and stood.

"Finished already?" Linc asked when he walked into the room.

"I'm about to find out." He turned on the faucet and crouched with his flashlight in hand to watch for water leakage. After the water ran for a while with no sign of dripping moisture, Mason turned off the tap. "Got it."

Linc clapped him on the shoulder. "You're a miracle worker. I owe you for doing the repair on short notice. Your services are in high demand."

Not always. Two years apparently wasn't long enough for him to earn the trust of some people around town and wondered if he'd ever be free of the stigma of prison.

"Are you off the clock?"

He'd been off the clock when Linc called. "I am."

"Have time for a glass of iced tea before you leave?"

A glance at his watch revealed he'd have just enough time to drink the tea, drive home, and shower before picking up Nicole for their date. "Sure. Thanks."

Linc motioned for him to take a seat at the breakfast bar. After filling glasses with ice, he poured a tall glass of tea for each of them. "I can cook although I don't do it often, but my specialty is iced tea."

Mason sipped, his eyebrows rising. "This is good."

Linc chuckled. "Told you."

"For a man who doesn't cook much, your kitchen looks well stocked."

"That's because my mother and sister drop in frequently to cook and freeze food." He rolled his eyes. "According to them, I have the food habits of a teenage boy. Doesn't matter to them that I'm 35 years old and capable of feeding myself."

"Didn't you hire Serena Blackhawk to prepare meals for you?" Serena, a personal chef, was also married to the police chief, the policeman Mason reported to once a week.

Linc nodded. "I told them about Serena. They insist on coming anyway. I think they're making sure I don't live like a slob. The Army drummed laziness out of me during boot camp."

Their conversation drifted to the upcoming baseball season, speculating on which major league team would make it to the playoffs. When their glasses were empty, Linc eyed Mason. "When will you start your own business?"

Shock held him immobile. "Why do you ask?"

"Buddy, you're a skilled artisan. I've seen your work. You have an impeccable work ethic. You're dependable and easy to work with. You should be running your own crew."

"Maybe." He hadn't considered that option too seriously. With his past hanging over his head, Mason wasn't as confident as Linc that he'd be successful as a small business owner. Plus, he counted himself lucky that Brian Elliott of Elliott Construction had taken a chance on hiring him as soon as he was released from prison. He owed his kind-hearted boss for extending the opportunity to work.

"Think about it. I can't be the only homeowner in desperate need of your repair services."

His cell phone rang. "Excuse me." Mason glanced at his screen, eyebrows soaring. Ethan Blackhawk. Was this a home repair request or a surprise check on Mason? He reported to Ethan every week per the judge's order. Not a hardship. The chief was a good man. Still, if Mason stepped out of line, Ethan would come down on him hard.

He swiped his screen and answered the call. "What can I do for you, Ethan?"

Linc's eyes narrowed, his attention locked on Mason's face.

"Drop whatever you're doing and go to 457 Ash."

At Ethan's sharp tone, Mason straightened. He'd been at Riva Kemper's home earlier in the afternoon. Had Riva filed a complaint against him for some reason? "What's wrong?"

"It's Nicole."

Blood drained from his face. What was his girlfriend doing at Riva's? "Is she okay?"

"She will be. An ambulance is en route to take her to the hospital."

Oh, man. "I'm five minutes away."

"So is the ambulance. See you in five." Ethan ended the call.

Mason shoved to his feet. "I have to go. Nicole's hurt."

"Accident?"

"Ethan didn't give details."

Linc pulled keys from his pocket. "Where are we going?"

"I can drive."

"We're wasting time." The instructor locked up and led the way to his SUV. "Where am I going, Mason?"

"To 457 Ash. Ethan said an ambulance was on the way to take Nicole to the hospital." Did she fall? Why was she at Riva's to begin with?

Seconds later, Linc raced toward Ash. "We'll be there in two minutes and find out what's going on."

"I could have driven."

Linc sent him a pointed glance. "You could. Doesn't mean you should. What kind of friend would I be if I let you drive while you're upset?"

True to his promise, Linc parked two houses down from Riva's place at the two-minute mark. Three Otter Creek police vehicles were parked in front of the house, leaving the lower half of the driveway for the ambulance.

Mason bailed from the SUV as soon as Linc stopped and sprinted toward the house. One of the cops moved to intercept him until Josh Cahill, a friend of his cousin Rio's, waved off the other officer.

He raced across the yard, up the porch stairs, and into the house. Mason pulled up short when Ethan turned toward him. "Where is she?"

"Upstairs, end of the hall, last room on the left. Don't touch anything."

He took the stairs two at a time and hurried into the room to see the woman he adored lying on the bed with Dawn sitting by her side and pressing a towel to the side of Nicole's head. "Nicole."

Relief gleamed in her eyes. "Mason."

He dropped to his knees beside the bed. "You're hurt."

"I keep telling Rod Kelter that I'm fine. He's not listening."

He glanced toward the master bedroom where the detective in question stood, speaking in soft tones to someone else. Not another cop. The other person shifted enough for Mason to see his profile. He frowned. Why was the coroner on site?

Uneasiness coiled in his gut. Where was Riva? When the two men separated, Mason noticed the dainty foot clad in a stiletto-heeled shoe, the same shoe Riva wore earlier in the afternoon. Oh, man. Was Riva...?

He shifted his attention to Nicole. "What happened?"

"I brought Cosmo here and found Riva on her bedroom floor, injured. I heard a noise. When I started to turn, someone clocked me on the head with a hard object. I woke up with Dawn leaning over me."

Alarm roared through him. "Someone hit you hard enough to knock you out?"

"I don't want to go to the hospital for a bump on the head. Will you ask Rod or Ethan how Riva is doing?" She shifted as though she wanted to get up and check on the other woman herself.

Dawn bit her lower lip, guilt and concern in her eyes as she glanced at Mason. "Stay still, Nic. You could have more serious injuries than you think."

Mason turned Nicole's head to see for himself, his movements slow and easy. He whistled softly at the injury marring the side of Nicole's head. "You need to see a doctor, baby. I'm pretty sure you need stitches."

She flinched. "Can't Rio take care of it?"

"He and Darcy are out of town until Monday."

"What about Matt Rainer?" she said, naming another medic teaching at PSI.

A siren outside abruptly cut off. "The ambulance is already here. See the doctor for my peace of mind."

The woman he adored scowled at him. "Dirty pool, Kincaid."

"I'll do whatever is necessary to ensure you're safe."

"Mason."

He turned to see Rod Kelter in the doorway, a thoughtful look on his face. "Yes, sir?"

"Ambulance is here for Nicole."

But not for Riva. The ball of ice in Mason's stomach grew larger. He'd been right. Riva was dead. What on earth had happened after he left this house to work at another job site?

"How is Riva?" Nicole asked.

Sympathy filled the detective's eyes. "I'm sorry. She didn't make it." He stepped back and motioned to someone down the hall. A moment later, EMTs entered the room.

When Nicole's breath hitched, Mason wrapped his arms around her. "I'm sorry," he murmured.

"I should have come sooner." Her voice cracked. "Maybe then she'd still be alive."

And maybe Nicole would be as dead as the real estate agent.

"I knew something was wrong. She'd never leave Cosmo that long." Nicole raised her head. "What am I going to do about Cosmo? Going to a shelter is out of the question. He hates to be caged."

"We'll figure something out. My first priority is you." Mason loosened his hold and nodded at the EMTs.

"But Cosmo is in my SUV."

"I'd take him home with me, but my apartment complex doesn't allow pets." Dawn moved aside.

"Can you take him with you, Mason?" Nicole gripped his hand. "Please?"

"I didn't drive here." He should have insisted. "I was repairing a leak at Lincoln Creed's home when Ethan called. Linc drove me."

Dawn's eyes widened. "He's here?" Her cheeks flushed.

Huh. That was interesting. Mason wondered if the groomer was interested in his friend. Linc's voice drifted up the stairs as he spoke with Ethan and the flush on Dawn's cheeks deepened.

Maybe Linc would help out with Cosmo. If that wasn't possible, he'd find someone else to foster Cosmo for a few days until he and Nicole found permanent accommodations for him.

Mason stood and kissed the back of Nicole's hand before releasing her to allow the EMTs access to her. "I might have a temporary solution for Cosmo. I'll be back in a minute."

He glanced into the master bedroom as he walked toward the stairs. His hands fisted when he saw the blood-splattered room and Riva's torn and bloody clothing. Who would do that to her, to any woman? Ethan and Linc turned toward Mason as he descended the stairs.

"How's Nicole?" Linc asked.

"She has a cut on her head that might need stitches."

"I'll drive you to the hospital so you can be with her. Nicole shouldn't be alone."

Mason stared at him as goosebumps surged up his back, and the truth hit him with the force of a blow from a sledgehammer. Nicole wasn't safe.

CHAPTER THREE

Mason moved closer to Ethan so his voice wouldn't carry upstairs to the women. "Is Nicole in danger?"

"She's a loose end."

A loose end a desperate man might kill to silence. What had Riva stumbled into? Mason's jaw clenched. No matter what it was, no one was going to hurt Nicole again. They'd have to go through him first.

"Smooth, Ethan," Linc muttered with a dark look at the police chief.

"He needs to know the truth. Nicole isn't safe. For that matter, her friend isn't safe, either."

The PSI instructor frowned. "Who's her friend?"

"Dawn Metcalf," Mason answered. "She works at Pet Palace. Dawn's upstairs with Nicole."

"She came with Nicole to bring Cosmo to Riva." Ethan glanced toward the open front door. Cosmo barked continuously. "I'll have to contact the humane association. We can't leave him in Nicole's vehicle."

Mason sighed. "You can't send him to the shelter. Cosmo hates being crated. Would you be willing to house Cosmo temporarily?"

Ethan shook his head. "My work schedule is too erratic, and I can't saddle Serena with more responsibility. What about Alex? He already has a Lab. He might be willing to take Cosmo in for a few days."

Alex Morgan was one of Rio's teammates. His Lab, Spenser, loved socializing with other dogs. "That's a great idea. Spenser would have a blast with Cosmo."

"I'll call him," Linc said. "If he agrees, would Josh be able to drop off Cosmo?"

"That shouldn't be a problem. Josh patrols that area anyway."

Rod descended the stairs. "The EMTs are ready to transport Nicole, Ethan. You want to assign an officer to stand guard?"

"I'll be with her," Mason said.

"Someone from Fortress will also be at the hospital." Linc slid his phone from his pocket. "Mason and Nicole are part of the Fortress extended family. We'll handle the security."

Rod nodded. "What about Dawn?"

"Nicole and Dawn are a package deal." Linc glanced at Mason. "I know you can handle yourself, but you'll be able to concentrate on her if someone else has your back."

"Thanks." He'd been on Fortress missions in the past and stood watch so operatives would be able to sleep for a few hours. Being on the recipient end was odd.

The EMTs assisted Nicole down the stairs with Dawn following close behind. Mason met them at the foot of the stairs. "We'll follow you to the hospital."

Linc walked outside, phone pressed to his ear.

"What about Cosmo?" Dawn asked. "We can't leave him in the SUV."

"We're working on arrangements for him," Ethan said. "I'll make sure he's taken care of. Nicole, leave your keys with me and I'll transport your vehicle to the house."

She passed him the keys. "Thanks, Ethan."

"No problem." The chief turned to Dawn. "You should be checked by a doctor as well, Dawn."

Mason frowned. "Are you hurt, too?"

Dawn waved off his concern. "I'm fine."

Nicole scowled. "Hey, if I have to go, so do you. You said the guy who came barreling out of the house manhandled you. I know you're bruised."

"Aww, come on, Nic."

Linc returned, his gaze locking on Dawn for a moment. Finally, he tore his gaze away and shifted his attention to Mason. "Alex will be here in ten minutes to pick up Cosmo. What's going on?"

"The man who hurt Nicole also put his hands on Dawn. She doesn't want to go to the hospital."

"We need to get going," one of the EMTs said and started toward the door with his partner and Nicole.

"I'm not that bad off," Nicole protested. "Linc, would you mind if I rode to the hospital with you?"

"Of course not." He glanced at the EMTs. "I'll take her. I know you have other duties."

The medical technician pointed at Nicole. "Don't try to talk your way out of going, Nicole. You need stitches."

Her cheeks flushed. "You can forget a discount the next time you bring Tiger in for a grooming appointment, Abel," she muttered.

"I'll be happy to pay full price if I know you're healthy."

Dawn's smile was shaky. "Couldn't have said it better myself."

After Abel and his partner left, Rod went back upstairs. "Time for you to go," Ethan said to Mason. "This is a crime scene. Rod and I will be at the hospital later to take statements from Nicole and Dawn. Until we identify and arrest the man who killed Ms. Kemper, you should be vigilant. If you notice anything amiss, call me immediately."

"Let's go," Linc said. He motioned for Mason, Nicole, and Dawn to wait, then he scanned the area before allowing them outside. "Straight to the SUV, Mase." His gaze settled on Dawn. "You, too."

"I'm fine. Honest."

"I'll feel better if a doctor agrees with you, and so will Nicole."

With a grimace, Nicole's employee gave a nod and walked outside with Linc.

"I hope the doctor doesn't make me stay overnight." Nicole leaned into Mason's side. "I hate hospitals."

He tightened his grip on her waist briefly. "We'll do what he thinks is best."

Mason steered Nicole to the backseat of Linc's SUV, leaving Dawn to sit in the front seat beside Linc. Although his girl acted like her injury wasn't bad, Mason didn't like the pallor of her skin. She was in a lot of pain.

On the drive to the hospital, Linc remained vigilant. When they arrived at Memorial Hospital, he parked in front of the emergency room entrance. "Wait until I tell you it's clear." He exited the vehicle and took his time coming around to open Dawn's door. When he did, Linc glanced at Mason and nodded.

Mason assisted Nicole from the vehicle, tucked her close to his side, and escorted her inside the building at a fast clip. As he approached the registration desk with Nicole, a woman's voice called out, "Nic, what are you doing here?"

He and Nicole turned to see her sister hurrying toward them. Grace St. Claire's gaze landed on the side of Nicole's head. "Oh, sis, what happened?"

"Long story better told in the privacy of an exam room. Any chance you can pull some strings and get us seen sooner?" Nicole motioned to the full waiting room. "I'm rather not be out here for hours."

"Us?" Grace's eyes widened. "Are you injured, Mason?"

He shook his head as Dawn and Linc walked up. "Dawn needs to be checked out as well."

"Wait here. I'll see what I can do." Grace leaned close. "I expect a full explanation." With that, she walked up the hall and around the corner.

In less than five minutes, Grace returned, spoke to the nurse at the desk, and motioned for both couples to follow her. She led them to an exam room. "Dr. Anderson will see you soon. I'm on break. What happened, Nic?"

Mason helped her onto the examination table while she summarized the events of the past hour.

When Nicole finished, Grace said, "You're lucky you weren't killed. Did you call Trent, Mason?"

"Not yet."

"I'll let him know what's going on. Are you on watch, Linc?"

"Yes, ma'am."

The door opened and a white-haired, blue-eyed man walked in. "Looks like we're having a party, and no one invited me."

Nicole snorted. "Some party. I'm the one who ran into a guy with a bad attitude and a nasty temper."

"Take good care of my sister, Doc." Grace squeezed his shoulder on her way out the door.

"Who am I treating first?" Dr. Anderson asked.

"Nicole," Dawn said. "She has a cut on the side of her head."

"Then you need to look at Dawn." Linc folded his arms across his chest. "The guy who hurt Nicole also went after her."

Anderson's white eyebrows winged upward. "I see. You ladies can tell me what happened while I examine you. Linc, Mason, wait in the hall, please." He smiled. "As you can see, there isn't another exit from the room so your women will be safe."

Mason brushed his lips over Nicole's, then followed Linc to the hallway to wait for the doctor's assessment.

CHAPTER FOUR

When the door closed behind Mason and Linc, Dr. Anderson's smile melted away. "Tell me what happened, my dear."

Nicole flinched as the town's favorite physician poked and prodded her injury while she relayed the story about taking Cosmo home, finding the door ajar, and discovering Riva on the floor, injured. "I heard something behind me, turned, and bam, someone clobbered me with a hard object. The next thing I knew, I was on the floor with Dawn leaning over me."

The doctor was silent a moment, then said, "The EMTs were correct. You need stitches to close this wound." He stripped rubber gloves from his hands. "I'll be back in a moment with the stitch kit. Before I go, I have to ask you one question. I want you to be absolutely honest with me, my dear. Will you do that?"

"Of course." She didn't make a habit of lying. "Ask your question."

"Is Mason responsible for your injury?"

Dawn gasped and clamped a hand over her mouth.

Shock held Nicole immobile for a moment. "You can't be serious. I thought you liked him."

"I do. However, he is capable of violence."

Because Mason had been in prison. The spike of temper burgeoning in her gut intensified Nicole's headache. The assumption was unfair. Mason had paid for one error in judgment with thirteen years of his life. Why wouldn't people take him at face value? "Mason didn't hurt me, Doc, and never would. It wasn't Mason."

"Did you get a good look at the man who hit you?"

Nicole scowled. She wanted to say yes and couldn't. "I only caught a glimpse of a man wearing a black ski mask before he struck me."

"What about you, Dawn? Is it possible the assailant you saw was Mason?"

"I think the man who ran into me was taller than Mase, but it happened so fast I can't be sure. He was still wearing a ski mask when he raced from the house."

"The masked man wasn't Mason," Nicole insisted. How could anyone think the man she adored was guilty of hurting her and killing Riva? What possible motive could he have for either act?

She forced herself to focus despite the pain in her head and thought through the events in the bedroom when she'd discovered Riva. Nicole knew the assailant wasn't Mason. Was it simply gut instinct or something she could prove?

A memory popped to the forefront of her mind. "Spice," she blurted out. When Dr. Anderson's white eyebrow rose, Nicole's cheeks burned. "I smelled a spicy cologne a second before the man hit me."

"You're sure the scent wasn't one of Riva's perfumes?" Dawn asked.

"Positive. It's a cologne some of our male customers wear. Mason doesn't wear cologne because all perfumes and colognes give me a headache. I told you it wasn't Mason, Doc."

Anderson patted her arm. "I'm sorry for distressing you, my dear. I have to ask these questions. It's my duty to report abuse. I've seen injuries like yours that were the result of an assault by friends or family. No matter how often Mason says he loves you, he's still capable of losing his temper and striking out in a fit of rage. If Mason hurt you, would you tell me?"

Nicole smiled. "If he hit me, you'd be treating him, too. I won't let a man use me as a punching bag."

"Good for you." Another pat on her arm. "I'll return in a moment."

When the door closed, Nicole growled. "Why do people persist in thinking the worst of Mason? He's a good man who would take a bullet for me." He'd already taken a bullet protecting Rio's wife.

"People know he's been in prison, Nic. That's a hard environment to survive without scars."

Oh, Mason had scars. He just hid them from public view and endured the continual stares and whispers behind his back. "The man in Riva's house wasn't Mason." The man she planned to marry soon wasn't guilty of something so heinous.

"I know one thing. I wouldn't want Rod Kelter or Ethan Blackhawk on my trail. Whoever is guilty had better watch their backs. Those policemen are relentless. They won't give up until they have their man."

Anderson returned. "All right, my dear. Let's numb your scalp and stitch you up. Once I examine Dawn, we'll talk about your treatment plan."

Nicole frowned. Surely Dr. Anderson would release her tonight. She just needed an ice pack and over-the-counter pain reliever.

The next thirty minutes weren't ones Nicole wanted to repeat anytime soon. Once Dr. Anderson stitched her cut, Nicole turned her narrowed gaze toward Dawn as she climbed off the exam table. "Your turn."

Her employee held up her hands, shaking her head. "I just have a scratch and a few bruises. I'll be fine."

"You're already here." The doctor patted the table and motioned for the groomer to climb up. "If you're correct, you'll be out of here in ten minutes."

With a scowl at Nicole, Dawn climbed on the table and answered all the doctor's questions. When he finished his exam and agreed with her assessment, she asked, "Are we free to leave now, Dr. Anderson?"

"You are. I want to keep you overnight, Nicole. Head injuries can be tricky."

Oh, no. Her stomach turned a nasty flip. "Aww, come on, Doc. I have to be at the grooming salon early tomorrow morning. We have dogs arriving at 7:00 a.m. I'm fine."

"You have ten stitches and will need pain medicine once the lidocaine wears off." He pointed at her. "You also have a headache."

She huffed out a breath. "How did you know?" Nicole muttered.

"You squint whenever you look toward the light."

"It's bright."

"Not that bright." Concern filled Dawn's eyes. "Maybe you should stay overnight in case a problem develops, Nic."

A light tap sounded on the door and Grace slipped into the room. "You have another patient waiting in exam room six, Dr. Anderson."

"Very well, my dear. Prepare Dawn's release papers. Nicole will be our guest for the night."

Nicole groaned. That was not what she wanted to hear. She wanted to sleep in her own bed. If she could sleep at all. Her headache was no joke. "Isn't there another alternative, Doc?"

"I'm off shift in three hours, Dr. Anderson. Nicole and Dawn can stay here under observation until then, then come home with me. Trent won't mind. I'll keep an eye on Nicole overnight."

Seeing the doubt on the doctor's face, Nicole said, "I'll do whatever Grace recommends." Most of it, anyway. "If she thinks I need to come back, I promise I'll come without arguing." Much. She really did hate hospitals.

Anderson watched her a moment, then slowly nodded. "Very well. Find a room for Nicole until you clock out, Grace. I'll reevaluate her in three hours. If I'm satisfied that she's doing well enough, I'll send her home in your care."

Grace waited until Dr. Anderson left before she said, "I know you're not seriously hurt, Dawn, but Linc and Trent will want you under their protection."

"Why? I didn't see anything."

"The man who killed Riva doesn't know that. He might want to make sure you and Nicole won't be a problem. It's better to be safe." She smiled. "Consider it a grownup version of a slumber party. We'll have fun."

Nicole wrinkled her nose. "The slumber parties I went to in elementary school didn't include men standing guard. And how much fun will we have if we arrive at your house just in time to go to sleep. Slumber parties aren't followed by a 14-hour work day."

Grace rolled her eyes. "Take it or leave it, Nic. The alternative is staying here all night."

She groaned. "All right. I'll take it. I hope you don't mind Mason staying because I have a feeling he'll refuse to go home."

"Of course. We have plenty of room for Mason and Linc."

Dawn's eyes widened. "Linc is staying, too?"

"Fortress operatives take their responsibilities seriously. You and Nicole are officially under their protection now." Grace turned to Nicole. "Sit tight, sis. I'll find a room for you to rest in for a few hours. Is it all right if I send Mason in? He's pacing the hallway like a caged tiger."

"Absolutely. Thanks for putting us up for the night."

"What are sisters for?" She flashed a sunny smile and left the room.

Within seconds, Mason entered followed closely by Linc. "What did Dr. Anderson say?" Mason asked as he wrapped his hand around Nicole's.

"Ten stitches and I either stay with Grace overnight so she can watch me for signs of trouble or I have to stay here. I opted for Grace's house. She's trying to find me a room so I can lie down until she's off shift."

"What about Dawn?" Linc asked. "She shouldn't be alone, either."

"She's staying at Grace and Trent's as well."

When her employee protested, Nicole narrowed her eyes. "If you insist on staying at your own home, you'll have a bodyguard watching over you, too. If you stay at Grace's with me, fewer bodyguards lose sleep."

"I don't need a bodyguard," Dawn insisted.

"I disagree," Linc said, voice soft. "The man who killed Riva won't have a problem taking out two women who might have seen too much and are a threat to his safety. It's only for a few days, Dawn. As soon as the killer is behind bars, you'll return to your normal routine."

"Trust Linc's judgment," Mason said. "A few nights of inconvenience is better than being injured or worse."

Dawn held Linc's gaze for a few seconds, her cheeks flushing. She sighed. "If you think it's best."

"I do. Thanks for giving me peace of mind."

A ghost of a smile curved her lips.

Amusement spurted through Nicole. She could almost see sparks flying between Linc and Dawn. Although having to be watched around the clock wasn't something Dawn wanted, the benefit of spending so much time with Linc could be interesting.

Grace returned. "I found you a room. Follow me. Linc, Trent's here to help with guard duty if you want to go to the cafeteria with Dawn. You must be starving by now. I imagine Mason might appreciate a meal, too."

"I could eat. Anything you don't like, Mase?" Linc asked.

He shook his head. "I'm not picky. Thanks for playing gofer." Mason grimaced. "Lunch was a long time ago."

"I hear you. I'll see what I can find. What room do we bring the food to, Grace?"

"Room 3217."

Linc escorted Dawn from the room as Trent entered.

"What did the doctor say about you?" he asked Nicole.

"I'll live. Ten stitches and a massive headache." She glared at Trent. "Dr. Anderson already knows about the headache. You can use the information for blackmail purposes."

The operative grinned. "I'll have to change my tactics. I'm becoming too predictable." He looked at Mason. "You all right?"

"What do you think?"

"That the perp is lucky he's not standing in this room or you'd pulverize him for what he did to your woman."

Nicole tightened her grip on Mason's hand. "I'm fine."

"He could have killed you, Nicole," Mason said.

"Let's get Nicole into a room for a few hours." Grace opened the hallway door and returned a moment later with a wheelchair. "Don't argue, Nic. It's hospital policy. If you want, I'll let Mason push you."

"This is embarrassing." Nicole sat, surprised at how tired she felt. Must be the heavy dose of excitement after a 12-hour work day. Wouldn't do to let Mason know, though. The knowledge would stoke his worry even higher.

By the time she was in her room, Nicole's stomach felt as though she would barf at any moment. Not good. "Any chance this high-class establishment has a soft drink for upset stomachs?"

Grace eyed her sharply. "Nausea?"

"Oh, yeah."

"I'll be right back." Her sister thrust an empty plastic container into Mason's hands and left the room. When she returned, Grace clutched a green can in one hand along with a straw, and an ice pack in the other. After positioning the ice pack behind Nicole's neck, she held the can for Nicole to sip the drink. "If the nausea doesn't ease up, let me know, and I'll ask Dr. Anderson about an anti-nausea patch."

"Only if he'll still send me home with you. I don't want to stay here, Grace."

"Matt is ten minutes away," Trent said. "He stocks those patches in his mike bag."

Nicole breathed a sigh of relief. Good to know that Bravo's medic was close if she needed assistance and Grace wasn't available.

"Call him." To Nicole, Grace said, "If your symptoms worsen, have Trent text me, Nic. I'll be back on my next break. If you need more ice or soft drinks, send one of the men to the nurse station. They'll take care of you. The nurse will bring your pain meds in a few minutes. Do yourself a favor and take the medicine. The headache will worsen before it improves. I'll have your prescriptions filled by the time we leave tonight."

"Thanks, sis."

After she left, Trent said, "I'll send Matt a text about the patch. Concentrate on your girl, Mason. I'm on watch. No one will get past me or Linc. Nicole and Dawn will be safe."

Alone again, Nicole eyed the grim expression on the face of the man she loved. She scooted over and patted the bed. "Come here."

"You need to rest."

"I'll rest better with you holding me." Although reluctant to admit it, the close call had scared her. She didn't know why the man didn't finish what he started, but Nicole was grateful that he ran.

"You'll tell me if I hurt you?"

That question reminded her of Dr. Anderson's inquiry. She frowned. "You would never hurt me."

Mason's brows knit. "What's wrong?"

Before she could answer his question, a soft tap sounded on the door and Trent peered inside. "Ethan and Rod are here. You up to talking to them?"

Could she get by with saying no? Nicole sighed. That was a coward's way out. She had to answer Rod's questions. Any information might make the difference between the killer escaping justice or growing old in jail. Hopefully, Matt would arrive soon with the patch. She'd heard Trent mention several times how well the patch worked. She hoped he was right. "How far out is Matt?"

"Five minutes. I can stall the cops until he arrives."

"Hey," Rod protested from the hall. "Every second counts. I need as much information as Nicole and Dawn can give me."

Trent waited for Nicole to decide. She knew without a doubt that he would keep them out of the room at her request. She couldn't do that to him or the policemen.

"Send them in."

Her brother-in-law moved aside to allow the Otter Creek law enforcement officers to enter the room, then returned to his watch position.

"What did the doctor say about you?" Ethan asked.

"Ten stitches and I'll live, although at the moment I'm beginning to wonder if Dr. Anderson is right. The headache and nausea are winning the battle." Hope Ethan and Rod didn't mind an episode of puking.

"We wouldn't be here unless we needed every detail." Rod pulled out a notebook and pen. "Tell me everything you can remember."

Nicole ran through everything again. "I wish I could remember more, but everything happened so fast."

"What can you tell me about the man who hit you?"

"He wore a black ski mask. His clothes were black, too. And he wore gloves." Joy. No fingerprints.

"Eye color?" Ethan asked.

She closed her eyes and replayed the second her gaze had connected with the killer's. "Brown."

"Did you see any part of his skin? Perhaps around his eyes or his hands."

"Yeah. He was Caucasian."

"You're doing great, Nicole," Rod said. "What about his height and weight?"

"I don't know. I was on my knees beside Riva."

"Guess."

Nicole swallowed a few more sips of the drink and prayed Matt arrived soon. She really didn't want to barf in front of Mason or the tough policemen. "Taller than Mason."

"As tall as Ethan?"

Her gaze shifted to the police chief. She shook her head and immediately wished she hadn't. "Maybe your height, Rod."

"Any characteristics that stand out?"

She started to say no, then remembered the cologne. "He wore spicy cologne."

Another tap on the door. This time, Matt entered. Nicole breathed a sigh of relief. Thank goodness.

"I hear you need a patch."

"As fast as possible."

The medic skirted the two policemen and pulled a small white packet from his pocket. "Turn your head to the right," he murmured and positioned the patch behind Nicole's ear.

"Please tell me this works fast," she whispered.

"At least half an hour."

She closed her eyes briefly. "Oh, boy."

Mason glanced at Ethan and Rod as Matt repositioned the ice pack to drape over Nicole's forehead. "Finish your questions. Nicole needs to rest."

"I'm okay, Mason."

"No, baby, you aren't. Undergoing intense questioning is making your symptoms worse."

"Just one more question." Rod pulled out his phone, tapped his screen, and turned it around for Nicole to see. "Do you recognize this?"

Mason grabbed the phone, color draining from his face.

Ethan stilled. "Talk to me, Mason."

"That's my pipe wrench."

CHAPTER FIVE

"Are you sure?" Ethan asked. "Pipe wrenches are common. What makes you positive this one is yours?"

Stomach twisting into a knot, Mason expanded the image on the screen and pointed to the marred surface of the handle. "I scratched the paint while fixing a leak on one of the sinks at Pet Palace last month. I'm sure the wrench is mine."

The police chief's gaze bored into Mason. "How did your wrench end up at a crime scene?"

"No, Ethan." Nicole glared. "He wouldn't hurt Riva or me."

The policeman's gaze never wavered from Mason. "Answer my question."

Mason squeezed her hand in warning. "I must have left it when I fixed her sink."

A muscle in Ethan's jaw twitched. "When were you at Riva's?"

He knew the suspicion his next words would spawn, yet he wouldn't lie to the man who invested himself into Mason's life over the past two years, and supported and mentored while drawing a hard line which Mason toed out of respect. "Around 2:00 this afternoon."

Nicole gasped.

Rod's eyes narrowed, suspicion glittering in the depths.

Mason fought the bitterness threatening to well up from the depths of his being. When would the shadow of his past disappear? Rod knew him. He'd repaired several things around the Kelter home and as well as spent time there as a guest. He hadn't broken any laws since he left prison. When would the debt he owed for a tragic mistake in judgment be paid in full? Weren't his nightmares and unrelenting guilt enough?

"Matt." Ethan inclined his head toward the door. When the medic left, the chief said, "Tell us everything, Mason."

"Why? You and Rod have already decided I'm guilty."

Temper sparked in Ethan's eyes. "Talk to us now or we'll take you to the station for formal questioning as a person of interest in Riva's murder."

If he was taken to the station for questioning, Mason wouldn't be allowed in any Otter Creek or Dunlap County homes. Worse, he couldn't protect Nicole. His gut told him that the man who killed Riva would view Nicole and Dawn as threats. Although Trent, Linc, and the other operatives with PSI and Fortress were skilled in protection, he loved Nicole. If staying by her side meant swallowing his pride and answering biased, insulting questions, he'd do it.

"Make your choice, Mason. Do we question you here or at the station?"

"Mason, please," Nicole whispered.

He kissed her palm. "Riva called during lunch and asked me to meet her at her home to repair a leaking faucet in the master bathroom. I arrived at 2:00."

"She called you specifically?"

A nod.

"Why not call Elliott Construction to request a repairman?"

"I remodeled her kitchen last year with Brian. From that point on, if she needed repairs completed around the house, she called me."

"Did Brian know you did repairs off the books for her?" Rod asked.

His blood ran hot. "They were billed through Elliott Construction. Brian knew I planned to stop at her house."

"Brian will confirm you were at Riva's on company business when we ask?"

When, not if. He sighed. "Yes, sir."

"What did you do when you arrived at Riva's?" Ethan asked.

"Texted Brian to let him know that I was on site and knocked on her door. When she answered, Riva sent me to the master bath while she finished a phone call on her cell."

"Do you know who she was talking to?"

"I don't know, but it sounded personal. She seemed unhappy with the conversation. I went upstairs. Brian called a couple minutes later to request I check on another job when I left Riva's."

Ethan motioned for him to continue.

"The sink in the master bath was an easy fix. I used my pipe wrench to tighten a nut. While I was there, I checked the rest of the pipe and the faucet and found them in working order."

"When did you leave?"

"Thirty minutes after I arrived."

Ethan and Rod stared. Yeah, he knew how that sounded.

"You spent that long tightening a nut?" Rod's disbelief rang loud and clear in his voice.

"Riva had other quick maintenance projects." Mason hated that he sounded defensive. He'd bet the detective would as well if someone questioned his integrity. "She's a repeat customer of Elliott Construction. I was already there and the repairs didn't take long. Once I finished her list, I drove to the Willow Run construction site and was there an hour before going to PSI to work on a sink in the kitchen. Nate will vouch for me."

"I want a list of people you talk to at the Willow Run site," Rod said.

"You're out of luck. The crews were at other sites today. I was alone."

"So, we only have your word that you visited Willow Run for an hour before heading to PSI."

Ethan held up his hand to forestall his detective from saying more. "Where did you go once you left PSI?"

"To Linc Creed's home. He had a leak under his kitchen sink, too." His lip curled. "This was a day for plumbing problems."

Rod scowled. "How did you fix the leak at Linc's if you left your pipe wrench at Riva's?"

"I have more than one wrench." Rod needed to finish the questions soon. Nicole's face was too pale. He prayed the patch would kick in soon.

"How was Riva when you left her home?"

Mason's hand tightened around Nicole's. In his mind, he heard the prison doors clang shut behind him. "Alive and well. Why are you interested in my wrench?"

"Evidence points to your wrench as the murder weapon."

Although he'd expected that answer, the news still hit him like a blow to the gut. Mason drew in a careful breath. He couldn't face prison again. He almost hadn't survived the first time around. If he was sent back, he would lose Nicole. What woman wanted to stick around and wait for her man to serve out time for murder. Tennessee was also a death penalty state. He could lose his life as well as the woman he adored.

"He didn't do it," Nicole insisted.

"You have proof?" Rod demanded.

"I told you the man who hit me wore cologne. Mason doesn't wear any. Colognes and perfumes give me migraines."

"That's not enough."

"Then get out there and find the real killer," she snapped. "Don't assume Mason's guilty because he has a record." Nicole grabbed the green can and sipped more of the soft drink as she glared at the detective.

Mason stood. "Nicole needs to rest. The questions can wait."

The detective scowled. "I have a murder to solve and you're the prime suspect."

"Why am I not surprised? I'll answer questions tomorrow. Right now, I'm more worried about Nicole than you."

"We'll go," Ethan said. "For now. Don't leave town."

"Where would I go? You can track anyone anywhere."

"You have friends with safe houses almost impossible to find. I don't want to go up against Brent Maddox, but I will if I have to."

"Think about this while you order his prison jumpsuit," Nicole said. "If Mason killed Riva, who hit me and shoved Dawn? I know beyond a doubt that it wasn't him."

Rod shrugged. "Mason spent years in prison. One of his cell mates or friends could have done the job for him."

"Are you kidding me?" Nicole's voice rose. "Maybe I gave you too much credit for intelligence, Detective Kelter."

"Enough, Nicole." Mason met her fiery gaze. "He has a job to do."

"He's doing a lousy job."

He couldn't argue with that, but she wouldn't do herself or Mason any favors if she continued to antagonize Rod.

"Same restriction applies to you, Nicole," Ethan said, voice soft. "Don't leave town."

Her mouth gaped. "I'm a suspect, too?"

"You're in love with the man at the top of the suspect list. You want to help him? Think about what happened. Any clue you pass along will help us find the real killer sooner."

Mason froze. "You don't believe I killed Riva?"

"In the past two years, you haven't stepped out of line once. In fact, you go out of your way to be an outstanding citizen. You didn't kill Riva. Now, we need to find the evidence to nab the man who did."

Some of the knots in his stomach untied themselves. Thank God. Mason shifted his attention to the detective. "What about you? Do you think I'm guilty?"

The corners of his lips lifted. "My job is to investigate every possibility."

"What does that mean?" Nicole said.

"I have to follow leads no matter if I believe a suspect is guilty or not."

A tap sounded on the door and Trent poked his head inside. "Food's here."

Nicole groaned, clutching her stomach. "Don't say that word."

Ethan glanced at Rod and inclined his head toward the door. "We'll let you rest. Be vigilant, Nicole. The killer is still out there, and I don't want you and your friend to be collateral damage."

"No problem. I'll have a shadow for a while anyway."

An eyebrow rose. "Fortress is providing a bodyguard?"

"The Fortress teams at PSI are in charge of security for Nicole and Dawn," Trent said.

"If you feel the need for a safe house outside of town, I need to know the location before you make the move."

"Yes, sir."

Ethan turned to Mason. "You have my number. Use it. If you need me, I'll be there."

"Thanks."

The police chief left the room followed by Rod.

"What do you want to do about your meal, Mase?" Trent asked.

"Go eat, Mason." Nicole gave him a wan smile. "I'm not going anywhere, and I don't want you to starve. Trent will watch over me."

"I'll be fine." His stomach chose that moment to growl.

"Don't be stubborn." She released his hand. "If it will make you feel better, send Matt in here. He can keep me company for a few minutes."

Knowing that she'd worry if he didn't take care of himself, Mason bent and brushed his lips over hers. "I won't be long." He turned and looked at Trent.

The operative smiled. "I've got her, Mase. No worries."

Why did he wonder when the next disaster would strike?

CHAPTER SIX

Nicole opened her eyes to slits to identify the person who slipped into her room and was relieved to recognize the dark-haired medic from the Bravo team. She'd had more than enough poking and prodding by the doctors and nurses at Memorial. "Thanks for staying, Matt. I figured you would abandon ship and go home to your wife."

"I have a soft spot for Otter Creek's favorite pet groomer. How's the nausea?"

"Starting to ease. I could use something for the headache, though. I feel like my head's going to explode at the next loud noise."

"Your nurse is making the rounds now with the med cart. She should be here soon." He removed the limp ice pack. "Mason seemed upset when he left your room."

"He has a right to be," she murmured, shutting her eyes again. She didn't have to be on guard with Matt at her bedside. "He's the prime suspect in Riva Kemper's murder."

"Kelter is a good detective. He'll find the real killer."

Nicole's lips curved, pleased the medic assumed Mason was innocent. Would other people in town give him the benefit of the doubt or believe the worst? "One of

Mason's wrenches might have been used as the murder weapon."

"Does he have an alibi for the time of the murder?"

She'd been too lost in a haze of pain to remember much about Mason's answers. "That depends on when Riva died. Part of the afternoon, Mason was on a job site by himself, inspecting work completed by construction crews."

Matt blew out a breath. "Too bad someone couldn't vouch for his whereabouts during that time."

No kidding. The timing couldn't be worse. Otter Creek wasn't that large, though. Someone had to see him going to the Willow Run site or leaving it, and verify the timeline for Rod and Ethan.

Nicole sighed. Even if they found someone, that wouldn't be enough to convince Rod to focus his attention elsewhere. Mason could have slipped away from the site and returned to Riva's place with no one the wiser if he was careful.

What Rod seemed determined to ignore was that Mason didn't have a motive to kill the real estate agent. Second, the construction worker would never lay a hand on Nicole in anger. In the past year, he had treated her with respect and gentleness, grateful that she'd given him a chance instead of condemning him for his wayward past. No, she knew in her heart Mason wasn't responsible for her injuries.

A light tap sounded on the door. Trent said, "The nurse is here with your medicine, Nicole."

"Hallelujah. Maybe I'll survive the next hour."

He chuckled and a moment later the nurse wheeled in a cart.

"I have the pain medicine Dr. Anderson prescribed for you, Ms. Copeland."

Nicole squinted at her, flinching at the bright light from the hallway. "I groom your poodle, Misty. You don't need to be so formal. Call me Nicole."

"Yes, ma'am."

After she swallowed the capsules, she thanked the nurse. "Isn't it about time for me to see Candy?" The standard poodle, a favorite customer, was a sweet girl with beautiful dark eyes and chocolate-colored fur.

"She's overdue for a haircut and bath. I'll call tomorrow to make an appointment." Her gaze drifted to the side of Nicole's head. "How were you hurt?"

"A guy whacked me with a hard object."

"Oh, wow. Do you know who it was?"

"No clue." Even if she did, Ethan and Rod wouldn't appreciate her spreading details about an ongoing investigation. She'd heard through the grapevine that they were prickly about such matters and didn't want to be on their bad side.

Misty looked troubled. "Are you sure you didn't recognize the man?"

Nicole stared at the nurse. "If you're wondering if Mason is to blame, the answer is a definite no."

"I'm sorry. I didn't mean to offend you, but we see a lot of domestic abuse patients in the ER."

She shoved aside her irritation. "I appreciate your concern, Misty. Rest assured, my assailant wasn't Mason."

"You'll tell someone if he ever hurts you?"

Seriously? She understood people were concerned and wasn't immune to the stares and whispers, but Mason was a good man. Why wouldn't people take him at face value instead of assuming he was a hardened criminal who had zero regard for human life or the people he loved? "Absolutely."

Misty relaxed. "Good. If you want anything, press the call button. I'll bring whatever you need."

"She needs another ice pack," Matt said as he handed her the warm one, his tone cool.

The nurse dropped her gaze. "Yes, sir. I'll bring a fresh one in a few minutes." A moment later, she was gone.

"You have to teach me how to intimidate with a stare. I have a feeling I'll need the skill before Ethan and Rod catch the real killer."

The medic moved a chair to the foot of Nicole's bed. "She won't be the only one to assume Mason is guilty and that you're covering for him."

"It's not fair. Why won't people give him a chance?"

"He's winning Otter Creek over. People who know him won't automatically think the worst."

"You didn't."

"Because I know him. Delilah and I also spend a lot of time with you both plus he's remodeled part of our home."

Unfortunately, not enough people had overcome their preconceived notions to see Mason as the man he'd become instead of the college graduate who made a poor decision to drink and drive, and paid for it by spending years of his life behind bars.

"The pain medicine should kick in soon. When it does, you'll be sleepy. Don't fight it. You'll heal faster if you rest."

Easy for him to say. He didn't have a nuclear bomb threatening to explode in his head. "Yes, Doctor."

Matt chuckled. "Still have the attitude, I see. Guess that means you'll live."

She snuggled deeper into the pillow. As the pain medicine kicked in, she let herself drift, registering muted conversations and the squeak of Misty's medicine cart, yet not focusing on anything. Although the headache still nagged at her, the nausea had subsided to a manageable level. Nicole hoped she made enough progress for Dr. Anderson to release her as promised.

A short while later, the door opened and she hissed when someone placed a new ice pack at the back of her neck.

"I'll remove it in twenty minutes," Matt murmured. When she shivered, he draped a blanket over her.

Later, the door opened again and a large hand with roughened skin wrapped around one of her own. Nicole's lips curved. "Mason," she whispered.

"I'm here. Rest. I'll watch over you."

"Dawn?"

"In good hands with Linc. They're in the waiting room down the hall. It's small and isolated. If anyone means to harm her, they'll have to go through Linc first."

The time with Linc would allow Dawn the opportunity to get to know the handsome PSI instructor. "Love you."

"I love you, too." His voice sounded thick.

"Two months, six days, and fourteen hours until our wedding."

A soft chuckle. "I can't wait to introduce you as my wife."

"Second best day of my life was the day you asked me to marry you. First day was the day I met you."

"I'm honored that you said yes when I proposed. I won't let you down."

"We won't let each other down. We're a team, Kincaid."

He squeezed her hand.

The pain medicine tugged her down again and the low-voiced conversation between Mason and Matt became background noise as she drifted to sleep. The next time she surfaced, Dr. Anderson entered the room. After talking to the medic, Anderson walked to her bedside.

"How is the headache, my dear?"

"Tolerable with the pain meds."

He patted her hand. "Excellent." The physician assessed her condition for himself and appeared satisfied with what he found. "If you still insist on leaving our fine facility, I'll sign your release papers."

"Thanks, Doc. You're the best. If you get yourself a dog, he or she will have free grooming for life."

A laugh. "I work too many hours to have a dog. If I ever retire and adopt a pet, I'll take you up on your offer."

"Deal."

"Misty will be in soon with your discharge paperwork and instructions although I don't suppose you'll need the instructions with Grace to watch over you. The main thing I want is your promise to return if your symptoms worsen. No hiding the truth from Grace."

"I promise." Anything to get out of here.

Twenty minutes later, Nicole and her entourage exited the hospital with Trent in the lead. Linc sat behind the wheel of his idling SUV near the ER entrance. Nicole climbed into the backseat with Mason while Dawn sat in the shotgun seat. When Trent signaled Linc, the operative drove from the hospital with Matt following behind them. The St. Claires brought up the rear.

Her stomach began to churn. Nicole closed her eyes and prayed she wouldn't barf in Linc's SUV. Talk about embarrassing.

Mason's hand tightened around hers. "How are you?"

"Praying we don't hit a traffic jam."

Linc's gaze shot to the rearview mirror. "You sick?"

"Trying not to be."

The SUV shot forward. "If you need to puke, tell me and I'll pull over." He drove through the center of town, then hung a right on Poplar Road. Thank goodness the St. Claire home wasn't much farther.

A mile before the turnoff, Linc slammed on his brakes and skidded to a stop.

"What's wrong?" Mason leaned forward to peer through the windshield and groaned. "You've got to be kidding."

Nicole stared at the big furry object standing at the side of the road, making a bush a late-night snack. "Oh, brother. Which camel is it?" A grizzled farmer who lived outside of town owned a couple of camels at the request of his granddaughter. One of those camels was a real Houdini who regularly slipped from the pasture where the animal normally grazed with cattle.

Linc glared at the animal. "Bonnie. Clyde is a homebody."

"We can't leave her here," Dawn said. "Someone might hit her."

"I know who to call."

A moment later, a familiar voice filled the cabin. "Yeah, Cahill."

"It's Linc. You're on speaker with Dawn Metcalf, Mason, and Nicole. I need your camel whisperer skills."

A growl came through the speakers. "I'll call old man Lawrence. Where's Bonnie this time?"

"Intersection of Blue Spruce and Dogwood. She's making a meal out of Mrs. Waterman's bushes."

"Great. Mrs. Waterman will have a fit."

"I'd stick around but Mason and I don't want Nicole and Dawn out in the open for long."

"I understand. I'm two minutes out. If Bonnie moves, she won't go far. Good thing I restocked the chips supply in my cruiser."

Dawn frowned. "Chips?"

"Yes, ma'am. Bonnie won't budge unless you bribe her with potato chips."

"Good to know for future reference."

"She loves people, but if you interact with her, watch out for your hair. Bonnie's been known to pull out strands with her enthusiastic attention. Linc?"

"Yes, sir?"

Nicole's eyebrows winged up at the deference Linc paid to Josh until she remembered that Josh was Linc's boss at PSI.

"You two have backup for the night?"

"Trent. We're staying with him and Grace. We'll be fine. No one will get past us to harm the women."

"I'll make it a point to drive by Trent's on my rounds. If anything happens, I want to know about it."

"Yes, sir."

"Nicole?"

She blinked. "Yes?"

"You're in good hands. Trust the men guarding you. They'll keep you safe."

She turned her head to smile at Mason who tucked her closer to his side. "I know. Thanks for watching over us tonight, Josh."

"Glad to do it. I'm one minute out, Linc. Get moving."

"Copy that. Bonnie hasn't moved." He ended the call, eased around the camel, and continued toward the St. Claire home. Five minutes later, he parked in the long driveway near the front door.

When Dawn reached for the door handle, Linc stilled her movement by laying his hand on her arm. "Wait until I'm sure it's safe."

The PSI instructor exited the vehicle and slowly circled the hood toward the passenger-side door, his gaze scanning the area as Matt and the St. Claires parked behind them. Linc stood beside the door while Trent escorted Grace to the house. Matt joined Linc.

"Why are we waiting now?" Dawn asked.

"For Trent to signal Linc that the house is safe." Mason kissed the top of Nicole's head. "Another couple of minutes and you can go to bed."

"How do you know so much about security?" Dawn asked Mason.

"Rio and Trent. I've been on several missions with them to help with night watch."

"Have you spent much time with Linc?"

Nicole smiled despite her churning stomach. Her friend was smitten with the PSI instructor. Nice.

"Not as much time as I've spent with Durango and Bravo, but we're friends. He's a good guy." He sent her a pointed look. "He's not dating anyone."

She whipped around to stare at him. "I didn't ask that."

"You wanted to," Nicole said.

"Maybe," she muttered.

Trent reappeared in the doorway of his home and signaled Linc and Matt. They opened the passenger-side doors of the SUV. "Let's go, Dawn." Linc assisted her from the vehicle and hurried her toward the St. Claire home.

Matt waited until the two were inside the house before saying, "Your turn, Nicole. Mase, get out on the other side and come around. Go to Nicole's left side. I'll take the right."

Mason joined Matt and held out his hand to Nicole. He gathered her against his side and hustled her toward the front door.

They arrived without incident, but Nicole felt as though someone watched them take every step. Ridiculous. How would the killer know she'd go to Trent's?

She shivered. Anyone who knew her would suspect the likelihood of her staying with her sister was high. After all, she'd been injured, and Grace was a nurse.

Only a fool would take on Trent St. Claire, though. Her brother-in-law was a skilled black ops soldier and a Navy SEAL. No one sane ticked off Trent.

Her gaze slid to Mason. Her husband-to-be was no slouch in the security department, either. He might not be an operative or allowed to carry a weapon, but he knew how to handle himself and protect her. She trusted him with her life as well as her heart.

Matt secured the door. He turned an assessing gaze on Nicole, then glanced at Grace. "Do you have a soft drink with ginger or chamomile tea?"

Nicole frowned. Did she have a sign on her forehead warning others she was sick to her stomach?

"Both. I know not to incur your wrath."

He snorted. "Brat."

Grace grinned as she headed for the kitchen.

"Your room is ready, Nic," Trent said. "Dawn has the guest room."

Dawn frowned. "What about Linc and Mason? Where will they sleep?"

"On the couch in shifts," Linc said. "The person on night watch will alternate between the living room window and the back door in the kitchen." He slid a glance toward Mason. "Although I suspect Mase won't be sleeping at all."

"Why not?" Nicole asked. Mason had to go to work early in the morning.

"He'll sit by your bedside and watch over you when he's not on night watch."

"No." She frowned at Mason. "You have to be at work early."

"So do you. I'll be fine. One night short on sleep won't hurt me."

Although she didn't like his reasoning, Nicole understood. If their roles had been reversed, she would have watched over him all night, too.

Grace returned with a soft drink. "Drink part of this and go to sleep if you can, Nic. I'll check on you in two hours."

"I have to be at work by 6:30 a.m."

"We both do." Dawn smothered a yawn. "I hope one of you doesn't mind dropping us off because our vehicles are parked in front of Riva's house."

Trent and Linc exchanged glances with Mason. "I'll be your chauffeur," Linc said.

Nicole frowned. Something was up. The men were hiding something. "What's wrong, Trent?"

"At the moment, nothing. We'll see what Rod and Ethan come up with overnight before we talk about further security measures."

"Trent..."

"Give it up, Nic." Grace nudged Nicole toward her room. "Mason is no less protective than Trent or Linc. Get some rest because I'll be checking you periodically throughout the night."

She leaned into Mason's side, barely managing to put one foot in front of another. "One of these days, I'll return the favor and keep you up all night."

Her sister laughed. "Deal."

Inside her temporary bedroom, Mason turned the lamp to the low setting. "Do you need help getting ready for bed? I'm sure Dawn or Grace will be glad to give you a hand."

"I need something to sleep in. I keep toiletries here for the nights I stay over when Trent is gone on a mission."

"I'll let Grace know. Call for me if you need me."

"Mason, I'll be fine if you want to sleep for a few hours."

The muscles in his jaw firmed. "I won't be able to sleep anyway if I'm not sure you're safe. Let me protect you."

Tears stung her eyes. "You'll always be my refuge in the storm."

He brushed his lips over hers in a gentle caress. "I'll be back in a few minutes. If you become dizzy, call out."

"I promise. Go."

Nicole held herself erect by sheer force of will until Mason walked down the hall. She braced her hand against the wall as she walked to the attached bathroom to brush her teeth and wash her face. By the time she finished her before-bed routine, she felt limp as a dishrag. Great way to convince the man she loved that she was healing.

A light tap sounded on the bedroom door and her sister walked inside with a pair of yoga pants and a tank top. "Figured you'd be more comfortable with clothes you could run in if necessary."

"Better not be necessary." She waved aside Grace's concern. "I'm just tired. I guess the extra-long day and the encounter with Wrench Man is catching up with me."

"Understandable. Need help changing clothes?"

"Nope. I've got it. Where's Mason?"

"Working out night watch shifts with Trent and Linc. Dawn is in her room with a mug of tea." Grace's eyes twinkled. "Is she sweet on Linc?"

"She hasn't said, but I have my suspicions. She blushes when he's mentioned in conversation. It's cute."

"Reminds me of you when you first met Mason."

"And now I'm going to marry that man in two months, six days, and," a quick glance at her watch, "twelve hours."

Grace grinned. "Not that you're counting or anything. I'll leave you to change. Open the door when you're ready for Mason to return. He's worried about you."

"For a couple seconds before I passed out at Riva's, I was afraid I wouldn't live to walk down the aisle. Believe me, I don't mind one bit that he wants to be close to me. The feeling is mutual."

Her sister's smile faded. "He won't let anything happen to you. Neither will Trent and Linc. You're in good hands." Grace handed Nicole the clothes and closed the door on her way out of the room.

Nearing the end of her strength, Nicole hurried to change clothes and open the door. She left the lamp on dim, climbed on the bed, and tugged the quilt over her legs.

When Mason returned to the room, he left the door to the hall open and moved a chair to her bedside.

"The bed's large. You could stretch out beside me."

A slow smile curved his lips. "No, baby, I couldn't. In two months and six days, I'll take you up on your offer." He sat, turned off the lamp, and threaded his fingers through Nicole's. "Sleep. I'll be right here."

Between one heartbeat and the next, Nicole dropped into the oblivion of sleep.

CHAPTER SEVEN

Dawn threw off the covers and sat up, frustrated by her inability to slow her mind enough to sleep. If nothing changed, she wouldn't be much help to Nicole in the morning. Every time she closed her eyes, she saw that masked man barreling toward her.

More tea, she decided. That was her only option unless she could find a book with a plot that moved at a snail's pace. Maybe a slow movie if she wouldn't disturb whoever was on night watch at the moment. Would it be Trent, Mason, or Linc?

What did it matter? The point was safety. Besides, Lincoln Creed was the bachelor of choice for every woman in town. How could she hope to compete with all of them? She couldn't let herself take his care and concern over the past few hours to heart no matter how much she was tempted.

Dawn slid her feet back into her running shoes, mentally thanking Grace for her foresight in providing workout gear to sleep in. She walked into the hall and glanced toward Nicole's room. No light. Hopefully, her friend was asleep. She suspected Mason was somewhere close.

Maybe one day, she'd be lucky enough to have a man as devoted to her as Mason was to Nicole.

She walked toward the living room and pulled up short when Linc turned from the window to look at her, concern growing in his eyes.

"You okay?" he asked, voice soft.

Why did he have to be the one on duty now? Dawn couldn't deny that familiar tug of attraction. So much for lulling herself to sleep on the couch. Wouldn't be happening with this man so close. "I can't sleep. I planned to make tea and hunt for a nice, slow book to read. Any chance Trent has an ancient history book I can borrow for the night?" That ought to be dry enough to bore her to sleep.

"Are you in pain or is your brain replaying the events at Riva's?"

Smart man. "Second option."

"The instant replay is your brain's way of coping with trauma. Your subconscious is searching for different options that were available to change the outcome. There aren't any."

His simple statement eased her discomfort enough for her to take her first deep breath since this nightmare began. How did Linc know just what to say?

He moved away from the window. "Come on. I'll walk with you to the kitchen. I need to check the back of the house anyway and refill my coffee mug."

"Since you're awake at this time of night, you must have drawn the short straw."

Linc glanced at her, eyebrow raised. "Short straw?"

"The first watch."

"I volunteered."

"Why?" She wouldn't have wanted to stay up half the night, waiting for the other shoe to drop. Riva's killer must be long gone by now. A shiver raced down her body. The killer had to be a transient. Otter Creek was a safe town, one full of highly skilled men and women trained to protect. Linc was a prime example.

He lifted the carafe from the coffeemaker and poured more of the steaming liquid into his mug. "Giving up a few hours of sleep is nothing I haven't done many times over the years. I have a hard time sleeping some nights. More important, I wanted to know that you were safe. The only way I'll be sure of that is to watch over you myself."

She stared. "Mason and Trent are in the house. My safety isn't solely your responsibility." Is that all he felt for her? A sense of responsibility? A wave of disappointment washed over her.

Linc glanced over his shoulder. "Trent's priority is Grace. Mason is focused on Nicole. My priority is you. Believe me, it's not a hardship on my part. I would gladly do that and more to keep you safe."

Her heart skipped a beat. He couldn't mean that the way it sounded. Could he?

The instructor drank a few sips of his coffee and set the mug on the counter. "I'm going outside to make sure everything is still secure. I'll be back in ten minutes. Make your tea and go curl up on the couch. You can keep me company while I'm on watch."

She smiled, the ball of ice in her stomach melting at not having to face the four walls of her bedroom for a while longer and perhaps getting to know the PSI instructor better. "All right. Thanks, Linc."

After a nod, he left the house by the kitchen door and disappeared into the darkness.

Dawn rummaged through Grace's tea collection. She selected one, dumped the tea bag in a mug filled with water, and nuked it. After refreshing the coffee in Linc's mug, she carried her mug and his into the living room, and curled up at one end of the couch with her tea in hand. When she finished her drink, Dawn draped an afghan over her legs and settled back to wait for Linc.

When Linc returned, she handed his coffee and asked, "Everything okay?"

"Exactly as it was thirty minutes ago. I also spoke to Josh for a minute. Bonnie is home with her boyfriend, Clyde. No mishaps or problems. According to Josh, she polished off Mrs. Waterman's bush and two family-size bags of potato chips on her adventure tonight. Daybreak will reveal other camel snacks because I'm sure Bonnie ate more than one bush. That girl has quite an appetite."

She grinned. "You're familiar with her?"

"Hard not to be. I run frequently at night, and that's Bonnie's favorite time to wander around the area." He grimaced. "She's also made off with several strands of my hair when I didn't move fast enough to evade her attention."

"You can't sleep at night?"

"That's part of it. The other part is running five miles or more a day is more comfortable at night because of the lower temperature. More peaceful, too. Less traffic." He stationed himself by the front window again and sipped his coffee.

"Is running that much required for your job?"

A soft chuckle. "It doesn't pay for trainees to be in better shape than instructors. To train them, we need to be better than they are. They respect strength and skill. If I let myself be a couch potato, I won't have as much impact. My job is to impart as much knowledge and training as possible to keep them alive on the job. I don't take that responsibility lightly."

"What did you do before you came to PSI?"

Linc paused, then murmured, "Military."

She noted his utter stillness. Sore spot? "How long were you in?"

"Seventeen years. I left for boot camp the day after my high school graduation."

"What branch?"

"Army." He was silent a moment, then asked, "Does it bother you?"

Dawn blinked, surprised at his question. "Of course not. I was an Army brat. My father served for 30 years."

"Are you going to ask what my job was?"

"If you're teaching bodyguards how to handle weapons at PSI, you weren't in charge of supplies like Dad."

The stiff lines of his body relaxed. "No, I wasn't. Thanks."

"For what?"

"Not asking me details."

"I wasn't born yesterday. It's obvious you don't want to talk about your military service and aren't allowed to talk about your work. I don't know anything for sure, but people around town talk and speculate about what really goes on behind closed doors at PSI. Many of the operatives in charge of PSI are something other than run-of-the-mill soldiers. You fit right in with them."

Linc snorted. "Gossiping is a favorite town pastime."

He didn't deny her assessment of him and his military service. Good enough confirmation for her to know that the PSI weapons master had been in Special Forces. The quiet man had hidden depths. "I'll listen with an open mind if you ever want to tell me about your work or service. Otherwise, I won't push."

"I believe you mean that."

Dawn lifted one shoulder. "I mean what I say. I don't know what you went through during your stint in the military, but I appreciate your service and sacrifice, Linc."

"Think you can fall asleep now?"

"Are you trying to get rid of me?"

Linc half-turned to face her, consternation on his face. "No, of course not."

She grinned. "Gotcha."

"You have a wicked sense of humor, Ms. Metcalf. I like it."

Did that mean he liked her? "Will it bother you if I stay?"

Although he shook his head, his attention stayed focused on something outside the window.

What did he see? "Linc?"

"Go into the kitchen. Leave the lights off."

Oh, man. Dawn whipped the afghan away from her legs and rushed toward the back of the house. She only made it a few feet before Linc shouted something and slammed into her, taking Dawn to the floor, covering her body with his. Before she drew in a breath, the living room window exploded.

Linc's arms tightened around her while the chaos continued unabated. After what seemed like a lifetime, the noise finally stopped.

"You okay?" he asked.

"I think so."

"Sit rep," Trent snapped from the hallway.

Linc jumped up, pulling a weapon from his holster. "One shooter in a black pickup. Watch over Dawn." His jaw hardened. "I'm going hunting."

"Go."

He raced out the kitchen door and into the darkness.

"Are you hurt?" Trent crouched beside Dawn and helped her sit up.

"I don't think so." She glanced down at herself and, not seeing any obvious injuries, counted her blessings. "What about you and everyone else?"

"We're fine." His cell phone rang. Trent stabbed the speaker button. "St. Claire."

"Security monitoring called me. Sit rep," a deep voice demanded.

"You're on speaker, boss."

"Understood. What do you need?"

Mason, Nicole, and Grace entered the kitchen.

"Have the tech geeks analyze the security footage and ask Zane to hack the traffic cams in my neighborhood. Someone driving a black pickup shot up my house."

"Security breach on our end?"

"Can't be ruled out but I doubt it." He summarized the events at Riva's home. "Mason, Nicole, and her friend Dawn Metcalf are here along with Linc Creed."

"How many black pickups are in Otter Creek?" The tone was dry.

"Too many to narrow down, sir."

"I was afraid of that. Hopefully, the security footage will give us something more definitive. Have the police arrived yet?"

Sirens sounded in the distance.

"Two minutes or less."

"They can have whatever they need. Tell Blackhawk that Zane will push his requests to the front of the line."

"Yes, sir."

"Let me know what you need. You'll get it. No questions asked." The call ended.

Dawn frowned. "That wasn't Josh Cahill, but you called this man 'boss.' Who is he?"

"Brent Maddox, the CEO of Fortress Security. PSI is the bodyguard training arm of Fortress. Bravo and Durango are employed by Fortress. Our secondary jobs are to train bodyguards."

What did that mean for Linc? Was he like Trent and his team, employed by Fortress first and PSI second?

After a knock sounded on the back door, Trent shifted to place himself between the door and the rest of the occupants of the room, gun in his hand and aimed.

"It's Linc. I'm coming in soft."

"Come." Grace's husband remained in position with his gun ready until Linc walked in alone.

"Anything?"

"Zip." Disgust filled Linc's voice. "By the time I got around the side of the house, he was long gone."

"Big head start."

"Cops will be here any second." Linc glanced at Grace, Mason, and Nicole. "You three are okay?"

"Thanks to you." Grace padded over and hugged him.

"We owe you," Mason said.

Linc waved that aside. "Want me to check your security footage, Trent?"

"The tech geeks are going to do that while Zane hacks into the traffic cams. With luck, we'll find enough information to help the cops wrap this up soon. I don't want Bravo deployed with someone still gunning for the women."

"I should go." Nicole sat at the kitchen table. "I'm bringing danger to Grace's doorstep."

Trent tapped the end of her nose. "Got news for you, Nic. Danger follows me like a shadow."

"Some yahoo shot up your house." She scowled. "You're the one who always says there is no such thing as coincidence in your line of work. Do you expect me to believe my close encounter with Riva's killer has nothing to do with this attack?"

"Doesn't matter, does it? The result is the same. I still have to replace my windows and patch bullet holes in the walls." His lips curled. "And when I find the shooter, I'll be taking the repair price out of his hide."

"Listen up, St. Claire. I'm not putting Grace at risk."

"We'll work out different arrangements for tomorrow night," Mason said.

A hard rap sounded on the front door this time.

Trent checked the peephole and opened the door. He gestured for Josh to come in and explained what happened. "I've already requested the techs look at the security footage, and Zane is checking for other footage."

The policeman's lips curved slightly. "Since the perp did a drive-by, I doubt Ethan will look too closely at information dropped anonymously into his email. I'll call it in and get more help out here. For now, stay in the kitchen. Do you have plywood to cover the windows?"

"I have several sheets in my garage," Mason said. "My truck is at Riva's. I'll need a lift to the house. I might be able to get the glass to repair the windows when our supplier opens for business tomorrow."

Dawn edged toward the barstools at the breakfast bar. She needed to sit before her legs gave out. She climbed on the nearest stool and prayed no one saw her swaying on the seat. When Dawn glanced around, she noticed Linc watching her. Busted.

"We'll work it out." Josh turned to Trent and Linc. "Either of you get a look at the driver?"

"Not enough to help." Linc grabbed three mugs from one of the cabinets, dropped a bag of chamomile tea in each, then added water before heated one in the microwave. "The guy was Caucasian and wore a baseball cap pulled low over his forehead. I wouldn't recognize my own mother dressed like that."

When the heating cycle finished, he handed the mug to Dawn and slid another one into the microwave. "Wish I could be more help. By the time I got outside, he was gone."

With a nod, Josh walked outside to make his calls.

By the time Linc heated the other two mugs of tea, Dawn trembled all over. She knew what it was. Her father had talked about adrenaline crash often while he was in the military. Still ticked her off even though she was entitled to a small meltdown. She also had a close encounter with a killer, and the same man had decided she and Nicole were a threat. The incident happened so fast, she wouldn't recognize him if she passed him on the street.

She eyed the mug. Dawn wanted the tea but was afraid she'd spill more than she managed to drink. Maybe she'd have better luck in a few minutes.

After Linc handed Grace the final mug of tea, he tugged Dawn to her feet and wrapped his strong arms around her. Surprised, she held herself stiff for a few seconds before the scorching heat of his body began to thaw her ice cold one. Wow. He was like a furnace.

By degrees, Dawn relaxed against him, soaking up the warmth as her body processed the shock. From the safety of his arms, she noticed that Trent and Mason were holding their women, too.

When the shakes subsided, Linc loosened his hold. "Okay now?" he murmured.

Dawn nodded. "Thanks."

"Did I hurt you?"

"I'm fine."

"You sure? I hit you pretty hard."

"A bruise is better than a bullet any day."

Low-voiced conversation drew her attention to the front room. Soon, Ethan Blackhawk strode in. "Is everyone all right?"

"No injuries," Trent reported.

"Sit rep."

While Trent spoke with Ethan about the events of the past few minutes, Linc urged Dawn to retake her seat and sip the tea. While she drank, he kept his hand on her back as though reminding her of his presence and protection. As if she'd forget. The PSI instructor hit all the marks for her.

When Trent completed his summary, Ethan turned to Linc. "Your turn."

"A black pickup drove slowly up the street, turned right on Dogwood, and kept going. I didn't think anything of it until the truck reappeared five minutes later, still doing a slow crawl. This time, however, instead of simply passing the house, the driver rolled down his window and aimed a weapon. I called out a warning to Mason and Trent, and tackled Dawn to get her out of the line of fire."

The police chief's eyebrows rose. "She wasn't asleep?"

"Too revved up to sleep," Dawn said. "I was in the living room with Linc."

"Did you see anything?"

She shook her head. "I sat on the couch until Linc told me to go to the kitchen. Halfway there, he tackled me."

Ethan glanced at the others. "What about the rest of you?" When he received a negative response from them, the police chief turned back to Trent. "You have a security breach I need to know about?"

"Zane's looking into it. He's at your disposal, whatever you need. Maddox's orders."

A nod, then Ethan turned his attention to her and Nicole. "Keep your cell phone charged and on your person at all times, even inside your homes. Don't go anywhere alone. Be aware of your surroundings. Keep your doors and windows locked. If you have an alarm system, use it."

"What is the chance that this is related to Trent instead of us?" Nicole asked.

"Slim to none. If you wondered whether the killer considered you a threat, you can take this incident as your answer. If he's bold enough to come after you here, he won't give up until we stop him or you're dead."

CHAPTER EIGHT

Mason and Linc positioned and secured plywood over the compromised living room window while Nicole and Dawn watched from the couch. His bride-to-be nudged her friend. "Nice view."

"Best in town."

Eyebrows arched, Mason glanced at Linc, then over his shoulder. He chuckled. "It's the latest trend in home remodeling."

"We're not talking about the plywood, baby. We're interested in the men hanging the plywood."

Oh, brother. He blew out a breath. Although glad Nicole felt good enough to tease him, his cheeks burned at the compliment. "What did you put in that tea?" he muttered to his friend.

"Nothing to cause that response." He shook his head when Nicole and Dawn laughed. "The women are enjoying this way too much."

"There's something about men with tools," Dawn said.

Definitely time for a change of topic. "We have three hours before we need to get moving. You should try to sleep. Linc and I will keep an eye on everything."

"How?" Nicole eyed the plywood-covered window. "We could have an army of terrorists setting up in the front yard and not know it."

"One of us will keep watch at the back door. The other will go to the security room to watch the monitors," Linc said. "We'll know if the shooter is making another attempt."

Dawn folded her arms over her stomach. "Do you think he will?"

"I think he'll regroup and come up with another plan."

"That doesn't make me feel better."

His gaze held hers. "It's the truth. Would you rather I lie to you?"

"Never."

Mason put in the last screw and stepped back, Linc's words sinking deep. Was his friend right? If so, Nicole was in more danger than he'd realized. How could he protect her from an unknown assailant?

He set his screw gun on the floor beside his toolbox and crossed to her side. "Couch or recliner?" Trent had purchased a high-end recliner that was almost as comfortable as a bed.

Nicole looked at her friend. "You mind if I take the recliner? Elevating my upper body might help with the headache."

"No problem."

Mason glanced at Linc. "I'll take the back of the house. You have more expertise with the security system and monitors."

The PSI instructor turned to Dawn. "If you leave the living room for any reason, stay away from the windows. I'll be in the security room if you need me."

Her gaze followed him as he left the room. Nicole smiled. Romance was blooming. Sweet.

"Do you need anything, Nicole?" Mason crouched in front of her. "Grace said you could take over-the-counter pain medicine now."

She brushed his lips with her own. "I'm okay. Please don't worry about me."

"I love you." More than he ever thought possible. She was an unexpected gift.

Her smile pushed away the last of the coldness that had settled in his body after the shooting. "Good thing since I intend to marry you."

"I'll be close if either of you need me. If something spooks you, come to me." He couldn't help but steal another kiss before he took up his post at the back door of the darkened kitchen.

For the next two hours, he watched as leaves and branches swayed in the breeze. At the one-hour mark, a neighbor's cat strolled through the yard. While he watched the sky lighten to a pearl gray, Nicole and Dawn began to stir in the living room.

Soon, Grace entered the kitchen. "Good morning, Mason." She smiled. "Again."

"At least this time, you weren't woken by a hail of bullets."

She opened a cabinet and grabbed supplies to make a fresh pot of coffee. "Are you working today?"

He'd been wrestling with that question during his vigil at the door. "Brian is depending on me and I don't want to let him down." Skipping work would bring Ethan Blackhawk down on his back, a problem he didn't need. The police chief was a tough taskmaster.

Trent walked in, hair still glistening from a shower. He was dressed in the typical Fortress uniform of black cargo pants and black t-shirt. "All quiet?" he asked Mason.

"The only movement I saw was a white cat out hunting."

"Snowball." Grace grabbed more mugs from the cabinet. "He loves to hunt at night."

"You're off duty, Mase." Trent clapped him on the shoulder.

He turned away from his watch position. "I'll let you know if I can't line up the glass replacement today."

Mason walked into the living room in time to see Nicole lower the foot rest of the recliner. He kissed her. "How do you feel?"

"Not bad considering a hard object collided with my head yesterday. No nausea this morning and my headache is manageable. I need to go home to get ready for work and so does Dawn."

The other groomer swung her feet to the floor in front of the couch and sat up. "Any chance you can drop us off before you head to work?"

"I'll take you ladies to your vehicles." Linc walked into the living room. "Josh checked them an hour ago. They're clean."

Nicole frowned. "Why would someone…" Her voice trailed off as she understood the implication of Linc's statement. "The killer might have circled back and either planted a bomb or tampered with something."

Linc nodded.

"How would the killer reach the vehicles with the police at Riva's place overnight?"

"I could do it. Bravo and Durango could slip in and rig the vehicles. It's not as hard as you think. Just takes a bit of luck and stealth."

"Comforting thought." Dawn grimaced. "Now I'll be paranoid every time I start up my truck."

"Caution is always wise," Trent said as he walked into the room with mugs of coffee for Mason and Linc. "Plan's the same?"

Linc glanced at Mason, eyebrow raised in silent question.

Mason nodded. He didn't like handing off responsibility for Nicole's safety to someone else, but he didn't have much choice.

His bride-to-be frowned. "What plan?"

"Linc will stay at Pet Palace until I'm off work at 3:00. I'll take over guard duty so he can teach a night class for the instructor covering Linc's day classes."

"I'm bringing lunch." Trent smiled. "A food delivery from That's A Wrap is acceptable for lunch?"

Nicole and Dawn looked at each other. "Babysitters." Nicole sounded disgusted. "That's not necessary, you know."

Mason wrapped his hand around hers. "While you're capable of defending yourself, that doesn't mean you have to shoulder the burden alone." Not while he drew breath. He wanted to shield her from danger.

Dawn smiled. "Nice dodge, Mason."

"Effective, too." Nicole narrowed her eyes at him. "I'll let you get by with it this time."

He'd take that for a start and come up with other angles to protect her as long as the threat to her life remained. "Are you hungry?"

"A little. Not much is open this early, though."

"I can stop at Delaney's, Perk, or the bakery for to-go breakfast for the four of us. Your choice."

Nicole looked at her friend. "Perk?"

"Fine with me. Linc?"

"Any of those options work for me."

"Good." Mason gave Nicole a gentle push toward the hallway. "We need to leave in 30 minutes." He waited until the women returned to their rooms before he faced Trent. "Did you talk to Ethan?"

"Yeah. So far, the cops haven't come up with much from their end."

"What about Fortress?"

"The tech geeks sent the security footage to Ethan along with still shots. Apparently, the shooter removed his license plate before he drove into town. His truck doesn't have distinguishing marks, and the camera never got a good shot of his face."

Not what he wanted to hear. "Anything from Zane yet?"

"A text to tell me he's working on a higher priority task and my request is next in line. He'll get to it in a few hours, Mase."

"The way our luck is running, he won't find anything."

"Have a little faith. If there's information out there, Zane will be all over it."

Easy for him to say. His wife wasn't the target of a killer. "I want to know as soon as you hear something."

"You have his number. Use it. You're part of the Fortress family, Mason, and by extension, so is Nicole. Z won't mind direct communication."

Zane Murphy, the communications and tech guru, was always busy. From what Mason had learned while serving as backup for night watch, the man didn't sleep much and was fiercely devoted to Fortress and his family. He'd also saved operatives lives several times over the years with his skill, including the life of Mason's cousin.

He gave a short nod. "I'll contact him when I'm on a break today. Hopefully, he'll have information to help Ethan and Rod with this investigation." At least this time, Mason couldn't be accused of shooting up Trent's home.

At that moment, Trent's cell phone rang. He checked the screen. "Z, you're on speaker with Grace, Linc Creed, and Mason."

"I only have a minute. The Texas team is in a hot zone. I ran a scan on you, Grace, Mason, Nicole, the rest of Bravo and Durango plus their wives. The teams and spouses are in the clear. No new activity to raise a red flag."

Mason's gut tightened.

"It's Linc," the PSI instructor said. "I'm still clear?"

"Someone in Otter Creek posted a picture of you on social media a few days ago. I removed that and haven't detected any elevated interest in you or your aliases. No surprises with your family, either."

That left him and Nicole. Mason braced for the inevitable. "Let's have it, Zane."

"Your name has popped up in several searches. I'm in the process of tracing the origination of the inquiries. Same with Nicole except the inquiries on her are a lot more extensive." A few seconds of silence, then, "I have to go. I'll contact you as soon as I have more." And he was gone.

"You don't know that you're to blame for this," Linc said to Mason, his voice soft. "Don't take that on unnecessarily."

"It's sure not Nicole."

"Are you saying you're responsible for Riva's death?" Trent folded his arms. "I'm not buying it."

His hands fisted. "Of course not, but you can't deny I'm the common denominator."

Grace laid her hand on his forearm. "All the facts aren't in, Mason."

"Rod Kelter is already mentally fitting me for an orange jumpsuit."

"You're not a killer."

"That's where you're wrong." He'd already killed a young mother and her toddler through his own stupidity, something he would never allow himself to forget. The course of his whole life changed the moment he'd climbed behind the wheel of his car after drinking heavily at his college graduation party. "Anyone tries to harm Nicole again, I'll defend her by whatever means are necessary." Even if he had to pay for his actions with more years behind bars.

CHAPTER NINE

Mason followed behind Linc's SUV as his friend drove to Riva's with Dawn, alert for trouble. He might not have all the specialized training of a Fortress operative, but he could run interference if trouble came calling.

He parked behind Linc and circled the hood of his truck to open Nicole's door. "Wait here until I'm sure your SUV is safe to drive." Although Nicole didn't have far to drive, Mason refused to allow her to crank the engine until he was positive someone hadn't tampered with her vehicle.

Nicole rested her hand over his heart. "Josh checked it two hours ago. I'm sure it's fine."

"I'm not. You mean more to me than anything or anyone else in my life. It's my responsibility to take care of you, a responsibility I don't take lightly. You are my greatest treasure, Nicole." Without her, his life had no meaning or purpose.

Her expression softened. "Have I told you how much I love you, Mason Kincaid?"

"Not in the past few hours."

"How remiss of me. I'm blaming the head injury for that lapse. I love you. Thank you for checking my vehicle and keeping me safe."

He relaxed his grip on the frame of his truck, relieved he wouldn't have to insist. His lady was independent and stubborn, and he adored her. Her safety, however, was an area where he wouldn't budge. "I won't be long."

After a brief kiss, Mason closed the passenger door again to better protect her and circled Nicole's SUV, searching for signs of tampering. Rio's teammate, Nate, was one of the best EOD men in the business and Mason had spent several hours with him over the past two years, learning the signs of sabotage in vehicles. Never thought he'd have to use the knowledge he'd gained to safeguard the woman he loved.

While he searched, he noticed Linc searching Dawn's vehicle. If anything was wrong, the PSI weapons master would know.

Mason dropped to his stomach and surveyed the vehicle's undercarriage. Nothing that shouldn't be there. Breathing easier, he returned to Nicole. "All clear. I'll follow you to work, then pick up breakfast."

"You're going to spoil me, Mason."

"I'm taking care of you," he corrected. "You'll stay in the shop today?"

"We have back-to-back grooming appointments until six o'clock tonight. I'll barely have time to eat lunch much less step outside of the shop."

"If you need to go out for any reason, don't go without an escort. If I'm not available, Ethan might have an officer available or Trent could send one of the bodyguard trainees with you."

Nicole pressed her lips to his. "Don't worry. I won't go anywhere without taking along a big, burly male I trust."

"Thanks."

"Hey, I don't want to be responsible for you slamming a hammer onto your thumb rather than a nail."

His lips twitched. "I appreciate that." He turned as Linc approached. "Clean?"

"No tampering. You?"

"Same."

Linc's brows knitted. "I'm surprised the killer didn't try to rig up something even with the police activity. He had the perfect opportunity after he shot up Trent's house. Most of the third-shift cops were securing the new scene."

It was curious. Maybe the killer didn't have the knowledge necessary. How could that be, though? A simple search of the Internet would yield directions for a bomb. Low-tech sabotage would have also been effective. Nicking a brake line or dumping sugar in a gas tank would make Nicole and Dawn vulnerable to another attack. "I'll follow you to the salon, then get breakfast."

"You'll be late for work," Nicole said.

"I'll call Brian and explain." Mason held out his hand. "Come on. You need to be at the salon soon in order to set up for your first customer."

That brought a smile to her face. "My favorite four-footed guy, Tank, is coming."

"Tank?" Linc's eyebrows rose.

"He's a big chocolate Lab with a heart of gold and the sweetest disposition ever. Don't rat me out, but I'd do his grooming for free just to have a chance to work on him."

He chuckled. "Can't wait to meet him."

A short time later, the entourage headed toward Pet Palace. On the drive, Mason called his boss. "It's Mason. I'll be a little late this morning."

"You forget to set your alarm?" Brian teased.

"No, sir." He summarized the events of the previous evening and early this morning. "Linc and I are escorting Dawn and Nicole to the grooming salon to be sure they arrive safely. Want me to bring you something since I'm picking up breakfast for the others anyway?"

"I wouldn't turn it down. I'm running late, too, which is why I'll be arriving at the Oakdale site with an empty stomach."

"Thanks, Brian. I'll make up the time."

"Mase, you work over frequently without turning in the extra time. If anything, I owe you. Are the cops hassling you about Riva's death and Nicole's injury?"

Trust his boss to cut to the chase. "They'll uncover the real culprit soon." Being Ethan and Rod's primary suspect in Riva's murder and Nicole's attack rankled. No question that he was innocent of the drive-by shooting. Of course, he could have had an accomplice pull the trigger. He grimaced. Yet more fallout from his conviction and prison sentence.

"If you need me to put in a good word for you with Ethan, let me know. I'll be happy to vouch for you."

"I'll see you in an hour with breakfast." He ended the call as he turned into the lot in front of Pet Palace and parked beside Nicole's SUV.

He opened the driver's door for her and walked Nicole inside the shop. While she and Dawn turned on lights and booted up the computer, he and Linc checked each room in the shop for signs of a break-in. Everything was normal. Excellent.

Back in the reception area, Mason cupped Nicole's cheek as he leaned in for a quick kiss. "I'll be back in a few minutes."

"Something light for me," she murmured. "I'm not up to a full meal this morning."

Concern knotted his stomach. "Are you feeling sick again?"

"A little. It's not bad. Maybe the patch Matt used is wearing off."

And maybe Nicole was downplaying how she felt so he wouldn't worry. He looked at Linc with a pointed glance. The PSI instructor's lips twitched as he inclined his head in acknowledgment of Mason's silent order to look after Nicole.

After another brush of his lips over hers, Mason drove to Perk and ordered food and drinks for five. When he returned to the salon, he placed the food and drink carrier on the counter.

He tapped the largest of the three cups. "Tea for you, Nicole. The other two contain coffee. I bought a bagel for you. Take it easy today. If you need me, call. I'll get here as soon as I can."

"I'll be fine. Go."

As he left the salon, Mason held the door open for Tank and his owner to enter.

"Tank!" Nicole leaned down and hugged the Lab. "It's about time JT brought you in. I've been missing you, buddy."

The dog's 80-year-old owner chuckled. "Tank and I have been visiting my grandchildren. We just returned to Otter Creek yesterday."

Mason smiled as he cranked the truck's ignition and backed out of the parking space. At least, Nicole's day had started off with a favorite customer. He'd have to call and check on her at his break time.

Another idea occurred to him, one that would be sure to irritate Nicole but give him peace of mind. As soon as he parked at the Oakdale job site, Mason called Matt.

"Rainer."

"It's Mason. I need a favor."

"Name it."

"If you have time between classes today, swing by Pet Palace and check on Nicole."

"She's worse?"

"I don't think so. Grace kept tabs on her during the night, but I'd feel better if you evaluated her yourself. Nicole is complaining about nausea again this morning."

"I have a break around 10:00. Is that soon enough?"

"That's perfect. Thanks, Matt."

"No problem. Everything quiet overnight?"

He told the medic about the shooting."

A soft whistle came over the speaker. "Brazen or desperate. You have someone watching over Dawn and Nicole today?"

"Linc. I'll take over at 3:00."

"I'll be glad to lend a hand if you need someone else to take a shift. The other members of Bravo and Durango will be glad to help, too."

"Thanks."

"Anytime, Mason." The medic ended the call.

Mason grabbed the bag of food from Perk along with the coffee. He sincerely hoped the extra-large coffee worked its magic on him. Although he didn't regret staying awake all night to watch over Nicole, Mason was feeling the lack of sleep already.

He found Brian at one of the Oakdale apartment complex buildings and handed his boss breakfast.

Gene Patton, one of Mason's co-workers, turned, nail gun in his hand. "Sucking up to the boss because you're late, Kincaid?"

Mason's friend, Dean Conner, caught his eye and shook his head slightly. Yeah, he was right. He couldn't let Patton's lousy attitude set him off over something so simple. The cantankerous worker would have plenty to rib Mason over before the day was out. Otter Creek's grapevine was sure to carry news of Riva's death and the police interest in Mason soon.

Brian frowned at Patton. "Knock it off." He turned back to Mason. "Nicole and Dawn are taken care of for today?"

"Yes, sir."

"Excellent. Let's get moving. Take Dean to Building 10 and finish the punch out." He handed Mason a clipboard with the checklists. "After that, go to Building 8 and do the same there. The inspector will be on site tomorrow morning at 7:00."

"Who's scheduled to do the inspection?"

"Noel Manning."

Mason blew out a breath. Great. Manning was notorious for finding fault no matter how meticulous their work. Made Mason doubly glad he'd purchased the largest cup of coffee sold at Perk. "We'll be ready." He glanced at his friend. "Come on, Dean. We have a boatload of work to complete."

Dean picked up his toolbox and followed Mason outside. "I'll meet you at Building 10." The dark-haired man climbed into his truck and cranked the engine.

Five minutes later, the two men carried their tools into the building and began to work down the list, checking off items as they completed each task. In the last unit, Mason noted several of the outlets weren't working. "Who worked on this unit?"

"Patton and Fisher."

Of course. Gene Patton and Ed Fisher were thick as thieves and lazy. "They missed a few things."

Dean snorted. "They always do. I bet the nuts aren't tightened enough on the pipes, either."

"You want the outlets or the pipes?"

"I'll take the outlets. You're the plumbing king."

Twenty minutes later, Mason found Dean still fixing the outlets. "Need a hand?"

"Yeah." Disgust rang in his voice. "None of the outlets work. They slapped on the outlet covers before they connected the wires. Maybe it was a mistake."

"More likely they did it deliberately to look good in front of Brian. Patton's angling for a promotion."

"If Brian can't see the truth about him, I might have to look for another job. I don't think I can work under him with his shoddy workmanship. Someone is going to get hurt if Patton keeps cutting corners."

Between the two of them, they connected wires in the outlets and tested them before covering them again. When they secured the last screw, Mason and Dean continued with the checklist, finding more mistakes and fixing them.

Two hours beyond the time Mason had allotted for the punch list, he and his partner drove to their next assigned building to check the work and do the finishing touches. Manning would check everything. Mason and Dean were determined to make sure the picky inspector didn't find anything to complain about.

They found more issues in Building 8. Mason scowled. "Let me guess. Patton and Fisher again?"

"Who else?" Dean sipped coffee from his to-go cup. "What are you going to do?"

"Fix their mess because I don't want Elliott Construction blamed for the lousy work, then report the issues to Brian." Mason glanced at his watch. "I'm not sure I'll have time to talk to the boss before I need to leave today."

"Doing something with Nicole?"

"Keeping her safe. Linc Creed is watching her and Dawn until I'm off."

Dean's eyebrows knitted. "What's going on?" When Mason finished his explanation, his friend dragged a hand down his face. "Good grief, Mase. Kelter and the police chief think you're guilty of murder and assault?"

His gut twisted at the thought. "They labeled me a person of interest."

"Do yourself a favor, buddy. Make sure you can account for every minute of your time from now on until they unmask the real killer. Otherwise, you may find yourself behind bars again. Plenty of people in town will point a finger at you."

Mason sighed. "The same people who refuse to let me inside their homes without someone else from Elliott Construction to make sure I don't steal the silver or family jewels."

"They're wrong about you."

He eyed his friend. "How do you know? Maybe I've snowed you like I have every other citizen in Otter Creek."

Sadness filled Dean's eyes. "I've met the worst of mankind. You aren't anything like them."

"Need to get something off your chest?" Mason had suspected for several months that Dean had a difficult past. Although he'd offered to listen before, his friend had never taken him up on the invitation. Would he this time?

The other man shook his head. "It doesn't matter now. Those people are in the past."

His face, drained of color, hinted that he couldn't talk about his background, that perhaps he'd slipped and told too much. Good enough for Mason. He was familiar with operatives who couldn't talk about their work. "If you change your mind, I know how to keep secrets." He smiled. "It's a necessity in my family."

That brought a short laugh. "I'll bet."

"Come on. Let's go to the next unit. I'm guessing we have more mistakes to fix and we're running short on time."

By the end of the workday, Mason and Dean had finished their punch lists as well as repaired or completed tasks that should have been done already.

Mason gave a brief verbal report to his boss about the shoddy workmanship and handed over the lists he and Dean had completed during the day.

Brian scowled. "Are you sure it was Patton and Fisher?"

He nodded. "Dean and I noted every task we either had to do from scratch or repair. Check the paper trail to confirm the responsible parties."

His boss rubbed the back of his neck. "I'll check into it after Manning's visit tomorrow. In the meantime, keep an eye out for anything that should have been finished and isn't. Don't go out of your way, Mason, but if you see evidence of a problem, I want to know about it."

"Yes, sir."

Brian waved him on. "Go. I know you're worried about Nicole. I need you on site tomorrow morning by six."

"I'll be here." With a vat full of coffee. Man, he was tired. How would he be able to stay awake to protect Nicole? With a wave, he climbed into his truck and drove toward town.

When he passed the Otter Creek B & B on the outskirts of town, he glanced at the man exiting a luxury SUV. Mason's breath caught when the stranger turned enough for him to see his face.

A ball of ice formed in his stomach. No, not now. Not when things were chaotic and he was under suspicion for another crime, this one he hadn't committed. The timing couldn't be worse.

Although he was tempted to turn around and confront the man, Mason continued into town. Nicole was his priority. His past could wait. Hands gripping the wheel, he vowed to track the other man down and find out what he was doing in town. Mason had served his time, and he wouldn't allow his past to hurt Nicole.

CHAPTER TEN

Nicole blew an escaped strand of hair out of her eyes and slipped the perky red collar back on Violet, the Australian Shepherd. "You are one beautiful girl, Violet. Your mom will be so happy to see you, especially now that you don't smell like a skunk."

"The new de-skunking shampoo is amazing." Dawn glanced up with a smile as she swept the last of the dog hair into a large dust pan and dumped the contents into the trash. "How many times has Violet been up close and personal with a skunk?"

"The score is five to zero. The skunks have won every skirmish."

"Ugh. I can only imagine how potent she was right after she was sprayed or how rank her owner's vehicle is now."

The grooming room had a faint skunk odor lingering in the air. Skunk scent hung around for a long time. "Gretchen took her SUV to be cleaned. Her ride home with Violet should be much more pleasant."

The bell over the front door rang as another customer walked inside the salon. Nicole frowned. "Did another appointment book? I thought we were ahead by 30 minutes." She'd been looking forward to a 20-minute power nap or an extra-large coffee or both.

Dawn shrugged. "Charlie is our next grooming appointment. Maybe Heidi is dropping him off early. Want me to check Charlie in?"

Uneasy for some reason, Nicole shook her head. "I'm finished with Violet if you want to put her in a holding crate. If we keep moving as fast as we are now, we might finish early today."

"Hey, I won't complain about that." Dawn covered her yawn. "We didn't sleep much last night. I'm glad we had Linc, Mason, and Trent on hand when the shooter showed up." She crossed to Nicole's side and attached a leash to Violet's collar. "Come on, sweet girl. Mom should be here soon."

Nicole opened the door to the reception area, thankful her part-time appointment setter had agreed to come in today to help out. Expecting to see Charlie, another Lab, and his owner, she came to an abrupt halt when she spotted a tall, dark-haired man in his late thirties, someone she'd never seen around town or in her shop. A new resident looking for a pet groomer? Pet Palace was the only business in town that fit the bill.

As she started forward, a furtive movement out on the street caught her eye. Her breath froze in her lungs. No. It couldn't be. Pedestrians walked between her shop and the blast from her past. When the crowd had moved on, the man she thought she recognized was gone. She must have been mistaken. Ivan had no business in Otter Creek.

Linc was watching the stranger in the shop closely from the other side of the lobby while Nicole's helper, Ryan, talked with him about their services. The shop assistant glanced her direction and smiled. "This is Nicole Copeland. She owns Pet Palace and can answer all your questions about the services we offer."

She stepped behind the desk to stand beside Ryan after catching Linc's warning glance. "May I help you?"

He studied her a moment, then appeared to come to a decision. "I'm here to help you."

Was this man a salesman? "If you're selling pet grooming supplies, leave me your contact information and website address. When I'm ready to order more product, I'll take a look at what you're offering."

"I'm not selling anything, Ms. Copeland. I'm offering you a friendly warning."

Linc moved closer to the stranger, ready to intervene if necessary.

Nicole glanced at Ryan. "Take a break. I'll cover the desk for a few minutes."

The college student glanced at Linc who gave him a slight nod.

Once Ryan was out of the room, Nicole turned back to the man staring at her with a wealth of sadness in his eyes. "Who are you?" she demanded.

"Todd Fitzgerald."

"Well, Todd Fitzgerald, here's the thing about advice. You can offer, but I'm free to accept or reject it. Say what you have to say and we'll both move on."

Fitzgerald glanced at Linc before refocusing on Nicole. "Is there a place where we can talk in private?"

"No," Linc said. "Here or nowhere."

"Say your piece, Mr. Fitzgerald." Nicole's hands fisted. "We're slammed today."

He shrugged. "Suit yourself."

"I usually do. Talk or leave."

"I understand you're involved with Mason Kincaid."

Her cheeks burned. She could understand friends and family expressing concern but not a total stranger. "We're getting married soon."

"You should rethink your decision."

"Because?"

"He's a murderer."

Fury exploded in her gut. "Do you live in Otter Creek, Mr. Fitzgerald?"

"I'm from a small town outside of Summerton."

She scowled. "You're from Liberty?"

Fitzgerald inclined his head.

This man must be related to the woman killed in Mason's accident. "I'm sorry for the loss of your family members, Mr. Fitzgerald, but Mason paid for his mistake. You can't keep harassing him because you're still hurting. The law says he has the right to a life. Do yourself a favor, and go home."

"You're still going to marry him? Even after what he did?"

"I love him. He's a good man who learned a hard lesson. I'm honored that he asked me to marry him."

"You're making a huge mistake. You can't trust him. What if the next time he drinks and drives, you're in the car with him or your kids? Think hard before you marry him. I don't want what happened to my sister-in-law and niece to happen to you."

"You don't know him, Mr. Fitzgerald. Mason is a man of honor and integrity. Go home and be with your family. They need you to be strong for them."

Cheeks flushing, he grabbed her wrist and squeezed. "You're a fool, Ms. Copeland. I'm trying to save you from my sister-in-law's fate. She was murdered by your boyfriend before she could watch her baby grow up. I don't want the same to happen to you."

Before Nicole could tear her arm from his grasp, Linc latched onto Fitzgerald's wrist with a punishing grip. "Leave now or I will throw you out."

The other man hissed and released his hold on Nicole. "I'm just trying to help."

Nicole held up her hand to hold off Linc's rebuttal. "I understand your motivation, but this conversation is over. If you don't have a pet for me to groom, I'll have to ask you to leave Pet Palace."

He stepped back. "I hope you don't regret your decision." Fitzgerald strode out the door as Heidi and Charlie came in.

Her eyebrows rose as she approached the desk. "Unhappy customer?"

"Just a man with an agenda." As Linc and Heidi exchanged greetings, Nicole came around the desk and rubbed Charlie's head. "Hey, buddy. How's it going?"

The dog barked.

"That good, huh? I guess Heidi and Quinn have been treating you like a prince." She turned to Heidi. "The usual?"

"Please. We've been on three S & R missions in the past three weeks. Charlie found two lost hikers and a lost child."

Nicole took his leash and led him toward the workroom. "Good job, buddy." To Heidi, she said, "I'll give you a call when he's ready. Probably three hours, though."

"No rush. See you soon, Charlie."

Linc remained silent until the door closed behind Heidi. "Are you okay?"

"I'm fine." Mostly. Fitzgerald had a grip on him.

"If you're not, Mason will take it out on me."

Nicole had started to turn but froze at the instructor's words. "You can't be afraid of him. You have tons more training than he does. Mason might get in a few punches, but you could wipe the floor with him. Don't do it, though. I'm partial to that handsome face of his."

"You don't know your husband-to-be very well, Nic."

"What do you mean?"

"What do you think he's been doing when you work late?"

"I assumed he was at home or running errands."

"Even though he can't have a weapon, he's been training hard with Bravo and Durango on self-defense skills."

No wonder he was in such good shape. Nicole had thought his prime physique was from the construction work. "Why?"

"To be able to protect you better. Haven't you figured out that everything he does is with you in mind?"

Tears stung her eyes. She should have known his reasoning. She'd seen for herself the lengths he went to for those he loved. Now, Nicole was the center of his world.

She grinned. "I think I'll ask him to let me watch the next time he joins a training session with them. I think it would be fun." Certainly entertaining.

Linc snorted. "Fun? Bravo and Durango don't spare Mase when they train with him. He's becoming as tough and skilled as they are."

Huh. Good to know.

Dawn walked into the reception area. She smiled. "Charlie! How's my buddy?"

The Lab barked.

She took the leash from Nicole. "I'll take him on back. Take a break and put your feet up for a few minutes. You're pale."

"Pain meds would be welcome along with a soft drink."

"I'll send Ryan back out. Relax for a few minutes while I shampoo this handsome boy."

Nicole answered two calls by the time Ryan arrived and took over the appointment desk. "Need anything, Linc?" she asked.

"I won't say no to a soft drink."

The next hour passed at a fast pace as she and Dawn groomed Charlie and three other dogs that arrived for baths and nail buffing. Nicole shook her head at the antics of the Silky Terriers, three sisters who livened the shop's back room with yapping and their attempts to escape the dryer. None of the three were fans of the noisy contraption.

Once they finished with the terriers, Nicole and Dawn tied a different colored scarf to each small neck and placed the dogs in crates to wait for their owner to pick them up. The din of their protest was deafening. Nicole was glad to escape the cacophony.

She poked her head into the reception area. "Call Tori and tell her the triplets are ready," she told Ryan.

"Yes, ma'am."

The bell over the front door rang and in walked Mason. Although he smiled, that sentiment didn't reach his eyes. Something was wrong. Nicole walked into his open arms and hugged him. "I'm glad to see you. I missed you today."

"I missed you, too." He raised her hand to his mouth to kiss the back. When Mason lowered her hand, he glanced down and froze. He shifted her arm so her wrist was in a patch of sunlight. "What happened?"

Rats. Nicole had hoped he wouldn't notice the bruises forming where Fitzgerald gripped her arm. Should have known that wouldn't be the case. Mason noticed everything. She hoped she was as observant about Mason. "It's nothing. Don't worry about it."

"Nic."

When she glanced at him, Linc shook his head slightly. She scowled. This wasn't a good idea.

Mason cupped her chin and turned her face toward his. "Tell me."

"Todd Fitzgerald."

Color drained from his cheeks. "Fitzgerald came to the shop?"

She nodded.

"What did he want?"

"He warned me not to marry you. I told him to leave."

Mason turned narrowed eyes toward Linc. "You didn't stop him from touching her?"

"Hey." Nicole poked Mason in the gut with her finger. "I can take care of myself. I was getting ready to break his hold on my wrist when Linc did it for me."

"Fitzgerald hurt you."

"You know I bruise easy. He gripped my wrist for a few seconds at most so don't blame Linc."

Linc shook his head. "Mase is right. It's on me. I should have been close enough to break his hold immediately." He looked at Mason. "I'm sorry. I won't allow that to happen again. You have my word."

Mason wrapped his arms around Nicole and pulled her close. He gave a slight nod to Linc, accepting the apology. "I've got the watch. You have a class soon."

"I'll text you when I'm finished at PSI. You can tell me where to meet you, and we'll figure out how to set up for tonight." With that, Linc left the shop.

"I'm fine," Nicole murmured. He had to believe her. Otherwise, Mason might confront Fitzgerald. That wouldn't be a good thing.

"I should have been here."

"You have to work, and so do I. The bruises will fade soon." She brushed her lips over his and stepped back. "I need to get back to it. We have two more dogs arriving soon. Dawn and I will have to work fast to finish on time. We would have been finished already, but we had a dog emergency earlier."

Mason frowned. "One of the dogs was hurt?"

"Nope. Violet decided to play with a skunk this morning."

He grimaced. "I hope your treatment was successful."

"De-skunking shampoo is a life saver." Another kiss, then Nicole turned toward the back room. "Ryan, we don't have time to work in any latecomers now. Unless we have another skunk emergency, the rest of the horde without an appointment will have to wait until tomorrow."

"Yes, ma'am. I'll pass the word."

She hurried to the back room and joined Dawn in bathing a gorgeous white German Shepherd named Annie. The sweet dog was a shy one who had taken a shine to both of her groomers and took every opportunity given to share doggy kisses.

The next two hours passed in a blur of activity. By the time the last pet left the salon, Nicole was about ready to drop from fatigue and Dawn didn't look in any better shape. "Let's clean up and get out of here. I hear takeout calling my name."

"Me, too."

The two women dragged themselves through the cleaning process and set everything up for the next day. Thankfully, the start time was two hours later. Maybe she and Dawn would be able to sleep in a little. With her head pounding, she couldn't think through the logistics of having a bodyguard stick around until 8:00. For Mason and Linc, that was late to begin their day.

Hopefully, Rod or Ethan would identify the killer soon and put him behind bars. She was ready for her life to go back to normal.

When the salon was ready for business the next day, Nicole closed the door to the supply closet with a snick. "Done. Let's get out of here."

She and Dawn walked to the reception area where Ryan was closing down the computer for the day. "Need me to come in tomorrow, Nicole?" he asked.

"Don't you have classes in the morning?"

His face flushed. "I have skip days available."

"You might be my future doctor one day. I'll pass on the offer of help until your regular shift tomorrow. We have fewer grooming appointments booked. We'll handle the load until you're free from class."

"If you change your mind, text me."

"Thanks." She wouldn't do that to him. He'd worked hard to get a scholarship to the community college in town.

From there, Ryan planned to transfer to East Tennessee State University for the rest of his studies, including medical school.

While she and Dawn waited in the office, Mason checked the windows and doors in Pet Palace. After he reported that everything was locked, he escorted them to their vehicles. "We're staying at my house tonight. Linc will split the watch shift with me and Matt."

"You asked Matt to stop by the shop to check on me today, didn't you?"

"If I couldn't be here myself, I wanted someone I trusted to look in on you. Since you weren't feeling well this morning, I preferred someone with medical expertise. He was happy to do it, Nicole."

Such a caring, thoughtful man. She laid her hand against his cheek. "Thank you for taking such good care of me."

"I'll do what's necessary to keep you safe."

CHAPTER ELEVEN

Refreshed from showering off the day's dirt and sweat, Mason stood at the front window keeping watch while Nicole and Dawn showered and changed clothes. As he studied the street in front of his house, he considered his options.

His hands clenched into tight fists. Those choices were slim. He was already under watch by the police. He'd spotted a cruiser tailing him more than once today. He understood their reasoning, but the action still made him angry. He wasn't guilty of anything, unlike 15 years ago. He'd made a lousy choice and paid for it long and hard, and now carried a load of guilt that nothing could ease. But he wasn't that same 22-year-old who believed himself capable of handling anything, including alcohol.

Mason couldn't let Fitzgerald's encroachment into Nicole's shop go unchallenged. He also couldn't let the confrontation become physical. If he did, he'd land in jail and leave Nicole defenseless. Fitzgerald's animosity should be directed toward him, not Nicole. The man had no right to drag her into the middle of this unwanted trip down memory lane.

He knew where Fitzgerald was staying if he hadn't left town already. If the man was still at the B & B, he'd ask him to leave Nicole alone.

Soon, a black SUV pulled into the driveway and parked. When Matt exited the vehicle with his mike bag in hand, Mason opened the door for the medic. "Thanks for helping out tonight, Matt," he said when his friend entered the house.

"No problem." He smiled. "Delilah will wait up for me. How is Nicole?"

"Still has a headache."

A frown. "Is it as bad as last night?"

"She hasn't said."

"I'll talk to her." Matt indicated his bag. "I planned to check her over anyway. I want to be sure she's improving."

"I am." Nicole walked into the living room and curled up at the end of the couch. "I'm able to control the headache with over-the-counter medicine and I haven't been as nauseated this afternoon."

"Good to hear. I still want to check your cut and your pupils."

She frowned. "Are you sure you shouldn't be a doctor?"

The medic chuckled. "Maybe when I'm ready to stop going on missions with Bravo. Fortress could use more doctors on staff."

"Isn't Linc coming?" Nicole asked Mason.

"His class ends at 10:00. He'll take over the watch from Matt. My shift starts at 1:00 a.m." He turned back to the other man. "I'm going out to pick up dinner. Is Delaney's special all right with you?" When he received a nod, Mason kissed Nicole and headed back to the town square.

Halfway to his destination, he turned right on Pine and drove toward the B & B. Wouldn't hurt to see if Fitzgerald's vehicle was in the lot. Five minutes later,

Mason turned into the lot and drove through slowly. No vehicles with license plates issued from his home county. Maybe Fitzgerald left town since he delivered his message to Nicole.

He snorted. Right. When had things ever been that simple for him? No, Fitzgerald had an agenda but he didn't know how far the man would go to make his point.

He mentally boxed up his frustration. Enough. He had hungry people to feed. If Fitzgerald was in town, he'd find Mason soon.

He walked into Delaney's ten minutes later. The deli only had a handful of customers in the dining area when he approached the register. "How are you, Cindy?"

A broad smile curved the lips of the grandmother of six. "Hi, Mason. I heard what happened to Nicole. How is she?"

"Better. Thanks for asking."

"If she needs anything, let me know. We love that girl and what she does for our precious fur babies. Now, what can I get for you, honey?"

That made him grin. "Five specials to go."

"Coming right up. You want some coffee while you wait?"

Did the coffee come in a gallon-size bucket? "Yes, ma'am. Thank you."

She snagged a white coffee mug and filled it with the fragrant, steaming liquid. "Have a seat, Mason. I'll put your order in. We'll have you fixed up in a few minutes."

He slid onto the padded stool and sipped the brew while listening to the quiet hum of conversation behind him. In between delivering meals and refilling drinks, he talked with Cindy about the progress on the Oakdale apartment complex.

"I can't wait for the work to be completed." She beamed. "My granddaughter is planning to rent an apartment there when she arrives for college in the fall.

She'll be sharing the space with her two best friends from high school."

"They'll enjoy living there. The complex features two nature trails, a full gym along with two pools, and plenty of green space. Your granddaughter needs to contact the leasing agent soon, though. I hear the apartments are filling up fast." He gave her the agent's name and number. He'd lost count of how many inquiries he and his boss had fielded since Elliott Construction began work on the site.

Cindy grabbed her phone and sent a text. "Thanks for the tip, Mason. I'll see if your order is ready." She hurried to the kitchen as Mason finished the last of his coffee.

A moment later, Cindy returned with a large bag. "Here you are. I added an apple pie to the bag. My treat."

After he settled the bill, Mason leaned over and kissed her cheek. "Thanks for the coffee and pie, Cindy."

"You bet, sugar. Come back and see us soon."

He turned to leave and pulled up short when he saw Todd Fitzgerald glaring daggers at him from two feet away, hands fisted, cheeks red.

Not the time or place, Mason reminded himself. He had an avid audience and didn't need citizens in the diner calling in a disturbance to Ethan.

"Fitzgerald," he said, voice soft.

"They don't know the real Mason Kincaid, do they?"

"Mason?" Cindy came out from behind the counter as conversation dropped to nothing in the diner. "Everything all right?"

He glanced at her with a wry smile. Nothing had been right since the night he graduated from college until he'd met Nicole. "Yes, ma'am. He's from my hometown."

Mason turned back to Fitzgerald. "If you want to talk, we'll go outside. Otherwise, I have meals to deliver." Noticing two people on their cell phones with their attention locked on the unfolding drama, he wondered how soon law enforcement would conveniently drive by this location.

The other man tipped his head toward the door.

Marginally better. Mason's truck was parked directly in front of the large diner windows where their eager audience could watch the action. Any action wouldn't be at his instigation.

He followed Fitzgerald outside. Once he stored the food inside the cab of his truck, Mason eyed the brother-in-law of the woman he'd killed. "Stirring up trouble for me won't bring your sister-in-law or your niece back."

"Did you get my delivery?"

The age-progressed pictures of his victims, the ones that haunted his dreams. "I got it."

"You killed them."

"Yes, I did."

The man stared. "No denials or protestations of innocence?"

"It would be a lie." He sighed. "Look, Fitzgerald, I understand you're hurting. I apologized to you and the rest of your family at the sentencing hearing. Nothing I say will make up for the loss of your family members."

"You stole their futures." His voice broke on the last word.

"I know," Mason said softly.

"You don't deserve to live when they're dead."

Pain pierced Mason's heart. "The law says otherwise. If I could go back and undo that one decision, I would do it in a heartbeat. I can't. You and your family have to live without your sister-in-law and her baby to love and cherish. I have to live with the knowledge that I caused the deaths of two innocent people, and deal with the guilt and regret every day of my life."

"You think that's enough penance, that the slate is wiped clean?"

"Nothing I do will make up for your loss or balance the scales of justice. The only thing I can do is be a man of honor and warn others of the dangers of drinking and driving."

He gripped the handle of his door. "Stay away from Nicole. She has nothing to do with the past. If you want to take your pain out on someone, come at me, not her. Like your sister-in-law, she's totally innocent. Leave her out of whatever you're planning."

Fitzgerald moved closer. "Ms. Copeland doesn't know you like I do. You're a no-good, lousy, stinking drunk. You should be wasting away behind bars where you can't kill anyone else."

Wouldn't do any good to tell Fitzgerald that he hadn't touched alcohol since the night of the accident and would never let another drop pass his lips. He didn't want to hear it, and wouldn't believe the words. "On the contrary, Nicole knows all about me, good and bad. By some miracle of God, she loves me anyway. I know it doesn't change anything, but I am sincerely sorry for my role in the loss of your sister-in-law and niece."

Fitzgerald growled, balled his hand, and slammed his fist into Mason's jaw.

CHAPTER TWELVE

Mason's head whipped sideways as pain exploded in his jaw. Blue-and-white lights lit up the night as he staggered back against the truck, hand to his jaw.

"What's going on here, Mason?"

Terrific. The police chief himself. "It's nothing, Ethan."

"Try again. I just saw this man punch you. Do you want to press charges for assault?"

He shook his head. Man, talk about pouring fuel on the fire.

"Are you sure?" Ethan pressed.

"Let it go."

The six-foot-four police chief pointed at Fitzgerald. "Step over to my vehicle. We're going to have a talk. Mason, be at my office tomorrow morning at 7:00. Don't be late."

Mason drew in a slow breath. He'd had his required meeting with Ethan the morning of Riva's death. Ethan scheduling another meeting wasn't a good sign. "Yes, sir."

Ethan motioned for Fitzgerald to precede him.

From the corner of his eye, Mason noticed a subtle movement to his right. Not far away, Gene Patton stepped back into the shadows. The confrontation with Fitzgerald ought to make Patton's day. He'd witnessed the punch and would be sure to spread the news about the fight. By the time the news spread, however, Mason was sure to seen as the aggressor.

Mason climbed into his truck and cranked the engine. His jaw ached. He'd had plenty of punches to the face and body during his years in prison.

Nicole would flip when she saw his jaw. At least he had the satisfaction of knowing that he'd warned Fitzgerald to stay away from her. She had enough to deal with without adding additional baggage from his past.

He arrived at home ten minutes later and walked into the living room with the to-go meals.

Nicole's smile of welcome faded. She scrambled to her feet as Matt moved closer to look his jaw and whistled. "What happened?"

"I ran into Fitzgerald at the diner."

Dawn frowned. "Who's Fitzgerald?"

He explained his history with the Fitzgerald family.

Matt handed him a chemically-activated ice pack, then took the bag of meals and handed them to Dawn. "Did you hit your head against anything?"

"I'm fine, Matt."

"Why didn't you defend yourself?"

Nicole threaded her fingers through Mason's. "How do you know he didn't?"

"His hands. Answer the question, Mase. You know how to deal with an attacker. Why didn't you use your training?"

"Besides the fact that diner patrons were watching from the windows, I figured he had a free shot coming. The anniversary of his sister-in-law's and niece's deaths is in two weeks."

"That doesn't give him the right to hurt you," Nicole insisted.

Matt scowled. "I know you couldn't be the aggressor without landing behind bars, but after that free shot, you should have ended the confrontation with him on the ground."

"If he'd tried to punch me again, I would have. As it was, I didn't have a chance to respond. Ethan was close enough to see what happened and lit up the night with his cruiser lights. He asked me if I wanted to press charges."

"Are you?"

He shook his head. "If he comes after me again, I will." Mason looked down at the woman he adored. "If he comes after you, all bets are off. I will take him down. No one is going to hurt you again."

"Together, Mason." She cupped his cheek with her palm. "We face everything together. We're a team. Don't forget that."

He turned and pressed a kiss to her palm. Invisible bands tightened around his chest. He didn't deserve her and never would.

"Enough mush for now. You're making me miss Delilah. What did Cindy send us?" Matt asked.

Mason tore his gaze from the woman he loved. "Chicken and dumplings, green beans, and an apple pie."

The medic rubbed his hands. "Fantastic. I'm starved."

So was Mason. Whether he'd be able to eat or not was the question. The ache in his jaw had intensified in the past few minutes. "I'll take the watch while I'm waiting for the ice to numb my jaw."

A nod. "I won't be long."

After Matt went to the kitchen, Mason pressed his forehead to Nicole's. "You should go eat, too." From the way she was leaning heavily against him, his bride-to-be was almost asleep on her feet.

She shook her head. "I'll wait for you."

No point arguing with her. Truthfully, he enjoyed holding her and, after the confrontation with Fitzgerald, Mason needed her gentle touch and comfort. The confrontation had left him scraped raw inside, ripping open wounds that never fully healed.

He guided her to the window and nudged her back against the wall to make sure she wasn't visible to anyone outside the house. With an arm around her waist, Mason eased the curtain aside.

The night was dark and peaceful. Hopefully, the killer would still be regrouping and leave them alone for the night. All of them could use sleep.

"Does it hurt?" Nicole murmured, her cheek resting against his heart.

"Oh, yeah. A kiss will make it better."

She smiled. "When you're not on watch, I'll give you as many as you want."

He groaned. "You shouldn't tempt a starving man, Ms. Copeland. I'm tempted to nibble on you instead of chicken and dumplings."

"I wouldn't protest."

A vehicle drove slowly down the street. Mason tightened his hold on Nicole. Had the killer come out of hiding after all?

When it continued past the house, he relaxed. Three other vehicles came and went before Matt returned.

"I'll keep watch from the security room. That way, I'll be able to keep track of anything happening at the front and back of the house."

"Good idea." His cousin, Rio, had installed a security room complete with a computer screen split into six sections corresponding to the security cameras mounted around the house. The room also included a weapons vault and some medical supplies. Most of his cousin's equipment and supplies were stored at the huge Victorian house where he and his wife, Darcy, lived.

After they finished their meals and cleared the table, he walked to the living room with the women.

"I'm too wound up to sleep," Dawn said.

Nicole rolled her eyes. "I think you want to wait up for a certain PSI instructor to arrive."

"I'm allowed to wait for a friend."

"A friend, huh? That's a change from a couple of days ago."

Dawn shrugged, cheeks turning pink. "Are you up for a movie while we wait?"

"I have several DVDs in the entertainment center," Mason said. "Pick what you want."

"Even a chick flick?" Nicole teased.

"Ha. I have a wide selection of good movies. No chick flicks allowed."

The women razzed him for a few minutes about his taste in movies before selecting one that he enjoyed but contained a romance storyline that he tolerated. Fifteen minutes into the movie, Nicole slept against his shoulder while Dawn snoozed in the recliner.

Smiling, he turned down the volume and switched the channel to a baseball game.

Matt went to the kitchen for more coffee during the fourth inning and smiled at the sight of the sleeping women. With a shake of his head, he returned to the security room. At 10:30, he returned. "Linc is here." He unlocked the door for the PSI instructor.

Linc walked in with his Go bag over his shoulder. His gaze tracked to Dawn, eyebrows rising. "Why didn't she go to bed?" he asked softly.

"She was waiting for you," Mason said.

Matt hoisted his mike bag onto his shoulder. "I'll leave you the watch, Linc. Delilah is waiting for me. If you need me, call." With that, he left.

Linc set his Go bag near the door and locked up behind the medic. He nodded toward the television. "Who's winning?"

"Braves."

He returned his attention to the sleeping women. "Do we wake them or let them sleep?"

Dawn stirred and opened her eyes. She smiled when she saw Linc. "Hey. You made it. Are you hungry?"

"I wouldn't say no to a meal." His eyes twinkled. "I didn't have time for dinner."

She lowered the footrest and stood. "Come on. Mason bought dinner at Delaney's."

"I see." He looked at Mason. "Is that where you got the bruise to the jaw?"

"Yeah. Long story. I'll fill you in later. Matt kept watch in the security room. Down the hall, first room on the left."

"I'll heat your dinner and bring it to you," Dawn said. "We have soft drinks, coffee, or water to drink. What's your preference?"

"Water's fine. Thanks."

She smiled and left.

"I'll be in the security room if you need me." With that, Linc walked down the hall.

Mason wanted to let Nicole sleep exactly where she was, but she'd be more comfortable in a bed. He eased away from her, then slid on arm under her knees and one behind her shoulders.

She woke with a gasp when he lifted her into his arms.

"It's all right. I'm carrying you to your room," he murmured.

"Two months and five days, and I get to sleep in your arms every night."

"I'm looking forward to that day." He kissed her forehead as he passed the security room and angled her through the doorway of her room.

He set Nicole on her feet at the side of the bed. "Need anything?"

"Kisses. Lots of kisses."

He gave a rough laugh. "I need the same thing, but I don't trust myself right now. Rain check?"

"Deal. The debt's due tomorrow."

"Copy that, Ms. Copeland," he murmured and brushed her lips with his before forcing himself to release her and walk out while he still could.

On the way to his room, he heard the low hum of conversation in the security room and realized that Dawn was going to keep Linc company for a while. Maybe Nicole was correct. There might be a romance brewing between Linc and Dawn.

He popped three over-the-counter pain killers into his mouth and swallowed them, then stretched out on top of the bed fully dressed. Although he didn't anticipate trouble overnight, he'd learned to be prepared for anything on missions. This one, however, was more personal than any other. He dropped off to sleep.

Mason woke when Linc walked in and said, "Mase, Ethan's here."

CHAPTER THIRTEEN

Nicole woke with a start when she heard Mason and Linc speaking in low tones in the hallway. She swung her legs over the side of the bed and shoved her feet into her running shoes, thankful she'd chosen to sleep fully dressed again. "Mason?" Looking at the love of her life, she saw the worry in his eyes. "What's wrong? Is it another attack?"

He shook his head. "Ethan's here."

Nicole glanced at her watch and frowned. "It's after 1:00 a.m. He should be at home in bed. Why is he here?"

"I don't know, but the reason can't be good."

She threaded her fingers through his. "Let's find out what he wants."

"You're tired and still healing, Nicole. Go back to bed."

"No way. Linc, I hope you have the Fortress lawyers on speed dial because if they arrest Mason, I want the toughest lawyer on the planet to have his back."

He grinned. "Maddox only hires barracuda lawyers to defend his employees and their families."

"Excellent." She headed for the living room.

The police chief turned to face them, a grim expression on his face. "We need to talk, Mason."

"About what?"

"Where you've been for the past four hours."

Mason stiffened. "What happened?"

"We can do this here or at the station. Your choice."

Nicole's hand tightened around Mason's. Not good. Something bad must have happened. If Ethan took him to the station to question him, Nicole wouldn't be able to hear the questions or offer Mason moral support. "Talk to Mason here. Would you like some coffee, Ethan?" Maybe sitting around a kitchen table for a question-and-answer session would take the formality out of Ethan's interrogation.

"I would appreciate a cup."

"Come back to the kitchen. I'll brew a fresh pot if we're out." She motioned for the men to take a seat at the table. A glance at the carafe revealed a full pot of coffee.

She grabbed two mugs, filled them, then set them in front of the men who faced each other across the table in silence. She sat beside Mason and wrapped her hand around his. "What's going on, Ethan?"

The police chief focused on Mason. "Where were you from 8:00 until midnight?"

"Here."

"I assume you have people who will verify your location?"

"I can," Nicole said immediately.

Mason kissed the back of her hand. "Your testimony wouldn't hold much weight in court since you love me. Also, you can only account for a few minutes. You fell asleep against me for two hours before Linc arrived. I could have slipped out without you knowing I was gone."

"I need a timeline, Mason," Ethan said.

"Why?"

"Someone is accusing you of assault."

Outraged, Nicole said, "That's ridiculous. Mason would never do that."

Mason squeezed her hand in warning. "Who's the victim?"

"Todd Fitzgerald."

He dragged a hand down his face.

"He's lying," Nicole insisted. "Look at Mason's hands, Ethan. No bruises or busted knuckles."

"In this case, it wouldn't matter. The perp used a hand tool. Missing any tools, Mase?"

He groaned. "I don't know. I didn't check when I left the job site at 3:00. I was more interested in taking over the watch at Pet Palace from Linc than counting my equipment. What tool was used?"

"Hammer."

Mason flinched. "I must have four or five hammers in my collection. Fitzgerald will recover?"

A nod. "He was lucky. A broken arm and a couple fingers. Other than that, bruises over various parts of his body. The perp didn't use the hammer on his head."

"He wanted Fitzgerald to live to accuse Mason," Nicole said, her pulse rocketing. Who was doing this and why? She thought she was the only one with a target on her back. Was the killer trying to hurt her by bringing harm to Mason or setting him up to be arrested? If Mason was out of the way, she would be vulnerable.

"Tell me where you went from the time you left the job site at 3:00," Ethan said, pulling a notepad and pen from his jacket pocket.

Mason summarized his activities with approximate times for each. "You were a witness yourself to the time I was at Delaney's."

"Your altercation with Fitzgerald hit the Otter Creek grapevine the minute you pulled away from the diner." The police chief's lips curved. "That grapevine is the most efficient communication system in town." His smile faded.

"We've taken fingerprints from the hammer, Mason." His voice was soft. "We'll run them to confirm, but my gut says it's your hammer."

"He didn't do it," Nicole snapped.

"Can you prove it?"

She thought fast, determined that Ethan would not arrest Mason for a crime she knew he hadn't committed. "I can't, but Linc might be able to."

"How?"

"The security system. Rio had cameras mounted all around the house. I know Fortress monitors the feed and the system here records the activity."

"Mason could have slipped out without detection."

Mason snorted. "You could have. Not me. I'm not trained in stealth."

"You've been training with Durango and Bravo."

Nicole's eyes narrowed. How did the police chief know that information? She hadn't known until today.

"Self-defense," Mason said evenly. "I want as much training as I can get to better protect Nicole."

"Why is Fitzgerald convinced you're the one who beat him?"

"You know why."

"Enlighten me."

"I told him to leave Nicole alone."

Ethan frowned. "Why?"

"He came to my shop." Nicole tightened her grip on Mason's hand. "He warned me to break things off with Mason before I ended up dead like his sister-in-law."

The police chief refocused on Mason. "You can't afford to be in trouble with the law, Mason."

"I didn't seek him out."

"You would have."

A shrug. "I had no intention of getting into a physical altercation with him, but I won't let him harass Nicole, either. She doesn't have anything to do with my past."

"You did end up in an altercation."

"I didn't touch him."

Ethan waited, gaze locked on his face.

"If Fitzgerald had tried to punch me again, I would have defended myself. If Nicole had been with me and he'd tried to hurt her, I would have done more."

Ethan sighed. "Lucky for you that I was parked close enough to see the whole episode outside the diner."

Nicole frowned. "Why does Fitzgerald say Mason was his attacker?"

"He doesn't know anyone else in town except you two, and he and Mason aren't on the best of terms. Mason is the only person with a reason to hurt him."

"Don't you think it's a little extreme for Mason to beat up a man for warning me to break up with him? I have people in town tell me that all the time."

Mason turned to her. "Are you serious?"

She squeezed his hand. "They don't know the real Mason Kincaid."

He gave a wry laugh. "Funny. That's exactly what Fitzgerald said when we were in Delaney's. Do you need any other information from me, Ethan?"

"I want a copy of the security recordings."

Mason got to his feet. "I'll be back in a minute."

Nicole waited until he left the room, then said, "You know him, Ethan. You know he isn't capable of doing this." She expected the police chief to agree with her since he'd met with Mason every week since his release from prison. She was disappointed.

"To protect the woman he loves, a man will do a lot more than beat an aggressor. Don't kid yourself, Nicole. If your life is in danger, Mason will do whatever is necessary to save you."

Mason returned to the kitchen with a flash drive in hand. "Six cameras. Six digital files. The recordings begin at 7:00 p.m. and end at 1:00 a.m."

Ethan stood and accepted the drive. "Anything you want to tell me?"

"Would you believe me if I told you I didn't touch Fitzgerald?"

"I have a job to do, and I'll do it to the best of my ability. That means I follow the trail of evidence wherever it takes me, no matter what my gut says."

"What does your gut say?" Nicole asked.

"Mason is telling the truth. Someone is out to set him up for a fall and willing to use innocent people to do it." He turned to Mason. "Between now and 7:00 a.m., give some serious thought to who might hate you enough to send you back to prison."

Nicole and Mason followed Ethan to the front door. With his hand on the knob, the police chief turned to Mason. "Bring a lawyer with you."

Ice water flowed through Nicole's veins as Ethan stepped outside and closed the door behind him with a quiet snick. She looked at Mason. At the sight of his pale face, she wrapped her arms around him and held him tight.

CHAPTER FOURTEEN

Mason strode out of the police station at 8:45 a.m. with the Fortress lawyer at his side. Andrea Esposito paused at the top of the stairs and glanced at him, her dark hair blowing in the breeze.

"Remember what I told you, Mason."

How could he forget? "Don't answer any questions without you or one of the other Fortress lawyers at my side."

"That's right. Blackhawk and Kelter will keep digging. They don't have the reputation of looking for easy answers. Unfortunately for you, someone is wrapping a bow around your neck, hoping the cops will take the gift being offered and blame all this on you."

Anger burned in his gut. "I haven't done anything, and I would never hurt Nicole, even if I was furious with her. I love her and need her more than I need to breathe."

A sour smile curved Esposito's mouth. "You know what they say about love and hate. A fine line separates the two. You can hate someone with the same passion as you once loved them."

That would never be the case with them. He knew it in his gut. Mason shook his head. "I have no life without her."

"A sweet sentiment, Mason, but we need facts to keep you out of the pokey."

"I'll find them." Whatever it took. He refused to go back to prison for crimes he didn't commit.

She scowled. "That's not a good idea. Law enforcement frowns on suspects chasing down leads, intimidating witnesses, and contaminating evidence."

"I'm not going to intimidate anyone or contaminate evidence. If your freedom was on the line, would you sit on the sidelines and let someone else do the work, especially if the person you planned to marry had a target on his back?"

"We don't know if the person who attacked Ms. Copeland is the same one framing you. For now, we have to assume these are two separate investigations. The police won't be happy if you interfere. You could find yourself in jail again."

The idea made him want to hurl, but what choice did he have? "I'll be careful."

"Not what I wanted to hear." Esposito sighed. "You have my number. Call me if there are further developments. If I can't shake free to get here, I'll have Maddox send one of the other lawyers on staff. Be careful, Mason. I'd hate to see your future plans derailed. I'd hate even more to learn you're dead."

"I'm not fond of either alternative myself."

With a few more instructions, the lawyer hurried to her car, and headed back to the airport in Knoxville where the Fortress jet waited to fly her back to Nashville.

Mason breathed in the fresh air for a minute and settled himself down before climbing into his truck. After sending a text to Brian about his approximate arrival time, he drove to Pet Palace. Nicole had asked him to stop by before heading to work. Truthfully, he needed a minute with her after the two-hour ordeal in an interrogation room with two cops at the top of their game. Both Ethan and Rod had hammered him relentlessly about timelines, details, and witnesses. Even though he counted the two men as friends, Mason wasn't sure whether they believed his story or not.

When he parked in front of the salon and walked inside, Nicole glanced up from the computer screen, phone pressed between her shoulder and ear. Relief shone in her eyes when she saw him. Man, every time she looked at him with just that expression on her face, he fell more in love with her.

After she finished booking a grooming appointment and ended the call, Nicole came around the desk and pressed her lips to his in a hard, heated kiss. When she eased back, she gripped his biceps. "You're okay?"

Not hardly. "Ethan and Rod don't use torture to obtain answers."

"The lawyer arrived?"

"Andrea Esposito is everything Maddox said she was. The lady is a ruthless shark and frustrated my interrogators from the first question asked."

Satisfaction filled Nicole's face. "Excellent. I owe Maddox a favor. I don't know how I'll repay him, but I'll find a way. What do we do if Ethan drags you back in for another grilling session?"

An accurate assessment of how he felt at the moment. Grilled evenly on every side. "I'm to answer no questions without one of the Fortress lawyers present."

"What's the likelihood of you going back into the interrogation room?"

He tucked her against his chest and breathed in the familiar scent of her shampoo. "The way things are going, a near certainty." Did someone hate him that much? If Fitzgerald lived in Otter Creek, Mason would point the police his direction. He and his family were the only ones that had a reason to come after him.

He frowned. Was it possible one of the other members of the Fitzgerald family was in town and carrying out a campaign to put Mason back in jail? Maybe Zane could help him figure out if the Fitzgerald family members were still in Liberty.

Much as he would like to go home to see his father, that wasn't an option, especially now that he was suspected of committing various crimes around Otter Creek. He'd been warned by Ethan not to leave town.

"We'll figure this out and move forward from here." Nicole held him tighter. "No one is going to take you away from me. Sorry, Mr. Kincaid, but I can't live without you now. I need you."

"I feel the same about you, Ms. Copeland." He dropped a quick kiss on her mouth before stepping back. "I need to go. We have an inspector coming to the Oakdale site in a few minutes. Who's keeping watch?"

"Alex Morgan. He went to the back to help Dawn with an Irish Wolfhound. That big, sweet girl isn't cooperating. She's not a fan of baths. Alex is in the grooming room, two seconds away if there's trouble."

The door opened and Durango's sniper walked into the reception area. "Daisy is all set but she's not happy about it." He squeezed Mason's shoulder. "How are you holding up?"

"I've been better." Understatement of the year.

"You can trust Ethan and Rod to find the right culprit." His lips edged up at the corners. "You can trust us to help them find the answers faster. You're not alone this time, Mason. You have many friends in this town who believe in you."

An invisible band tightened around his chest. He gave a short nod. "How is Cosmo?"

A chuckle from Alex. "Having a blast with Spenser. Savannah loves him and so does Ivy. He acts like he's always been a member of the family."

At least some good had come from such ugliness. Maybe the sweet dog had found a new home. "I need to go."

"I've got your woman and her friend, Mason. An attacker will have to go through me to get to them." A cold smile. "And I'm hard to kill."

"Thank you for watching over them." He lifted Nicole's hand to his mouth and kissed her palm. "I'll be back as soon as I can."

"We'll be fine. Watch your back, Mason."

With a nod, he made himself leave the shop and climb into his truck. Fifteen minutes later, he arrived at the job site as the inspector strode toward Brian with his clipboard in hand.

Brian directed him to the right buildings, then came to stand beside Mason. "How did it go this morning?" he asked, gaze locked on the inspector making his way to Building 8.

"About like I expected. Brutal. You don't want to be in an interrogation room with Ethan Blackhawk and Rod Kelter."

"I'll take your word for it. Dean is in Building 7." He gave Mason a long list of tasks to complete. "By the way, Patton and Fisher are on notice." He eyed Mason a moment. "Have you given any thought to what we discussed last week?"

"I haven't had much time between grilling sessions and dodging bullets."

Brian gave a bark of laughter. "Well, when you have time to breathe, give it some thought. I think it might be time. Our workload is becoming too heavy."

"You must have employees who are more qualified without my complicated background."

"You're the man I trust, Mason. You've proved yourself over and over for the past two years. Anyway, get going. You and Dean have quite a list to knock out today."

"Yes, sir." He climbed back into his truck and drove to Building 7. Mason found his partner on the second floor. "What have you finished so far?"

Dean rattled off the tasks he'd completed and the two men split the remaining tasks on the list and got to work. At lunch, Mason and Dean ate their lunches under the shade of a nearby maple tree.

"I hear you had a visit from Ethan in the middle of the night."

Back pressed against the tree, Mason glanced at his friend. "The town grapevine is nothing short of amazing. Yeah, Ethan showed up after 1:00 this morning." He explained about Fitzgerald and the man's accusation.

Dean scowled. "Why would you be stupid enough to do something like that? You'd be the first suspect."

"Definitely the most obvious one."

"Did Fitzgerald see who attacked him?"

He gave a rough laugh. "Sure. A muscular man dressed in black from head to toe, complete with a convenient ski mask, and a hammer with my fingerprints on it."

"Huh. That's the second tool of yours used in a crime."

"Believe me, I know."

"How is the man getting your tools, Mase?"

He dragged a hand down his face. "I have no idea. I lock the tool box in my truck bed every afternoon before I leave the job site."

"But it's open all day?"

"I'm in and out of the box several times a day."

"Lock it from now on. The hassle of having to unlock the box when you need another tool is better than having another one of your tools used in a crime."

"I'll lock it when we return to work. Might be a moot point, though."

"Why?"

"The person who stole the pipe wrench and hammer may have stolen more items but not used the remaining tools yet." And wasn't that a cheery thought. If he hadn't had an alibi for the time of Fitzgerald's attack, Mason would be in jail now.

Dean grimaced. "Let's hope that's not the case. Someone's doing a good job setting you up for a hard fall."

"If they succeed, I'll lose everything I've worked to achieve. More important, I'll lose Nicole." Mason could rebuild his life if Brian cut him loose to protect his company's reputation. He couldn't ask Nicole to wait for him to be released from prison if he was tried and convicted. It wouldn't be fair, especially since he might not leave the prison except in a body bag.

"You think she'll dump you? She loves you. I can't see Nicole walking away when you're at your most vulnerable."

"She wouldn't. I'll break the engagement. I won't take her down with me."

His friend looked amused. "I think the lady will have several things to say about that. A blistering tirade, in fact. I don't believe it will be as easy as you assume."

Easy? No, doing the right thing for Nicole wouldn't be easy. Severing ties with the woman he adored would gut him and destroy his last vestige of hope. But what choice did he have? At least she'd have a life while his would be over the moment he stepped foot behind those prison walls again.

"Maybe we're looking at this from the wrong side."

"What do you mean?"

"What if this isn't about you, but about Riva? This whole chain of events started with her death. You said you were at her home earlier in the afternoon. You probably did leave your pipe wrench which made a convenient murder weapon."

He frowned. "It's possible. But the killer made it my problem by trying to frame me and hurt Nicole. He came after her, Dean. Twice. I'm not going to forget that."

"He's probably afraid she saw too much and might recognize him."

"She saw almost nothing."

"The killer doesn't know that, and you can't take out an ad and announce that fact to the world. Maybe you should think about who had something to gain from Riva's death if you can't figure out who has it out for you."

Mason punched Dean lightly on the shoulder. "I should have thought of that before now." While he'd grown up, his father had repeatedly told him to go at a problem from a different angle if he hit a wall. This was a definite wall. Time to go around the immovable object instead of trying to beat his head against the wall and coming up short. Dean was right. This all started with Riva's death. Maybe this wasn't a vendetta against him. He could have been a convenient scapegoat. So, why didn't he believe that? "Thanks."

Dean glanced at his watch. "Break's over. Lock your toolbox, and we'll get back to work. Have you heard anything about the inspection yet?"

"Nope. Manning is taking his sweet time going over everything. If he can find something we need to fix in Building 8, we'll make his day."

"We checked everything ourselves and fixed the items Patton and Fisher skimped on or did wrong. That building is as perfect as we can get it."

Two hours later, Brian strode into Building 7. He handed Mason a list. "Manning's correction list."

Mason scanned the items, his frown deepening as he read. "Dean and I fixed about half of this list yesterday. The rest of the items on the list were working perfectly."

"They aren't now. Your fixes have miraculously undone themselves. We have another inspection in a week."

"Want a suggestion?"

"Lay it on me."

"Let Dean and me change the locks. You keep the keys. The only way someone will be able to get back in here to create mischief is to break in."

Brian smiled. "I like it. Go to our hardware supplier for the locks. Don't tell anyone else what you're doing. Let's see if we can thwart our troublemaker. Leave the list I gave you this morning. I'll keep an eye on things and give Dean a hand."

"Yes, sir." He motioned for Dean to follow him outside. When they were far enough away from the apartment building to not be overheard by Brian, he said, "Stay with him. I don't think the person who's been messing with me will go after Brian, but I don't want to take any chances."

"No problem. We'll install the crown molding while you're gone." Dean rolled his eyes. "We have about a zillion square feet to install."

"I'll be back soon to give you a hand." Mason drove to the hardware supplier thirty minutes away, purchased the necessary locks, and returned to the job site.

He grabbed the box of supplies and carried them inside the building. Brian and Dean were both on ladders, nail guns slamming nails through the molding and into the wall. "Looks good."

Brian snorted. "Whose idea was it to have this much fussy trim work in each apartment?"

Mason grinned. "Wait until we have to paint it."

A groan. "Don't remind me. Did you get the locks?"

"Yes, sir." He handed his boss the receipt and purchase order.

"Excellent. You two pause the molding work and change the locks in Building 8. I want the hardware changed out before you leave the site today, no matter how long it takes."

Mason glanced at his watch. He and Dean had at least four hours of work ahead of them and Mason was due to take over the watch in another hour. Guess he would have to call someone to cover his guard shift until he could shake free. "We'll take care of it, sir."

"I'll try to give you a hand after everyone else knocks off for the day." With that, he left.

Mason and Dean gathered their tools, then checked the doors and windows, and locked up behind themselves.

Mason led the way to Building 8 and set down the box of hardware on the living room floor of the first unit. "I need to call someone to watch over Nicole and Dawn."

His partner grabbed his own cell phone. "I need to call my wife and let her know I'll be late. She worries when I'm not home on time." Dean walked to the back door with his screw gun and a new door knob to match the one Mason was ready to install in the front door.

He set his own screw gun on the floor along with the knob and called Linc.

"Is Dawn okay?" was Linc's greeting.

Huh. Looked like Nicole was correct. The PSI instructor was sweet on Dawn. "Alex Morgan is on watch at the shop. As far as I know, Dawn's fine."

"What do you need?"

"A favor. I'll be tied up for a few hours at the Oakdale site and I'm supposed to take over for Alex in an hour. Can you take part of my shift?"

"No problem. Take your time. I'll find out what the ladies want for dinner and have food waiting for you. We're still planning to be at your house tonight?"

"You have a different suggestion?"

"Yeah, my place. My windows are bullet-resistant glass."

"Sold." He could still hear the glass shattering as bullets smashed into the windows at Trent's home. "You sure you don't mind having three guests in your home?"

"Nope."

"Thanks, Linc. I owe you."

"No debt between friends. See you when you get off."

Mason shoved his phone into his pocket and got to work. Four hours later, he and Dean checked the last unit to be sure the windows were secure, and locked the door.

"I thought we'd never finish." Dean opened the toolbox in the bed of his truck and stored his tools before locking his equipment. "Did you notice some of those original locks had scratches on them?"

He nodded. "I saved the ones I found to show Brian. It's possible the cops can pull prints off them." He wasn't holding his breath, though. Any self-respecting thief would wear gloves.

His friend grimaced. "The only fingerprints they'll find will be ours."

"Probably." He clapped Dean on the shoulder. "Good work today. Hopefully, we'll thwart any further sabotage. I'll see you tomorrow."

Mason unlocked his toolbox and put away his tools before locking the box and double checking that no supplies had been left outside by accident. When he didn't find anything, he drove to the Oakdale clubhouse where Brian was working.

His boss turned as Mason entered the building. "All finished?"

"Yes, sir. I sent Dean on home." Mason handed Brian the key ring with the apartment keys identified by unit. "When we changed the hardware, we noticed some of the knobs had fresh scratch marks."

Brian's eyes narrowed. "Like someone had picked the locks?"

He nodded. "The new locks are reputed to be more difficult to pick."

"Looks like we're going to find out if that's true. Good job, Mase. Go home. I know you're anxious to check on Nicole."

"Yes, sir. I'll wait until you're ready to go."

Brian's eyebrows soared. "You're worried about my safety?"

"Is there anything I can do to help you finish?"

"I'm just packing up. I won't be more than ten minutes."

Mason helped his boss store nails and screws, and pack tools. Once Brian climbed into his truck, Mason opened his vehicle door and climbed inside.

After cranking his engine, he finished half the soft drink in a bottle in his cup holder, and started the drive to Linc's home, thankful he carried his own type of Go bag with changes of clothes and survival supplies in case of trouble. Rio had stressed being prepared for anything since Mason began training with the teams.

Halfway to his destination, fatigue hit him in a hard wave. He blinked as dizziness assailed him and the world spun.

Lights flashed in his rearview mirror, blinding him momentarily. Something was wrong. Seriously wrong. Shouldn't drive. He finally managed to slide his foot off the accelerator. Steering to the side of the road took an enormous amount of effort and too much time.

Gear. Put the truck in park. Couldn't drive anyway. Four tries later, he shoved the gear into park. Vision blurring, he fumbled for his cell phone. Stared at it, confused. Nicole. He needed Nicole.

Mason squinted, straining to read the names on his list. He touched a finger to her name.

When she answered with a cheery, "Hi, sweetheart. Are you on your way to Linc's?"

He couldn't respond. Tried three times before he finally said, "Help me." The phone slipped from his grasp and the world went black.

CHAPTER FIFTEEN

Alarm roared through Nicole. "Mason?" Nothing. "Mason, answer me." Wide-eyed, she spun to stare at her current bodyguard who watched her with increasing concern.

Linc took the phone from her hand and tapped the speaker button. "Mase, it's Linc. What's going on?"

Silence.

"Mason, answer me," he snapped, sounding like a drill sergeant in the military.

Still nothing. Terrified for Mason, Nicole clutched Linc's arm. "The truck's engine is still running. I can hear it. We have to help him but we don't know where he is. What can we do?"

Dawn wrapped her hand around Nicole's free one. "We'll find him. He was probably on his way here from the job site."

"Sure, but how many different routes could he take?" They had to find him as soon as possible. If Mason was critically ill and they chose the wrong route, he could die.

Her breath froze in her lungs. No, she couldn't think that or she'd fall apart. That wasn't an option. Mason needed her to be strong, to think logically. "Can Fortress help?"

Linc grabbed his cell phone. When his call was answered, he said, "It's Linc Creed. You're on speaker with Nicole Copeland and Dawn Metcalf. Mason Kincaid's in trouble." He rattled off Mason's cell phone number. "Ping his cell signal."

"Hold."

While they waited for the man to return with information, Linc turned to Nicole. "What did Mason say before I put him on speaker?"

"'Help me.'" She frowned, fighting to think past the panic threatening to swallow her whole. "He sounded off."

"Explain."

"His words were slurred." She narrowed her eyes at Linc. "He'd never drink and drive." Not after the accident that took the life of a mother and child. Her groom-to-be still grieved the loss of life from his decision years ago.

The Fortress tech's voice sounded over the speaker. "Linc, I sent the coordinates to your phone. Anything else I can do?"

"Not right now. Thanks." He ended the call and checked his text message for the coordinates. After scrolling rapidly through several screens, Linc studied one and frowned. "He's seven miles from here. I'll find him and let you know what's going on."

"We'll all go," Nicole corrected. "You can't leave us here unprotected, right?"

"It's not safe, Nic." Dawn squeezed her hand. "You'll be out in the open and a likely target since this involves Mason."

"I have an alarm system I'll activate until I return with Mason," Linc said. "You have my word that I'll bring him back to you. Just stay here where it's safe."

Nicole shook her head. "Either you take me with you or I'm driving myself." She yanked her hand free from

Dawn's hold, snagged her purse, and headed for the door. If Linc thought he was going to leave her in safety while Mason was at least sick if not injured, the PSI instructor was fooling himself.

He sighed. "Hold it, Nicole. Wait until I tell you it's safe." Linc passed her to open the door and step onto the porch. After scanning the area, he signaled Nicole and Dawn to join him. "Straight to the SUV." He unlocked the vehicle with his remote and hurried the two women to safety.

Nicole climbed into the back while Dawn slid onto the shotgun seat. Even though Linc drove faster than the posted speed limit, she mentally urged him to flatten the accelerator to the floor.

While he drove, Linc made another call.

"Blackhawk."

"It's Linc Creed. Mason's in trouble. He called, asking for help. I'm going to him now with Nicole and Dawn."

"Where?"

He gave the police chief Mason's coordinates.

"I'm not far from there. I'll meet you on site."

"Be careful, Ethan. After Mase asked for help, he hasn't responded to any questions. This may be an ambush."

"Copy that." He ended the call.

An ambush? Nicole clutched her phone like a lifeline. The call from Mason was still active. She'd heard some odd sounds, but nothing from him. Tears burned her eyes. Was he sick? Had he been in an accident? What if the killer had forced Mason off the road and hurt him?

She had to hold it together until they had all the facts. The most important thing was to find Mason and get him help.

Five minutes later, Linc rounded a curve, slowing when he spotted the swirling blue-and-white lights of a police SUV parked behind Mason's truck. The driver's door was open with a large figure leaning into the cabin.

When Linc skidded to a stop, Nicole threw open the door, jumped to the ground, and ran toward the truck.

The police chief glanced over his shoulder and backed away from the door with a bag in his hand containing a bottle. "I called an ambulance. ETA is two minutes."

"What happened? Is he sick?"

"He appears to be drunk."

Cold fury filled her. "Mason doesn't drink."

Ethan held up the bag in his hand. "How do you explain this?"

She glanced at the contents. Her mouth gaped. "I can't, but I know that's not his. Mason doesn't drink period. When he did drink in college, it was only beer. No hard liquor."

"You need to step back, Nicole."

"I'm checking on Mason. If you want to arrest me for it, go ahead." She hurried to the passenger side of the truck and opened the door.

As soon as she climbed inside, the overwhelming scent of alcohol assaulted her nose and made her cough. No matter what Ethan thought, Mason wouldn't be blind drunk and driving, not with his history. She'd find a way to prove that he was innocent no matter what she had to do.

Mason lay slumped over his center console. At least he was breathing steadily. Nicole stroked his hair away from his forehead. "I'm here, Mason. You'll be okay. An ambulance will take you to the hospital. Just hold on for me, sweetheart. I can't lose you." Her voice broke.

The ambulance siren cut off abruptly as the driver parked in front of the truck. Two EMTs rushed to Mason with their equipment bags in hand. After determining he didn't have any obvious injuries, they shifted him to a gurney, and strapped him down to transport him to Memorial Hospital.

"Tell the doc on duty to do a blood test on him immediately," Ethan said.

One of the EMTs snorted. "From the way he smells, he's way over the legal limit. Your case ought to be a slam dunk."

"Do what I told you," the police chief snapped, and motioned for them to get going.

With a scowl, the man and his partner rolled the gurney to the ambulance and loaded Mason inside.

A strong hand squeezed Nicole's shoulder. "Come on. We'll follow Mase to the hospital. When he comes around, he'll need you." Linc steered her toward his SUV.

"What happened, Nic?" Dawn asked. "Mason looked like he was unconscious when the EMTs loaded him in the ambulance."

Nicole waited until they were underway again before she answered her friend. "He was unconscious. Ethan believes Mason was drunk. How could he think Mason would risk going back to prison? He spent two years investing his life in Mason as a friend and making sure he toed the line as a law enforcement officer. Why would he assume Mason would throw his life away a few weeks before our wedding?"

"The circumstantial evidence against Mason looks bad." Linc glanced at her in the rearview mirror.

"Ethan should know better. Mason has been sober for over 15 years. Why would he go back on the promise he made me?"

"I don't believe the evidence, either, but many men wouldn't be able to handle the pressure he's under right now without sliding back into old habits. Don't assume Blackhawk is gullible, Nicole. He'll investigate everything."

"Will it be enough?" The evidence was damning. Even the EMTs believed Mason was driving under the influence of alcohol.

"You heard Ethan. He demanded a blood test first thing. If Mason sucked down a bottle of booze, the blood test will show his blood alcohol level."

Nicole scowled. "I'm telling you he didn't."

He held up a hand to forestall more of her vehement protests. "It's possible Mason is ill."

"That fast? He just left work. Worse, that doesn't explain the alcohol."

"We don't know what happened. If he wasn't drunk, someone went to a lot of trouble to make it look like he was three sheets to the wind."

She sucked in a ragged breath. "If that's true, that same person might have drugged him. Aside from the bruised jaw where Fitzgerald punched him, Mason didn't have a mark on him that I could see."

Linc glanced in the rearview mirror again. "Let's not get ahead of ourselves. Wait for the blood test results. Prepare yourself, Nicole. Mase won't get the benefit of the doubt, not with him smelling like a brewery."

The medical staff of Memorial better treat her man with respect or they'd be hearing loud complaints from her. She also planned to file formal complaints if necessary. Mason deserved better than their disdain.

Fifteen minutes later, Linc dropped her off at the ER entrance. She rushed after the EMTs and the gurney bearing the unconscious form of the man she loved.

"Exam 5," one of the nurses said. She wrinkled her nose and waved a hand in front of her face. "Whew. Smells like he took a bath in whiskey."

The EMTs pushed the gurney into the room and were quickly followed by a nurse and a Memorial technician.

Nicole glared at the nurse standing in front of her. "Where's the doctor?"

"With another patient. He'll be here soon. Are you a family member?"

Close enough. "Yes."

"I have forms for you to fill out since the patient isn't able to answer questions."

"If you bring them to me, I'll take care of it while I wait for word on Mason's condition."

The nurse walked to the desk and returned with a clipboard and pen. She handed both to Nicole as a man in a white coat walked out of one exam room and headed for Mason's.

Nicole took the clipboard and hurried to intercept the doctor. Before she reached him, Rod Kelter jogged into view, his expression grim.

"I need a blood test completed on the patient just brought in by ambulance," Rod said. "As fast as you can, Dr. Thomas."

"DUI?" the physician asked.

"No," Nicole said, hugging the clipboard to her chest. "He smells like someone poured a bottle of booze on him, but Mason hasn't touched alcohol in years."

"Alcoholics can have relapses," Thomas said, his tone gentle.

"That's not the case here."

Although he nodded, the doctor obviously wasn't taking her word in assessing Mason's current state. He pushed open the door and walked inside.

Rod glowered at Nicole. "Still convinced Mason is alcohol free?"

"Yes. You will be as well when that blood work comes back. I know him. He wouldn't lie to me. If he'd been tempted to drink, he would have told me so we could deal with it together."

"No man wants to appear weak in front of his woman, Nicole. Alcoholics lie to everyone, especially themselves."

"Stop saying that," she snapped. "Mason is not an alcoholic. You're going to eat your words, Kelter."

"Believe it or not, I hope I do. I just know that particular habit is a daily battle to kick."

Nicole blinked. Rod didn't sound as though he spouted platitudes. "Personal experience?"

He gave a short nod. "It's not a history I'm proud of." Rod's lips curved. "That part of my life is over and has been since I married Meg. Let's just say that my wife won't look the other way if I slip up and disappoint her."

The newspaper editor would have some strong words to say to her husband if he fell off the wagon. Nicole would hate to make that woman mad. She was one tough lady.

In silence, Nicole worked on the forms and Rod watched the exam room door until Linc and Dawn joined them. "Any news?" Linc asked.

"The doc is in there with him now," Rod said. "As soon as he wakes and I'm allowed in, I have to question him." He glanced at Nicole. "I'll give you two minutes first, but I have to be in the room."

She strode to the desk to return the forms. What did she care if the detective listened to their conversation? What concerned her was the possibility that Mason might not remember what happened if he'd been drugged. Would the detective believe him? If not, Mason might be spending part of the night in jail.

She clenched her jaw. If he spent one minute in jail for a crime he didn't commit, she'd have Ethan's and Rod's heads on a silver platter. Nicole looked at Linc. "We might need Andrea."

"Already contacted her."

Rod scowled. "Kincaid is not under arrest."

Nicole folded her arms. "I want to keep it that way."

Another employee went into the room and exited a few minutes later with vials of blood. He hurried down the hall.

Soon, Dr. Thomas opened the door and left the room followed by another member of the medical staff. The doctor nodded at Rod in greeting. "He's coming around, but still groggy and disoriented."

Rod straightened. "He's in good enough shape for me to question him?"

"I don't know how much help he'll be. He's in and out."

"Did he tell you what happened?"

A frown. "Ask him your questions, Detective."

Rod scowled. "Can you at least tell me if he's intoxicated?"

"I won't know for sure until I receive the results of the blood test, but I don't believe he consumed alcohol."

Relief swept through Nicole. Now maybe Mason would have a chance to stay out of jail. "He was drugged, wasn't he?"

"I believe so. Again, the blood test results will give us more information." Thomas looked at Rod. "No more than ten minutes. Mr. Kincaid is still recovering. He'll be our guest for the night. An orderly will transport him to his room in a few minutes. Ask your questions, then leave him to rest for the night." With that, he entered the next exam room.

"You owe me and Mason an apology." Nicole's chin tilted up.

"I'll hold off until all the facts are in." Rod motioned for her to precede him into the room.

"Dawn and I will wait in the hall," Linc said.

Dawn squeezed Nicole's hand in silent support and stationed herself by Linc's side.

Anxious to see Mason, Nicole walked into the room with the detective hot on her heels. Mason lay on his back, clothed in a hospital gown, eyes closed and skin pale.

She wrapped her hand around his. "Mason."

A small smile curved his lips. "Nicole." Beautiful brown eyes looked into hers. "Come here." He freed his hand and lifted his arms toward her.

That was enough encouragement for her. She wrapped her arms around him. "I've never been so afraid in my life," she whispered in his ear.

"I'm sorry, baby." His hold tightened.

"I'm just glad you're okay." After another moment, she eased back. The detective must be growing impatient. "You are all right?"

"I will be. Having a hard time focusing for long." He finally noticed the Otter Creek detective. Mason frowned. "Rod, why are you here?"

"I have questions for you."

Nicole threaded her fingers through Mason's. Maybe they'd get answers. A gnawing worry assailed her. What if he didn't know anything? Rod wouldn't accept that explanation.

"Now?" His lids were drooping again. "Not sure I can hold a conversation that makes sense but I'll try."

"Do you know how you got here?"

A frown. "No."

"Ethan found you passed out on the side of Danbury Road. Do you know why you passed out?"

A slight head shake. "Can't remember much."

"Tell me what you do remember. Where were you working today?"

"Oakdale site."

Rod slid a notepad and pen from his pocket. "What time did you leave there, Mason?"

"Late. Seven o'clock."

"Why were you working so late?"

"Changing out locks on a building."

"Did anyone work with you this afternoon?"

"Dean."

Rod glanced up. "Dean Conner?"

A nod.

"After you left the site, where did you go?"

Mason frowned. "To Linc's. Staying with him tonight to protect Nicole and Dawn."

"But you didn't make it to Linc's place. Ethan found you on Danbury, passed out behind the wheel. Your truck was still running. I need you to be honest with me, Mason. Did you stop somewhere to buy alcohol?"

His grip around Nicole's hand tightened. "No. I don't drink. Ever."

"You plan to tell that to the judge when Ethan testifies that he detected a strong odor of alcohol when he checked you for injuries?"

Shock filled Mason's eyes. "That's not possible."

"How do you explain the alcohol, Mason?"

"I can't. I didn't stop anywhere to have a drink or buy a six-pack of beer. I started feeling funny on the drive to Linc's so I pulled over. The last thing I remember was hearing Nicole's voice. Then I woke up here."

"You felt funny? Explain that."

"Dizzy, sleepy." He sighed, eyelids closing again. "Couldn't think. Sluggish."

"How do you explain the empty bottle of whiskey Ethan took from your hand?"

A frown. "What bottle?"

"Did you drink anything on the way to Linc's?" Nicole asked him.

Mason turned his head to look at her, eyes filled with hurt and disappointment.

She cupped his cheek. "I know you didn't drink alcohol. However, you usually drink something on the way home. Water, tea, a soft drink. You work outside and in hot buildings all day. What did you drink, Mason?"

The hurt faded from his eyes as he nuzzled her hand. "Soft drink. Tasted odd."

"What do you mean, odd?" Rod paused with his pen hovering over the notepad.

Mason shrugged. "Just off. The drink was hot. Been sitting in my truck for several hours. Forgot to take it inside with me."

A short knock sounded on the door and Linc poked his head inside. "Orderly is here to take Mase to his room."

"I'm staying?" Mason blinked and struggled to sit up. "Why?"

Nicole squeezed his hand. "The doctor wants to keep an eye on you overnight."

A scowl. "I'm fine." He swayed, leaning to one side.

Rod steadied him with a hand to his shoulder. "I don't think so."

"For my peace of mind, let's make sure." She leaned down and brushed her mouth over his. "Do it for me."

"I have to work tomorrow."

"If you do well overnight, you'll be released." Nicole glanced at Linc. "Send the orderly in. Detective Kelter has finished his questions for the moment." Mason was beginning to fade out again. Whatever he'd ingested was potent.

Rod scowled at her. "I have more questions."

"You heard the doctor. The questions will have to wait until tomorrow. He's finished for the night." She glared at him. "Mason will be right here. You don't have to worry that he'll skip town to escape justice."

Linc whistled softly and left only to return a moment later with a linebacker-sized orderly.

Nicole grinned at the newcomer. "Carlos, how's Tinkerbell?"

A broad smile curved his mouth. "Needing a grooming."

"Call the salon and set an appointment. I need some Tinkerbell time."

He chuckled. "Yes, ma'am. I'll call soon." Carlos positioned a wheelchair close to the side of the bed. "Hey there, Mason. Ready for a ride to your room, buddy?"

"Slow ride, please. The room's still spinning."

"Gotcha."

Knowing Mason would be more comfortable without Rod watching him shift from the bed to the wheelchair while wearing a drafty hospital gown, Nicole said, "Come on, Detective. We'll wait in the hall." She led the way from the room. Once the door closed behind them, she rounded on Rod. "You aren't going to ask him anything else tonight. His body's been through enough trauma today. Whatever you want to know can wait a few hours."

"Even if the delay might mean a killer roams free another night?"

"The only person who matters to me is Mason. The doctor said he needs to rest. Mason will rest even if I have to ban you and any other antagonistic person from his hospital room to be sure he gets it."

He gave her a wry grin. "Yeah, I got that. You and Meg are cut from the same cloth, Ms. Copeland."

"I'll take that as a compliment."

"Oh, trust me, I meant it as one. Just know that I will get my answers, even if I have to drag Mason back into an interrogation room to do it. I'd rather not handle it that way."

Her eyes narrowed. "Fair warning. The next time he'll have his lawyer by his side." And her, too, if she could somehow wheedle her way into the room.

The detective grimaced. "Great. Just what I wanted. Another session with a legal shark. I'll catch up with Mason tomorrow, with or without his lawyer." Rod nodded at Linc and Dawn, then left.

"He seriously thinks Mason is guilty of drinking and driving?" Dawn asked as she watched the detective walk down the hall.

"So much for innocent until proven guilty," Linc muttered.

"The blood test will exonerate Mason. Even Dr. Thomas thinks something else was the cause of Mason's behavior."

Soon, Carlos pushed the wheelchair bearing Mason into the hallway and led the entourage down the hall to the elevator. Minutes later, Mason was settled into his room on the fourth floor.

After Carlos left, a nurse came in to change the IV bag. "Mr. Kincaid, if you need anything, push the call button. I'll be around to check on you in a few minutes."

"How do you feel, Mason?" Dawn asked.

"Like I need a long nap."

"Go ahead and sleep," Linc said. "I'll be outside the door. No one will get in without being cleared."

"You can't stay awake all night."

"I could, but I won't have to. I have backup coming in a few minutes." Linc squeezed his shoulder briefly. "I've got your back."

Mason gave a slight nod as his eyelids sank down. Between one heartbeat and the next, he was sound asleep.

Linc glanced at Dawn. "Will you stay with Nicole or come with me?"

"If I can sit and keep watch like an operative, I'm game to go with you. My feet hurt too much to stay on them for much longer."

He smiled. "I'll find chairs for us."

"Deal." She turned to Nicole. "Do you need anything? A soft drink or tea? I'll be glad to bring you a drink or snack."

"I'm fine, but thanks." All she wanted was to curl up next to Mason and listen to him breathe.

"If you change your mind, let me know." Her friend followed Linc into the hall.

Seeing them together made her smile. Maybe things would work out for them. Nicole turned toward Mason. He slept near the edge of the bed, leaving room for her to settle beside him. Moving carefully so she wouldn't disturb him, Nicole stretched out on her side and rested her hand on his chest. His steady heartbeat reassured her enough to ease the tension that had wracked her body since his phone call two hours before.

She settled down to wait for the love of her life to wake.

CHAPTER SIXTEEN

Mason woke to a semi-dark room with Nicole sleeping beside him, her hand resting over his heart. He was blessed to have this woman stand by his side, one who loved him with her whole being. He didn't think he'd have someone as special as Nicole in his life after his release from prison. She was a beautiful gift, one he wouldn't take for granted.

Someone shifted in the shadows. "Need anything, Mason?" Ethan approached the bedside.

"Water," he croaked out. He felt as though he'd been in the desert for a week. Why was Ethan here? Maybe to make sure he didn't skip town and escape justice. Mason couldn't stand up without assistance much less run from the law.

The police chief grabbed a pitcher and plastic cup from the nearby rolling table along with a straw. He held the cup steady for Mason to drink before setting it aside. "How do you feel?"

Like a cornered rat watching the trap slowly closing around him. Admitting that to the police chief wasn't an option. "Wiped out."

"You should."

Mason blinked. Unexpected. "Why?"

"You were drugged."

Stunned, he stared at Ethan. "How? I don't remember taking so much as an aspirin yesterday."

"Someone dumped ketamine into the soft drink you left in your truck. The drug acts fast and causes the symptoms you described. You were lucky."

"How do you figure that?"

"You stayed conscious long enough to pull to the side of the road and call Nicole. If you passed out while driving a quarter of a mile further down the road, you could have died."

Danbury Road followed the outer edge of a mountainside with a steep drop off and no guard rail. Ethan was right. He shuddered to think what might have happened if he'd lost consciousness on that stretch of road. "I'll give you that one."

His gaze dropped to Nicole, fury simmering in his gut. "He endangered Nicole with his vendetta."

"Why do you say that?"

"She could have been with me when I finished that drink. If we'd been on a dangerous stretch of road and I couldn't pull over in time, both of us might have died." Someone would pay for this.

"Let us do our job, Mason," Ethan warned. "You don't want to take the law into your own hands."

"Would you stand by if someone targeted you and endangered your wife and son?"

His expression hardened. "I'm a cop. I can and will arrest anyone who is a threat to me or mine. It's my job to stand between you and Nicole and danger. You've built a good life in Otter Creek, including winning the heart of a beautiful woman of character and courage. Don't make a misstep now and lose it all, especially the woman you love."

"I didn't start this fight, but if he comes at me or Nicole head on, I'll finish it."

A frown. "Self-defense only to keep yourself out of prison."

He didn't accept the stipulation. He'd do anything necessary to protect Nicole and himself. He had plans and goals. The first challenge was to stay alive and keep his woman safe.

"Mason?"

Nicole's soft voice drew his gaze to her. "Right here." He slid his arm around her shoulders and tucked her tighter against his side. "You okay?"

"I'm better and alert enough to know this bed isn't comfortable."

She sent him a sleepy smile. "I agree. Two months and four days, and we'll be sleeping in our own bed." Nicole shifted her attention to Ethan and frowned. "Why are you here? Mason isn't answering questions tonight. I already told Rod he'd have to wait until morning. Same stipulation applies to you."

The police chief chuckled. "I heard. Not many people have been able to force Rod to back off."

"You didn't answer my question. Why are you here at this time of night?"

"I'm part of the team protecting you. Josh is on the door."

"Where are Linc and Dawn?" Mason asked.

"Staying with the St. Claires. Grace brought a change of clothes for Nicole. I found your Go bag in the truck and stashed it in the bathroom."

Excellent. At least he'd walk out of here in his own clothes instead of hospital scrubs. "Thanks."

Surprise flashed across Nicole's face. "A Go bag like the Fortress operatives carry?"

"I picked up the habit from Bravo and Durango. Mine has a change of clothes and survival gear we need in case of an emergency." Mason kissed her forehead. "Don't worry. No weapons in mine."

He turned back to Ethan. "Tell Nicole what you told me."

She stiffened. "You have news, Ethan?"

"Mason's blood test came back. No alcohol in his system."

"I knew it. I told you he wouldn't drink and drive. What caused him to pass out?"

"Someone dumped ketamine into the soft drink Mason left in his truck."

"Ketamine? Isn't that a drug used by veterinarians?"

"Yes, ma'am."

"How would someone other than a vet obtain a supply?"

"Ketamine is a party drug. You can buy it on the street if you know the right person."

"Do you know who is selling it?"

"Not at the moment."

"You owe Mason an apology."

Ethan's eyebrow rose. "I don't recall accusing him of drinking and driving. I told you it appeared he'd been drinking based on the whiskey bottle in his hand and the overwhelming scent of alcohol on his person. The blood test confirmed what we both already knew."

The ball of ice in Mason's stomach melted. "You didn't believe I was guilty."

"I watched you reclaim your life. When you were shot protecting Darcy, you didn't turn to alcohol to dull the pain. You followed every rule I laid out for you from our first meeting, built a reputation as an excellent, dependable employee who cares about his work, and made a place for yourself in the Otter Creek community. A man of character like that wouldn't be easily persuaded to bury his woes in a bottle. No, I didn't believe what I saw on Danbury Road. I did, however, have to follow the letter of the law. This time, the law worked in your favor."

Ethan folded his arms. "Whoever drugged you must have followed you, hoping for a different outcome. When the worst didn't happen, he took advantage of your unconscious state and set the stage to make you appear drunk."

A memory sparked in Mason's mind. "Lights. I saw headlights in my rearview mirror before I pulled to the side of the road."

"Let's keep that to ourselves. We'll use that information when we arrest the perp."

"It could have been another driver who thought I pulled to the side of the road to make a phone call."

"I don't think so." She glanced at Ethan. "If I'm right, the driver following had a bottle of whiskey that he poured on Mason. He reeked of the stuff when I climbed into the truck."

"We're lucky he didn't pour the alcohol down Mason's throat. With ketamine in his system, the whiskey could have killed him." Ethan shifted his gaze to Mason. "Lock your truck from now on. Don't take any more chances with your life."

He held up a hand. "Don't worry. I've learned my lesson. I also started locking my truck bed's toolbox."

"We ran the prints on the pipe wrench and the hammer. Both tools have your prints plus several smudged prints, indicating someone with gloves used the tools recently."

"The killer?"

"Probably." He dragged a hand down his face. "I could use some coffee. Do either of you want anything? Soft drink, water?" When they both turned down the offer, Ethan left, promising to return within a couple of minutes.

Josh knocked and walked in. "Good to see you're awake, Mase." He sat in the chair Ethan had vacated. "You gave us a scare, buddy."

"Scared myself. Thanks for standing watch."

A shrug. "You're family. I'm standing in for Rio."

Mason sighed. "You called him, didn't you?"

"He and Darcy will be back tomorrow."

"I'm fine. They don't need to cut their vacation short."

"Try telling that to your cousin's wife. She insisted on coming home."

Not surprising. Darcy treated him like she did her brother, Trent. "You staying all night?"

Josh shook his head. "I'm in charge of PT tomorrow at PSI. Quinn and Nate take over at 2:00." He smiled. "They wanted to help because volunteering gives them a pass to skip PT."

"I appreciate the help in protecting Nicole."

"We're happy to step in until you're able to take over yourself."

When Ethan came back, Josh returned to his post. "Sleep, Mason," Ethan murmured. "You and Nicole are safe."

Mason urged Nicole to lay her head against his shoulder. Two more months and he could hold her like this every night.

Two hours later, Mason roused when Ethan stood. "Shift change?" he whispered.

A nod. "I'll check on you tomorrow. Watch your back."

Seconds after he strode from the room, Nate slipped in, nodded at Mason in greeting, and settled into the chair Ethan had vacated. The rest of the early morning hours passed with the night nurse checking his vitals at two-hour intervals. At five, traffic in the hallway picked up.

Within another hour, Dr. Thomas checked his progress and appeared satisfied that the ketamine was out of his system. "You might have some residual fatigue, Mr. Kincaid, but that should disappear in the next two days. Once the nurse brings your discharge papers, you're free to leave."

"Thanks, Dr. Thomas."

"I hope I don't see you again as a patient."

That brought a rough laugh. "No offense, but I don't want to see you again unless you need repair work done to your house."

"You're a handyman?"

"I work for Elliott Construction. We also do home repairs and remodeling."

"I'll keep your company in mind for my next DIY project. I can treat patients, but I'm all thumbs when it comes to repairing things around my home." He grinned. "My wife is better at repairs than I am."

Mason found one of his business cards in his wallet and handed it to the physician. "Call me if you or your wife need help with a repair."

Thomas pocketed the card and, after shaking Mason's hand, left the room.

Nicole poked her head around the door frame. "Well?"

"I'm cleared to leave as soon as I have my release papers."

"Yes!" She hurried inside, threw her arms around his neck, and pressed a hard and fast kiss to his mouth. "What's the plan for the day?"

"Same as usual. Work, dinner with my beautiful bride-to-be, and maybe a movie if I can stay awake long enough." He wouldn't take bets on that last part of the plan, though. The way he felt at the moment, finishing the work day may be the extent of his grand plan.

"Will you be able to work today?"

"We're on a deadline, and I don't want to let Brian down." He pressed a kiss to her mouth. "Thomas said I'd be tired for a couple days, but I'll be back to normal after that."

Mason released her. "I need a shower and real clothes. This hospital gown is drafty."

She grinned. "I'll be in the hall."

When he'd showered and dressed, Mason came out of the bathroom to see Nate with one shoulder propped against the wall, waiting for him. "I thought you would have gone to work by now."

"My bodyguard assignment doesn't end until you leave the hospital."

"Do I hear weeping and wailing coming from PSI?" Nate, a professional chef as well as Durango's EOD man, kept the trainees and staff at PSI well fed.

"Serena Blackhawk is covering for me this morning. The staff and trainees won't miss me."

As a personal chef, the police chief's wife was also in high demand. "Thanks for keeping an eye on us overnight."

"No problem, Mase." Nate looked at him a moment. "Someone has a target on your back. Who is the most likely culprit?"

He snorted. "The possibilities are endless." Not everyone was happy that he'd moved to Otter Creek for a fresh start on life. Several people would be happy if he went back to prison.

"Think hard. This latest attempt to harm you could have had a tragic outcome."

"I know."

"Stay alert, Mason. This guy won't give up, and next time he might succeed."

CHAPTER SEVENTEEN

Nicole hid a yawn behind her hand. Good grief. She'd never make it through the day at this rate. And to think she used to stay awake all night studying for tests in college. Those days were long gone.

Although she wanted to call Mason to check on him, she resisted the urge. He was fine. If he wasn't, Dean would have called her.

Nicole wished Mason had agreed to let a PSI trainee shadow him today. What if the person who drugged him tried to hurt him again?

She blew out a breath. Mason could take care of himself, and Dean and Brian had his back. Trusting the man she adored to take extra precautions, Nicole dragged her attention back to sending out reminders for upcoming grooming appointments.

Good thing the appointments were further apart today. Otherwise, she'd be guzzling caffeine by the barrel to keep going without giving a bad haircut to someone's pet.

"Should I go to Perk and ask Sasha for her strongest coffee?"

At Rio's good-natured teasing, Nicole rolled her eyes. "Not all of us have spent a week lounging on the beach in the sun with our sweetheart." She grimaced. "As much as I want that coffee, I'm not sure my stomach could handle it right now."

He sobered. "Still having trouble with nausea?"

"No, thank goodness. My stomach feels like it's tied in knots, though. I'm worried, Rio. Ethan and Rod have been looking for Riva's killer for days but it seems they're no closer to making an arrest."

"I'm concerned for you and Mason. Whoever is targeting you won't give up until he succeeds or he's stopped."

"You think it's the same person attacking both of us?"

"I'm not ruling anything out. What are the odds that you're both being targeted at the same time without the attacks being connected?"

"Slim to none." Great. Had she started this whole thing by going to Riva's home to deliver Cosmo?

Mason called during his lunch break. "I'm fine although I am tired," he said.

Thank goodness. Nicole leaned back against the counter, a smile curving her mouth. "Nothing that a good night's sleep won't cure?"

He chuckled. "Maybe a couple of nights. That ketamine packs a wallop. Listen, I wanted to let you know that I'll be late again. Brian needs help in one of the buildings before the inspector comes back."

"I understand. Not too late, right?" He'd just admitted to being tired. Working overtime wouldn't help.

"Dean and I will leave by seven o'clock. I'll pick up dinner for the four of us after I leave the job site. Delaney's okay again?"

"Pet Palace is a couple of blocks from the town square. I'll pick up dinner." She'd ask Linc to stop by Delaney's on the way to his home. The day's special of roast beef with mashed potatoes and gravy sounded heavenly.

"I don't mind stopping."

Mason wouldn't think twice about inconveniencing himself to take care of her. This time, it was her turn to run the errand. "I know. Makes more sense for me to do it. Besides, I have a good chance of finishing my workday early."

"Business is slow?"

"It's usually slower in the middle of the week. The pace will pick up after tomorrow. In the meantime, Dawn and I are enjoying the break." She heard someone speaking in the background.

A moment later, Mason said, "I have to go. I'll see you in a few hours."

"Mason?" Rio asked when Nicole slid her cell phone back into her pocket.

She nodded. "He's tired but sounds good."

"Excellent progress. He'll be back to normal soon."

Couldn't be fast enough for her. Under normal circumstances, Mason could outwork her. Today, however, she might give him a run for his money.

The rest of the day passed without drama. Linc arrived a few minutes after three, relieving Rio. The medic kissed Nicole's cheek. "If you need me, I expect to hear from you."

"You just returned from vacation. I don't want to disturb you on your first night back."

"I want to help, Nic. Mason is my cousin. Family takes care of family. Promise you'll call if you need me."

She sighed. How could she refuse? "You have my word. Go take care of your PSI responsibilities so Darcy won't be alone tonight."

With a grin, Rio tapped her nose gently. "I'll check in with you and Mase later." He clapped Linc on the shoulder and left the salon.

"Where's Dawn?" he asked.

"In the workroom. She's almost finished with an Australian Shepherd named Gracie. Do you mind stopping by Delaney's on the way to your house tonight? I'm craving their special and it keeps any of us from having to cook dinner."

"You won't get an argument from me. I love their food. Have you talked to Mason?"

"At lunch. He's tired and is going to be late again."

"I understand. I'll be glad to make the detour."

By the time the salon closed for business and they cleaned the workroom, Nicole was more than ready for a meal. She hadn't been able to eat all day.

After she locked up, Linc drove her and Dawn to Delaney's. The three of them trooped into the crowded restaurant. When a friend of Linc's hailed him and Dawn from one of the booths, Nicole waved them on. He had a clear line of sight to her and if trouble broke out, was only a few feet away. Besides, who'd be crazy enough to come after her in this press of people?

Nicole placed her order and turned when a familiar voice called her name. She smiled at the middle-aged woman. "Hi, Greta. How are my favorite fur babies?" The woman had three Chihuahuas that were a delight to work on.

"They're wonderful. Thanks for asking." Her gaze shifted from Nicole's face to the side of her head. "How are you? I heard what happened at Riva's. Such a terrible tragedy."

The knot that had slowly disappeared through the day was back in full force. "I'll be fine. No more headaches or nausea, all good signs of healing."

Greta eased closer, sympathy filling her blue eyes. "I'm so sorry you had to find out that way."

Nicole's brows knitted. "Find out what?"

"About Mason, of course."

"I don't understand." Surely Greta didn't believe Mason was guilty of murder.

The woman paled. "Forget I said anything." She started to turn away but Nicole caught her arm.

"You've already raised my curiosity and I'd rather hear the news from you. What are you talking about?"

Greta whispered, "Mason's affair."

Stunned, Nicole stared at her friend. "Are you saying Mason had an affair with Riva?"

A nod. "He and Riva spent a lot of time alone together in the middle of the day. I'm sorry you had to find out this way."

"Keep your apology. I don't need it. Mason wasn't having an affair with Riva. He repaired items around her house. Brian Elliott assigned him the jobs."

"My home is over 100 years old, and I don't need that many repairs from a handsome handyman."

Greta was right about one thing. Mason was handsome. No matter what the grapevine said, Nicole knew beyond a shadow of a doubt that Mason would never cheat on her.

"There's no doubt that Riva was seeing someone. She bragged to anyone who would listen. It's been the talk of the town for weeks."

"Did she say who?"

Greta shook her head. "She always went on and on about Mason's kindness and attractiveness. It was obvious she had a thing for your man. I heard she sabotaged things around her house to have an excuse to see Mason alone."

"No matter what Riva might have wanted, Mason wouldn't betray me."

"How do you know? A lot of men have wandering eyes and hands."

"Not Mason. You can inform the gossip queens on the grapevine that they're way off base with this theory."

"Order up for Nicole," the cashier called.

"I won't keep you." Greta squeezed her hand. "Guard your heart, okay? I don't want to see you hurt."

Too late. The accusations and untruths about Mason ripped her heart into jagged pieces. Why wouldn't anyone give him the benefit of the doubt? Mason Kincaid was the finest man she knew aside from her adoptive father. She was honored to be his.

Nicole took the large bag from the cashier with a nod of thanks and turned to see Linc striding toward her, Dawn on his heels.

"I'll take that," he said. "You okay?"

She shook her head. "Let's get out of here." The last thing she wanted was to spend another minute in a restaurant full of people who believed the worst of Mason and her. By their estimation, Mason was a two-timing louse and Nicole was naive.

Linc ushered her and Dawn to his SUV. The ride to his house was silent as Nicole brooded.

Once they were inside Linc's house with the door locked, Linc led them to the kitchen where he unloaded the bag. "Do we eat now or wait for Mason?"

"Wait." Nicole couldn't handle food at the moment. "He should be here in a few minutes."

"I'll go clean up," Dawn said. With a glance at Linc, she left.

"I should do the same," Nicole murmured. She smelled like wet dog, a hazard of the job.

"Tell me what's wrong, Nic. Did Greta say something to upset you?"

An understatement. "Yeah, she did. She meant to protect me, not hurt."

"What did she say?"

"It's not what she said so much as what the town grapevine is saying. The general consensus around town is that Mason and Riva were having an affair, and that's why he spent so much time at her house."

Linc stared. "Do you believe her?"

"No. If Mason was unhappy with our relationship, he'd tell me straight out. No lying or slinking around for him. That's not who he is. For that matter, I wouldn't stay in a relationship where I didn't feel valued and loved." Been there, done that, and burned the t-shirt.

"Tell him before he hears it somewhere else."

"Not tonight."

A snort from the PSI instructor. "Good luck with that. You can't lie worth anything. He'll see right through you."

"Smart aleck," she muttered.

"Just calling it like I see it." He unpacked their dinner and opened one container to check out the contents. "Oh, man. One of my favorite meals from Delaney's. Good choice, Nic." He dug into the bag again for the pie she had requested. His eyebrows rose. "A cherry pie, too? I'll have to run a couple extra miles tomorrow."

"I figured your friends from Bravo or Durango would help you burn any excess calories you consumed. They seem to have a pretty aggressive PT program going at PSI."

"Those boys aren't joking around. Their PT is more intense than what I went through in the military." Linc's phone signaled a text. "Perfect timing. Mason is here. Get your game face on."

CHAPTER EIGHTEEN

Mason stared into the yard draped in shadows of night as he sat on the outdoor couch, his arm around Nicole's shoulders. One look at her face when he walked into the house after work and he'd known something was wrong. Although he pressed her to tell him what was troubling her before the meal, she insisted the conversation wait until after dinner.

When she remained stubbornly silent, Mason tucked her closer to his side. "Tell me what upset you, Nicole." Had she decided he wasn't worth the risk after all? No, he decided. She would have said so rather than draw out the drama. A strong, capable woman, Nicole Copeland said what was on her mind. If she'd concluded she was better off without him in her life, she would have made a quick, clean cut.

"I spoke to Greta today."

He kissed the top of her head, scrambling to remember who she was. "Three chihuahuas, right?"

"Cutest dogs ever." She relayed the conversation.

The more she talked, the more incensed he became. "Do you believe her?"

"Never."

The quick, certain response lessened the tension wracking his body. "Good, because it's not true. I love you. There is no other woman for me. If you broke our engagement, I'd do my best to win back your heart or go through the rest of my life alone. No other woman could take your place."

She pressed her fingers against his mouth to still his words. "I feel the same way about you. There is no one else for me, Mason. I adore you. I also trust you to be honest with me. If your attention had wandered to another woman, you would break our engagement, not two-time me."

"If you didn't believe I was guilty of cheating, why were you upset?"

"Because the accusation and gossip aren't fair to you. You've done nothing wrong, yet people are quick to find fault and point fingers. When will it stop?"

"With my prison record, some people may never give me a fair shake."

"Not learning who the real Mason Kincaid is will be their loss." She rested her head against his shoulder. "What can we do to quell the wagging tongues in town?"

"Ignore the gossips. Even if I took out an ad in Megan Kelter's newspaper to declare my innocence, people wouldn't believe me."

"This is a small town, Mason. Someone must have heard or seen something to help the police discover who killed Riva."

Mason glanced down at her. "What are you suggesting?"

"What could it hurt to ask questions?"

He scowled. "A lot if the killer finds out you're poking into Riva's murder. The police also prefer we not interfere in their investigation."

"I'm not going to sit by and do nothing when Riva's killer is targeting us. Are you?" Her eyes narrowed. "Wait a minute. You're planning to investigate on your own, aren't you?"

Busted. "Maybe."

"Definitely. You aren't investigating Riva's murder by yourself."

"It's dangerous."

"All the more reason why we investigate with backup. What's our first step?"

"Sleep."

She glared. "Not funny."

"I'm serious. We're both tired. We'll start tomorrow. In the meantime, think through what happened at Riva's. See if you remember more information. We'll figure out a game plan and start asking questions tomorrow."

Mason captured her mouth in a heated kiss, enjoying the heat and texture, the sweet taste that was uniquely Nicole's. When they were both holding on to their control by gossamer strands, he stood and held out his hand. "I'll walk you to your room."

Cade Ramsey, a member of Bravo, glanced over his shoulder as they passed the security room and smiled. Linc would take the watch at 1:00 a.m.

Outside her room, Mason held Nicole for long minutes. Finally, he forced himself to step back. "See you in the morning."

"Sleep well, my love."

When she closed her door, he went to his own room, showered, dressed in fresh clothes, and fell onto the bed. Mason sank into a dreamless sleep.

He woke well before his alarm went off, threw back the covers, and stumbled down the hall, praying the hot spray would wash away the dregs of fatigue still dragging him down.

Minutes later, he entered the kitchen and poured himself a mug of coffee. The first bracing sip infused much needed caffeine into his system. Maybe after consuming a gallon of the black elixir he'd be able to function. He carried his mug into the security room and sat beside Linc.

"I'm surprised you're awake."

"Everything quiet overnight?"

"Unless you count a stray dog and two cats, we didn't have visitors."

"Just the way I like it." Mason glanced at him, noting the fatigue on his face. "Dawn was okay during the night?" Mason had left his door open overnight in case Nicole needed him. He didn't have to ask if the Linc had left his door open to respond quickly if Dawn needed him. Something was definitely brewing between the two.

"Not really."

"What happened?"

"She sees the killer's masked face every time she closes her eyes." Anger burned in his eyes. "Dawn won't improve until she knows who he is and that he's behind bars. At the moment, every male in Otter Creek except for the two of us are potential suspects."

"Nicole feels the same except she lumps Bravo, Durango, Ethan, and the OCPD detectives in with us. You up for a little nosing around?"

Linc glanced away from the computer screen to stare at him. "You're going to hunt for the killer?"

"I have a vested interest in identifying this guy. He's a threat to Nicole."

"You're also a target."

"We have no idea if Riva's killer is the person coming after me." He sighed. "We also can't forget my less-than-savory past and the fallout from it. The Fitzgeralds have long memories, and I don't blame them."

"You paid your debt to society. The Fitzgeralds don't have the right to demand more. What will you do if you find the killer?"

"Call Ethan. I won't confront him myself. I just want him off the streets and away from Nicole."

"You telling me you don't want payback?" Linc shook his head. "I'm not buying it. If some thug came after my woman, I'd want a couple minutes alone with him for putting his hands on her."

Mason gave a wry laugh. "Oh, I want to point out the error of his ways so bad I can taste it, but I want to attend my own wedding in two months and three days more."

"What if he comes after you again?"

"I'll be happy to demonstrate the skills Bravo and Durango drilled into me."

Satisfaction gleamed in Linc's eyes. "If you want help hunting for Riva's killer, I'm in. I owe him for shoving Dawn to the ground and wreaking havoc in her life."

He couldn't do better than to have a Special Forces soldier for backup. "Thanks."

A shrug. "That's what friends are for, Mason. We have each other's backs, no matter the circumstances."

When a door opened close by, Linc rose and walked to the hallway. His face brightened when he saw Dawn. "You okay?" he murmured, cupping her cheek with the palm of his hand.

She smiled, humor dancing in her eyes. "I slept great when I sat beside you on the couch, but I only slept in short spurts after you carried me to bed."

His expression softened into one of tenderness. "I'm glad I helped you get some rest."

Mason cleared his throat. He didn't want to witness the kiss Linc looked ready to plant on Dawn's mouth.

Dawn's eyes widened. "Good morning, Mason. I didn't realize anyone else was awake. I hope I didn't interrupt anything."

"I couldn't sleep, either, so I decided to fuel my caffeine craving." He looked at Linc. "I'll take the watch. Enjoy your coffee and the sunrise with Dawn before you have to leave."

The other man linked his fingers with Dawn's. "Thanks, Mase." He led her toward the kitchen.

With a grin, Mason settled in front of the computer and sipped his coffee as he watched the screen. Nearing sunrise, the street traffic began to pick up and lights appeared in various windows in nearby houses.

Linc returned to the security room. "I need to go." He told Mason the alarm code. "Set the alarm when you leave. Matt will be waiting at Pet Palace to watch over Dawn and Nicole. We have the women covered, Mason. Watch your back today. We'll stir the pot tonight and see what rises to the top."

"I have an idea on that."

"Don't investigate on your own. You need an alibi and backup in case of trouble. As volatile as emotions are in this situation, there will be trouble."

"I hear you."

A scowl. "You better. So far, you've survived the attempts on your life and Nicole's. If the attacks continue, you won't be so lucky."

"The incidents might be an attempt to separate me from Nicole, not a threat to my life."

"Don't bank on that. Whether he meant it or not, the person who poisoned you could have killed you. Dead is dead, Mason." Linc's eyes grew shadowed. "I've lost too many friends. I don't want to lose another one." After a quick, low-voiced conversation with Dawn at the front door, Linc left.

As Mason continued to watch the computer screen, he considered what his first move should be. He glanced at his watch. Was it too early to call Zane? From what he'd observed, the Fortress tech wizard was usually up early because of his wife's schedule and his infant son. This might be the perfect time to catch him before the day's craziness at Fortress cranked up.

He grabbed his cell phone and tapped Zane's name.

A moment later, Zane answered his call. "How do you feel, Mason?"

Huh. Guess someone had told the Navy SEAL about the poisoning incident. "Better."

"Good. What do you need?"

He closed his eyes a second. No qualifications or questions. Just acceptance and an offer of help. "If you have time, can you run a check on the Fitzgerald clan to see if they're still in Liberty?"

"You have reason to believe they aren't?"

"I'm eliminating possibilities. I need to narrow my focus. The Fitzgerald family has the most reason to harm me although I don't think they'd hurt Nicole. I know Todd Fitzgerald is here. I have a fist-sized bruise on my jaw from our confrontation two nights ago. I need to know if other Fitzgerald family members are here as well."

"Copy that. I'll get back to you when I track them down." Zane ended the call.

"Is there something you aren't telling me?"

Mason shoved back from the computer console. He crossed to Nicole's side and kissed her. "Good morning, beautiful. You know everything I know. I called Zane at Fortress to request assistance in locating the rest of the Fitzgerald family. They have the most reason to cause me harm. Since we aren't sure whether the poisoning is connected to Riva's death, I figured we'd be wise to eliminate the rest of the Fitzgeralds from the suspect pool if we can."

Nicole leaned against him, arms wrapped around his waist. "What suspect pool? Right now, we don't have any suspects aside from Todd Fitzgerald. Even with a broken arm, he could have dumped ketamine in your drink."

True. He tightened his hold. "I hope he's not responsible. His family has suffered enough because of me."

"You didn't do anything to incite him. In fact, you've gone out of your way to avoid him and his family by staying away from Liberty, and I know you want to go home to see your father."

"He's been here several times as has Rio's family."

"At some point in the near future, that won't be enough. Your father is growing older. One day he won't be able to travel to see you. I want you to have the freedom to go home, Mason. Your father will need you."

He rested his forehead against hers. "Dad and I discussed this. When the time comes, he'll move to Otter Creek. In fact, he's talking about moving in the next couple of years."

Her eyes widened. "He doesn't mind leaving the town he's lived in all his life?"

"After the way the townspeople turned against us, he feels no loyalty to Liberty. His best friend has incurable second-stage cancer, though. When Roy passes away, Dad will sell the house. He's already doing repairs and considering remodeling the kitchen and bathrooms."

"When did you talk about this?"

"The night before Riva died. I planned to tell you, but you ended up in the hospital and I forgot about it."

She peeked at her watch and grimaced. "I need to leave for work soon. Is Dawn awake?"

"For a couple of hours. She had coffee with Linc before he left." He leaned down, nuzzled the side of her neck, and murmured, "I don't think we need to give those two a nudge to get together. They seem to be making fast progress all on their own."

"Are you sure?"

"You'll have to see them for yourself, but I'd say Linc and Dawn are well on their way to becoming a couple."

"Yes! Perfect news to start off another day with you."

Mason released her. "Get your gear together. We'll leave in fifteen minutes."

After driving Nicole and Dawn to Pet Palace, he headed for the Oakdale construction site. He and Dean were assigned to work on Building 9.

"Here." Brian handed over the itemized list. "First thing I want you to do is change out the locks like you did on Building 8. Everything else comes after that job's done." His expression was apologetic. "I need the list completed today, Mason. The inspector is coming tomorrow to check this building."

He eyed the two-page list and mentally calculated the amount of time each task would take. Unless things went quicker than he anticipated, Mason and Dean would be working until well after dark. The hunt for Riva's killer would have to wait. "Yes, sir."

"I'll get started on the list," Dean said. "When you return, we'll change the locks, then knock out the rest of the work."

On the way back from the hardware supplier, Mason's cell phone rang. He checked the screen readout on his dashboard and answered the call. "What do you have for me, Zane?"

"All the members of the Fitzgerald family are in Liberty except for Todd and one other. I traced the other man's credit card activity. He's in Otter Creek, Mase."

Ice water ran through his veins. "Who is it?"

"Gage Fitzgerald."

Oh, man. What was the husband of the woman he killed in the accident doing in town?

CHAPTER NINETEEN

Mason's hands tightened around the steering wheel. Did Gage come to cause him trouble? What was the point? Making him miserable wouldn't bring his wife and daughter back. If Gage intended to cause trouble, Mason preferred to face it head on rather than be blindsided. "Where's he staying?"

"The Otter Creek Bed and Breakfast."

Not surprising, he supposed. "When did he check in?"

"Yesterday afternoon."

Plenty of time to hunt down Mason and dump ketamine into his drink. The muscles in his jaw twitched. "He's a veterinarian."

Zane was silent a moment. "He'd have a ready drug supply handy, including ketamine. What will you do?"

"Have a talk with him if I run into him."

A snort. "You'll find a way to cross paths with him."

Smart man. "Otter Creek is a small town."

"You might sell that to Blackhawk, but don't bet on it. Anything else I can help with?"

"I meant to call you earlier about the security footage and haven't had a chance. Did you get more information from the recording?"

"A tattoo on the driver's left hand. Couldn't clean up the image enough to really see it, but you can at least be on the lookout for the marking. Sorry I can't tell you more."

How many men in town had tattoos on their hands? He could think of at least eight off hand, including Patton and Fisher. "Pass the information on to Ethan Blackhawk." The longer Mason delayed seeing the police chief in person, the better his chances of talking to Gage before Ethan warned him to stay away from the man.

"I'll take care of it. If I can help further, let me know."

Mason ended the call, tossing ideas around in his head. Should he confront Gage and ask him if he'd poisoned Mason's drink?

A lot of good that would do. If he was guilty, why would Gage admit it? At the moment, the police had nothing to go on and no reason to suspect Gage of a crime.

Mason considered his options. Going to the B & B would be asking for Ethan to come down on him hard. However, if he happened to be in the same place as Gage at the same time, no one could accuse Mason of instigating a confrontation.

There were only so many places a visitor could eat dinner in Otter Creek. Gage wasn't one to visit fast food places so that left the higher end restaurants. Maybe Tennessee Steakhouse on the other end of town.

Gage could also drive to Cherry Hill or one of the other towns nearby where he'd find a greater variety of restaurants. He might have left town already. As brothers, Gage and Todd were close. He might have driven to town to check on Todd and lend him a hand until he was ready to return to Liberty.

Mason parked in front of the supply store and went inside. He nodded at Bill, the sales clerk behind the counter. "How's it going, Bill?"

"Can't complain. You back already?"

"More replacement locks. Same amount as yesterday."

The older man's eyebrows rose. "The original ones we sold you didn't work?"

"They're fine. We've had a rash of vandalism in the apartment buildings and needed the higher end locking system."

Bill came around the counter and led Mason through the store to the appropriate aisle. "Don't know what the world's coming to. In my day working construction, we didn't have to worry about such things." He held up his hands to showcase the swollen joints of his fingers. "I'd still be working construction if I didn't have arthritis. Creating something beautiful and useful out of raw materials is more satisfying and a lot more fun that working on this end of the business."

Minutes later, Mason stowed the new locks in the cab of his truck and climbed behind the wheel. When he strode into Building 9 with the box of locks in one hand and his tool box in the other, Dean glanced at him from his perch on a ladder.

"Did you see your friend?"

Frowning, he set the boxes down. "What friend?"

"You must have missed him. He didn't leave his name, but said he was from your hometown."

"Was he wearing a cast or a sling on his arm?"

Dean's eyebrows rose. "Nope. You have more than one friend from home in town?"

He wouldn't call them friends. "The guy with the arm injury is the one who punched me in the face. I didn't know the second man was in town until a few minutes ago."

"Not a friend, either?"

"Not even close. He'd be happy to see me buried six feet underground. He's the husband of the woman I killed in the accident."

Dean whistled. "Why is he in Otter Creek?"

"That's the million-dollar question. I don't have an answer at the moment, but I will soon."

"Watch your step, Mase."

He held up a hand. "I know. I get it. I'll take precautions, but I'm finished taking whatever the Fitzgeralds dish out."

"If you need help from the police, you can trust Stella Armstrong."

That made Mason pause in the act of opening the first box. "You sound like you know her well."

"We go back. She bailed me out of a jamb. I would trust her with my life and Leah's."

There was a story here, but he knew from past questions that Dean would veer away from divulging details. People had a right to privacy, except for him apparently. His life was an open discussion forum on the grapevine around town. "I'll keep that in mind."

The two men worked quickly to replace the knobs and locks throughout the apartment building. When they finished, they returned to the first unit and worked through the list of repairs and jobs to complete.

They found unexpected damage in the first two units that slowed them down. By the time they broke for lunch, he and Dean still had eight units to complete work in.

Sitting beneath the closest tree, he slid his phone from his pocket and called Nicole. "I'm going to be late again. I'm sorry, sweetheart. The inspector is coming tomorrow. Everything has to be perfect."

"I understand. You've rearranged your plans often enough to accommodate my crazy schedule. It's my turn to return the favor."

"I'll make it up to you."

"Hmm. Sounds promising. I'm looking forward to it."

The laughter in her voice made him smile. "No problems at the salon?"

"Not unless you count another dog who roamed too close to a skunk."

He groaned. "Oh, man. That's a smelly job."

"Oh, trust me. I know. Our whole shop smells like skunk at the moment. Everyone who walks in gets this funny look on their face."

"I can imagine."

"Delaney's for dinner again?"

"Tennessee Steakhouse stays open late. What about a double date there with Linc and Dawn?"

"I like it. I'll talk to them when Linc arrives although I won't classify this as a double date. I don't want to scare them away from each other if they haven't figured out where their friendship is headed. I'll text you and let you know what the verdict is about the steakhouse. I love you, Mason."

"Love you, too, baby." More than she could possibly know.

"Nicole and Dawn are okay?" Dean asked when Mason ended the call.

He took a bite of his wrap and swallowed before he replied. "They're fine. Matt Rainer is keeping an eye on them until Linc takes over this afternoon."

"Why would Riva's killer come to the shop? It's broad daylight."

"Didn't stop him from attacking Riva."

Dean scowled. "True. I'm worried about Leah. That's A Wrap is close to Pet Palace."

"Police patrols have stepped up in a big way during business hours."

"Sounds great until you remember that no one knows who this killer is. He could have already walked into the grooming salon or That's A Wrap, and no one would know."

"The killer has to be someone who lives here."

"You don't believe the killer is a random stranger passing through town?"

"Not a chance. How would this guy zero in on Riva's house and happen to catch her at home without Cosmo? Riva worked crazy hours, and her schedule was never the same from one day to the next." He shook his head. "Too many coincidences for my taste."

"Is there another reason why you think the killer lives here?"

"Riva's door wasn't forced."

Dean paused with his sandwich halfway to his mouth. "She knew the guy and let him in. You saw the doors?"

"No," he admitted, "but Ethan and Rod never asked me what tool I used to force a door open or demanded my boots to compare them to prints found at the scene. I might be able to find out from Josh." More likely, Rio could call in a favor with his team leader. Every member of Durango owed Rio their lives several times over. As long as it didn't compromise the police investigation, Mason doubted Josh would balk at answering the question. "I'll text Rio and have him ask."

After sending the text, he focused on eating. Within a couple of minutes, his phone signaled an incoming text. Mason checked the screen. "No forced entry into Riva's home. She either admitted the killer or she left the door unlocked."

They finished lunch early and went back to work. Halfway through the afternoon, Brian walked into unit five. "How's it going?"

"Making progress although not as fast as we want. We keep finding items to repair, things that were in perfect working order two days ago." Mason glanced over his shoulder at his boss. "Need anything?"

The construction owner scowled. "Same kind of problems as in Building 8?"

"Yes, sir."

"The locks have been changed?"

"We finished installing the new hardware hours ago," Dean said. "If our vandal is planning to strike tonight, he'll have to break windows or bust doors to do it."

"Let's hope that doesn't happen." He turned his attention to Mason. "You'll be able to complete the work tonight?"

"We'll get it done, even if we have to stay all night." Although he prayed that wouldn't be necessary. He wanted to see Nicole and hold her.

"Great. I owe you both. I'd stick around and help but I have a meeting with a potential client. Big housing development that will keep us busy through the next 18 months. We have an excellent chance of getting the contract. The meeting is likely to go late, though."

"Not a tempting prospect. This is the fun part of the job." Dean moved to the next outlet. "I'd rather be working with my hands than sitting in meetings with clients."

"Same here," Mason said.

"It's not my favorite thing to do, but someone has to market the business to clients."

"Hire someone to take care of the marketing and do what you love."

Brian looked thoughtful. "Maybe. I'll give it some thought. Because of the security issues around here, I'm thinking about hiring a security guard to keep an eye on the property until we turn it over to the client."

"Got a company in mind to provide the service?" Mason asked.

He shook his head. "I need a company that's top notch but cheap. Know anyone that fits the bill?"

"Contact Josh Cahill. PSI is always looking for training opportunities for their students. Josh might be willing to work something out on a temporary basis."

A broad smile curved Brian's mouth. "I like it. I'll give Josh a call when I'm heading to the meeting. Thanks for the suggestion. I'll get out of your way. Listen, even if another member of the crew volunteers to give you two a hand, I don't want anyone else in this building. Manning is looking for an excuse to write us up."

"Yes, sir."

After clapping Mason on the shoulder, Brian left the unit.

"What do you think the chances are that the vandal is someone on the construction crew?"

"Caught that, did you?" Mason gave his partner a nod of approval. "I didn't see signs of forced entry in Building 7."

"Patton and Fisher worked in there almost exclusively." Dean scowled. "You think those two are responsible for the rash of vandalism in this building?"

"I wouldn't be surprised. No proof, though."

"If they're guilty, what's their motive?"

He thought about that for a minute, then shook his head. "I don't know. Fisher is bucking for a promotion. Doesn't make sense that he would sabotage his chances of moving up."

Dean flicked him a glance. "Makes perfect sense if he's sliding pieces into place to blame you for it."

Stunned, Mason stared at his partner. "That's crazy. Why would he do that?"

"You're Brian's go-to man. If something has to be done and done right, he turns to you first. That's why he's pressuring you to take over the home rehab side of Elliott Construction."

"I didn't realize you knew about the offer."

"The whole crew knows. Brian hasn't been quiet about his desire for you to take over."

Mason grimaced. "No wonder Patton and Fisher have been prickly. Fisher wants that job."

A snort. "He might have more time on the job with Elliott, but he's definitely not the most qualified for the position. That would be you."

Uncomfortable, he shook his head. "Plenty of other men on the crew have better qualifications."

"Not from where I'm sitting, and the boss agrees with me."

Two hours later, Patton and Fisher wandered into unit 7 and looked around. Patton smirked. "Having to redo your work, Kincaid? Guess you're not so perfect after all."

Mason refocused on the coat closet hinges, tightening a screw that had mysteriously backed out of the hole. "What do you want, Patton? We're pressed for time."

"Thought you might need a hand fixing what you screwed up."

"No, thanks. I'm sure you have plans for the night that are a lot more fun than this. I don't want to hold you up."

The other man's eyes glittered. "Our help not good enough for you?"

"Brian told us to take care of the tasks ourselves." Dean flashed him an impatient glance. "You have a problem with his orders, take it up with him."

"You think you're better than we are?" Fisher growled. "We've been with Elliott longer than you have and have more experience."

"It's not about either of those things." What was their problem? He and Dean didn't have time for this contest of wills. "Brian trusted us with the responsibility. We won't let him down."

Patton glared at each of them. "You better enjoy the work while you have it."

"What's that supposed to mean?"

"When Fisher's promoted, both of you slugs will be out on your butts."

"I guess we'll see what happens." If Brian promoted this guy to be Mason's supervisor, Fisher wouldn't have to fire him. He'd walk out. Hopefully, Ethan would give him time to find a new job before coming down hard. If he had to, Mason would start his own business. Not his first choice, though. He liked working for Elliott Construction and didn't want to go into competition with Brian.

Fisher nudged his friend with his elbow. "Come on. Let's get out of here. I hear an ice-cold beer calling my name. If Kincaid and Connor don't want help, let them work all night to finish. Serves them right."

Once they left, Dean sighed. "That could have dissolved into an ugly confrontation."

"Oh, yeah." He was afraid it would come to that if he accepted the position Brian offered.

CHAPTER TWENTY

Relief swamped Nicole when Mason parked in Linc's driveway. She'd been tense from the moment Mason told her he was leaving the job site. Now that he was here, she could relax.

When he stepped onto the porch, she rushed out of the house and into his arms, breathing freely for the first time since he left for work early this morning. She kept waiting for another attack. For the moment, she concentrated on the joy of being with Mason.

He captured her mouth with his. Minutes later, he eased back, stroking his thumb over her bottom lip. "I craved your kiss all day."

She smiled and led him inside. "If you're too tired to go out for dinner, we can order takeout."

Mason squeezed her hand. "I appreciate the offer, but after thinking of steak all afternoon, takeout would be a huge disappointment."

Nicole laughed. "We'll go when you finish your shower."

"I'll hurry. I'm starved."

Forty minutes later, Tennessee Steakhouse's hostess seated them at a corner table in the back. Despite lively conversation and laughter during the meal, Mason and Linc frequently scanned the crowded dining room.

Frowning, she glanced at the patrons in the restaurant. Faces turned away when the people staring at Mason noticed her glaring at them. Two men at the bar, however, stared and smirked, refusing to look away when she zeroed in on them.

They looked familiar. She thought for a moment, then remembered she saw them at the Oakdale construction site two weeks earlier when she had lunch with Mason.

Nicole turned toward him to confirm her suspicions but noticed the wariness in his eyes. "What's wrong?" she whispered.

"Does the staring bother you?"

"Staring is rude, and ticks me off." She narrowed her eyes. "But I'm not a fragile princess who folds at the first sign of trouble. I can handle foolish gossips. I can't handle losing you."

He leaned close and kissed her with a tenderness that brought tears to her eyes. "I don't know what I'd do without you."

"You won't have to find out. I'm in this for the long haul."

Mason trailed the back of his fingers down her cheek. "I'm blessed."

"Ready to go, Mase?" Linc asked.

Mason stood and held his hand out to Nicole. His strong fingers closed over hers, sending a shiver of awareness through her body. She loved his controlled strength. Any woman who didn't appreciate the roughened, calloused hands of a working man was missing out.

As they walked through the restaurant, her skin prickled. People watched them leave, their conversations dying off when she and her dining companions passed their tables. In their wake, the noise level rose.

Nicole squared her shoulders. The citizens of Otter Creek would eat their words when the truth came out. Mason Kincaid was innocent, and Nicole looked forward to facing down his accusers in the near future. All Nicole had to do was identify the killer. Too bad she didn't have more to go on than a spicy cologne and ham-sized fists.

Mason stayed close to Nicole's side as they walked to the SUV. Her lips curved when she noticed Linc doing the same with Dawn. Sweet. Unless she misread the situation, those two were becoming emotionally involved, and she loved it. Dawn deserved the best, and Linc might be the right guy.

Halfway to Linc's SUV, another vehicle circled the side of the building and parked a few spaces away.

Linc slowed, stared at the car, then glanced over his shoulder. "Mason."

At his low-voiced warning, Nicole crowded closer to Mason, her pulse spiking. What was going on? She glanced around but didn't see a threat. What was she missing?

When the car's occupants climbed from the vehicle, Mason stiffened. He nudged her behind him.

She recognized Todd Fitzgerald but not the driver. Based on his body language, Mason did.

Todd noticed Mason and elbowed his companion. The stranger spotted Mason and stopped abruptly, his expression hardening. "Kincaid," he said, voice flat.

"Gage." He glanced at Todd. "How are you?"

"Trying to convince me you care?" he snapped.

"Are you responsible for Todd's injuries?" Gage stalked toward Mason.

Mason pushed Nicole further behind him. Seconds later, she found herself standing beside Dawn, looking at Mason's and Linc's backs. The two men stood side by side, providing a wall of protection.

As the tension ratcheted up, Nicole slid her phone from her pocket, ready to call 911 if things got out of hand. She eyed Mason and Linc again, noting their confidence, and returned her phone to her pocket. Todd was in no shape to take on anyone much less men trained in self-defense. Mason and Linc could handle Gage without difficulty.

"Should we call the police?" Dawn whispered to her.

Nicole shook her head. "Our men can handle this without breaking a sweat." Hopefully without throwing punches.

"What good would it do me to harm Todd?" Mason's voice was quiet.

"Payback for your prison term."

"And end up behind bars again? No, thanks. My future plans don't include another prison term."

"A lot of men might believe the price of revenge was worth the cost."

"I'm not one of them." Mason folded his arms. "What about you?"

Surprise flickered on Gage's face. "Me? What are you talking about?"

"I'm the reason Stacey and Allison are gone. No one would blame you for avenging your family. Are you responsible for what happened to me?"

The other man's gaze swept over him. "Doesn't look like you have injuries."

"By the grace of God, I don't. But someone wanted me out of commission or dead. Two night ago, a soft drink I left in my truck was doctored with ketamine."

Understanding dawned in his eyes. "I wondered why the police questioned me regarding my whereabouts on the afternoon I arrived in town. I figured you sent them to harass me."

"What did you tell them?" Linc asked.

"I was with Todd at the pharmacy to pick up his pain medicine. After that, we ate dinner in Cherry Hill at an

Italian place highly recommended by the proprietress of the B & B."

"Your story can be verified?"

A shrug. "I haven't heard from the police again. They must have followed up." Gage shifted his attention to Mason. "How do I know you're telling the truth?"

"Same reason. The Otter Creek PD is thorough."

"You live here now. You might have friends on the force. Who's to say they aren't covering for you."

"If my alibi hadn't held up, I'd be in jail. Yes, I have friends on the force. They'd hate to arrest me, but would anyway if they had proof I committed a crime."

"Did you hire someone to poison Mason?" Linc cocked his head. "You have access to ketamine. You could have provided the drug to a free agent who doesn't mind getting their hands dirty for the right price."

He shook his head. "I could have, but I didn't."

"We only have your word for that."

The vet lifted one shoulder in a shrug. "That's not my problem. I don't have to defend myself against something I didn't do. By the way, I also don't travel with veterinary medicine in my car. And, yes, the police searched the car and the room."

"Why did you come to my work site today?" Mason asked.

Nicole's eyes widened. That was a bold move on the other man's part. Did he show up to cause Mason trouble with Brian, perhaps toss more accusations at him and convince the construction owner to kick Mason to the curb? If so, he was doomed to disappointment. Brian wouldn't fire Mason without irrefutable proof of wrong doing.

"I wanted to see your face when you answered my questions about Todd's injuries. You're the only person he knows in town. No one else would have the motivation to hurt him."

"How do you know it wasn't a robbery gone bad?" Dawn asked.

Todd frowned. "The guy who attacked me didn't demand my wallet, watch, or cell phone. He just went after me with that hammer."

"I doubt you'll believe me," Mason said to Gage, "but I don't have ill will toward Todd or you. My prison time was justified. I apologized at the sentencing hearing, and I meant every word. I'm sorry for your loss and my role in taking the lives of your wife and daughter."

"You're still breathing. From where I'm standing, an apology isn't good enough," Todd snapped.

"No, it isn't," Mason agreed. "But an apology is all I have to offer. That and a promise that nothing alcoholic will ever touch my lips again. I've kept that promise for fifteen years. If I slip up, I guarantee my wife will have strong words to say about it."

"You're married?" Gage seemed surprised by that.

"Not yet. In two months."

Todd cursed softly as he turned his gaze toward Nicole. "I warned you how dangerous he is."

"You're wrong."

Gage frowned at Todd. "You warned her off?"

"What did you expect me to do? Leave her vulnerable to this drunk? Look what happened to Allison and Stacey. I'm not letting another family suffer like ours if I can prevent it."

Linc's eyebrow rose. "Hard to call a man a drunk when he doesn't consume alcohol."

"That you know about. What he does in private, who knows?"

Mason snorted. "The police keep close tabs on me and with the way the grapevine works in Otter Creek, law enforcement would know if I bought alcohol in this town. More important, I won't disappoint Nicole by breaking my promise to her."

Todd sneered. "Too bad you weren't a teetotaler fifteen years ago."

"You're right. I made a stupid choice, one I'll have to live with the rest of my life."

"At least you have a life. Stacey and Allison don't have one." His voice broke. "They died on the side of the road. It should have been you."

Nicole slid her hand into Mason's, hurting for everyone involved, especially Mason who had fought to rebuild his life and overcome the stigma attached to his past. He'd made all the right moves and chosen the path of honor and dignity, and still people wouldn't let him move forward.

"Enough, Todd." Gage sent him a quelling glance before turning back to Mason. "Look, this isn't getting us anywhere, and I've said all I intend to say to you. If you crossed the line into vengeance, you'll pay. I'll throw every bit of influence I have into making sure you never see the light of day again outside of prison."

"A waste of time," Todd muttered, his hate-filled glare locked onto Mason. "No two-bit hick cops will hold him accountable."

Mason tightened his grip around Nicole's hand. "One more thing, Gage. How did you know where to find me?"

Gage frowned. "Your father speaks highly of you and this town. We knew you would be here with Rio."

"How did you find me when you arrived in town? I work at several different job sites around the county. How did you narrow your visit to Oakdale?"

"I received an email telling me where to find you."

"Who sent it?" Linc asked.

"I don't know. The sender didn't identify himself."

Mason and Linc glanced at each other, then Mason asked, "Would you forward the email to me? I have a friend who might be able to trace it to the sender."

"You think it's important?"

"I believe a murderer is using you to get to me. Worse, I'm afraid he's setting up both of us."

CHAPTER TWENTY-ONE

"You expect us to believe that?" Todd's voice, filled with derision, carried in the still night air. "You're a liar and a con artist, Kincaid. And your woman? She deserves whatever she gets if she doesn't dump you and run as far away from you as possible." He looked at his brother. "Let's get out of here. I need some clean air."

Fury burning a hole in his gut, Mason analyzed Todd's body language and pushed Nicole further behind him. He didn't trust Todd. If the guy threw another sucker punch, Mason didn't want Nicole hurt by accident.

To his left, Linc motioned for Dawn to move back. Guess the PSI instructor interpreted Todd's body language the same as Mason. Despite the injuries, the man was spoiling for a fight.

"Lay off," Gage snapped. "We're finished."

"Whatever." Todd strode directly toward Mason, balled his fist, and took a swing at his face.

Mason shifted enough for the strike to miss by less than an inch, throwing the other man off balance. He took advantage and shoved him onto the nearest car, face down.

Todd grunted with pain as his injured arm connected with the car's trunk.

Easily controlling the other man's struggles, Mason said, "Enough. You had your free shot at me. You don't get a second one."

"You're a dead man."

"More dangerous men than you tried and failed to kill me in prison." He had the scars to prove it. "Go home, Todd. If you stay in Otter Creek, you'll be used as a murderer's pawn. Your family has suffered enough. Get on with your life. Stacey wouldn't want you to wallow in hatred and misery. You'll only end up hurting yourself. Nothing you can do to me is worse than the knowledge of my own guilt."

He stepped back and away from the man struggling to regain his balance, alert for another potential attack. Gage gave his brother a hand. Once Todd was steady on his feet, Gage gave Mason a short nod and herded the swearing man toward the restaurant.

"Nicely done," Linc murmured as they watched until the men turned the corner of the building and disappeared from view.

"Thanks." Although he appreciated the compliment, Mason wished he'd agreed to takeout. The confrontation had left him with a boulder the side of Montana in his stomach.

The skin at the back of his neck prickled as though spiders crawled along his hairline. He scanned the area, looking for the source of his unease. A shadow moved at the very edge of the lot.

He focused on that spot, but he couldn't make out who watched from the darkness.

"What is it?" Linc murmured.

"Watcher at 10:00 o'clock."

The operative unlocked his vehicle, then pressed the remote into Mason's hand. "Get the women into the safety of the SUV. I'll find out who's interested in us." Linc walked to the opposite side of the building and disappeared.

"Let's go." Mason urged Dawn and Nicole ahead of him to the SUV. He opened the door for Dawn, then tucked Nicole into the backseat before sliding behind the wheel in case he needed to get them out of danger in a hurry.

"What's going on?" Dawn asked. "Where's Linc?"

"Someone was watching us from the trees. He's trying to identify him."

"Go. He might need help." Her hands gripped the edge of the seat with a white-knuckled hold.

Amusement zipped through him. "Linc doesn't need a hand. He's well trained and armed."

"What if the person watching is armed, too?"

"He can handle himself." How much did she know about Linc's training?

She groaned and relaxed against the seat. "Of course he can. I forgot the extent of his training."

"What am I missing?" Nicole asked. "Linc's better trained than a regular Army grunt?"

Mason twisted in his seat to look at Nicole. "Special Forces. He knows what he's doing."

He scanned the parking lot again, focusing on the shadowed area near the trees. Nothing. Had Linc caught the watcher before he or she disappeared?

Two minutes later, Linc walked toward the SUV. Mason asked the women to stay inside, then met the instructor away from their hearing. He handed Linc the remote. "Any luck?"

"Do the names Gene Patton and Ed Fisher mean anything to you?"

Mason groaned. "They're on the Elliott construction crew. Why?"

"They were watching from the shadows and weren't happy that I insisted they answer questions."

"What did they say?"

"They heard raised voices and wanted to be sure their coworker didn't need help."

Mason snorted. "They wouldn't lift a finger to help me if I needed an assist."

Linc's lips curved. "I got the impression they'd prefer to watch you beaten to a pulp rather than help."

"They were in the bar while we ate dinner. I noticed them keeping an eye on us."

"They smelled like they bathed in a vat of beer."

"Great. They won't be worth anything tomorrow." Mason sighed. "I wonder how much of their work Dean and I will have to redo."

"I'd steer clear of them. Those boys weren't cooperative at first, but I convinced them that answering my questions was best for their continued good health."

"You threatened them?" Oh, man. That wouldn't be good. He was sure to hear about that at some point tomorrow.

Linc shrugged. "Dawn's safety is at stake as well as Nicole's. I don't care who I offend." He opened the driver's door and climbed behind the wheel.

A moment later, Linc drove them from the lot and toward his home. Once there, Mason escorted the women inside while Linc checked the perimeter of the property for signs of incursion onto his property.

"Stay near the door while I check the house."

Nicole brushed her mouth lightly over his. "Be careful."

With a nod, he searched each room, checking every hiding place along with doors and windows for signs of tampering. He found nothing.

By the time he finished, Linc had returned. "Clear," he told his friend.

"Same. Anyone want coffee?"

"I can't handle that right now, but I'm sure whoever is on watch will need it." Dawn headed for the kitchen. "I'll start a pot."

Linc watched her go, concern in his eyes. "I'll be back," he murmured and followed her.

Nicole slid her arms around Mason's waist. "Any chance you have time to star gaze on the deck tonight?"

He dropped a quick kiss to her forehead. "For you, I'll make time. Besides, my watch shift doesn't begin until 1:00 a.m." Mason eased back from her. "Wait here a minute." He went to his room, snatched a quilt from the end of the bed, and carried it to the living room. "Come on. Let's see how many constellations you can identify."

Wrapping his hand around hers, he led Nicole to the kitchen. His eyebrows rose when he saw Dawn with her face pressed into Linc's neck, holding him tight.

Linc gave him a slight head shake and motioned for them to go on.

Hmm. The parking lot incident must have upset her more than she let on. Mason ushered Nicole into the yard. He scouted for an open area sheltered enough to protect Nicole.

He spread the quilt on the ground and stretched out beside Nicole. She propped her head on his arm and gazed skyward.

"The sky is clear tonight," she murmured. "You can see many constellations." She named one after another. Mason wouldn't be able to identify them without her pointing them out.

Nicole looked at him. "Do you think Dawn is all right?"

"She will be. It's the first time she's come face to face with what Linc's trained to do."

"He's an instructor."

"Linc has the same training as Durango. When Fortress needs him, he goes. If Dawn is in a relationship with him, she'll have to accept that part of his life."

"Why would he risk his life? He's a trainer now."

"Linc is a warrior and always will be."

When they returned to the house, they discovered Linc and Dawn sitting on the couch, holding hands and speaking in low tones. Quinn Gallagher monitored the security screen.

After escorting Nicole to her room and kissing her goodnight, Mason closed himself in his room and called Zane. "I apologize for calling so late," he said when the tech guru answered his call.

"What do you need?"

"I forwarded an email to you. The person who sent pointed Gage Fitzgerald my direction. I want to know who sent the email and why."

"I'll let you know what I learn."

"Thanks, Zane."

"Yep. Later." He ended the call.

That done, Mason got ready for bed. An hour before his alarm sounded, he woke in a cold sweat after dreaming of losing Nicole to Riva's nameless, faceless murderer.

A few minutes after midnight, Mason walked to the kitchen, hoping Quinn made fresh coffee recently. He needed something to wash the bitter taste of fear from his mouth. A breath of relief whooshed out when he saw the half-full carafe. He poured a mug and sipped half the liquid before refilling it and heading for the security room.

Quinn turned as Mason crossed the threshold. "Couldn't sleep?"

"Nope. Go home and get some sleep, Quinn."

"I don't mind staying if you need someone to keep watch with you."

"I'm sure Heidi would appreciate having you home."

Quinn flashed a grin. "I'll have to nudge Charlie out of my spot. He keeps her company when I'm gone."

After the operative left, Mason wondered if Nicole would like a dog for their home. She loved her four-legged customers and they loved her.

That conversation would have to wait until Riva's killer was behind bars, though. He refused to endanger an innocent dog.

"Two months and two days to go," a soft feminine voice murmured from the threshold.

Mason spun to see a sleepy-eyed Nicole dressed in her yoga workout clothes. He clasped her upper arms. "Why are you awake? Are you okay?"

She hugged him. "I'm fine. I woke up thirsty and saw you in here." Nicole made a soft sound of contentment. "Two more months, Mason. I'm looking forward to the day I become Nicole Kincaid. The name has a certain panache to it."

He chuckled, joy filling his heart. "Get your water and go back to bed. You need rest."

"You sent Quinn home early, didn't you? It's not time for your shift."

"Couldn't sleep. I'll be fine." He dropped a soft kiss on her mouth. "Get your water and quit distracting me from my job."

"Yes, sir." Nicole snapped off a quick salute and went to the kitchen.

Smiling at the smart-aleck attitude, Mason settled in front of the computer screen again and scanned the sectors around Linc's house. All but the view of the back of the house looked the same.

He stared at the screen. Something was off, but what? Mason frowned. A second later, he sprinted toward the kitchen. Nicole's scream shattered the silence.

CHAPTER TWENTY-TWO

"Nicole!" Mason raced into the kitchen.

"Someone was looking in the kitchen window. When I screamed, he ran."

"Did you recognize him?"

She shook her head.

Linc ran into the room, a Sig in his hand. "Sit rep."

"A man looked in the window and scared Nicole. Stay with the women." Mason slipped out into the night. He noted boot prints in the dirt under the window and followed the trail of flattened grass through the yard to the edge of Linc's property.

He grasped the top of the fence, hauled himself over the structure, and landed in a crouch. No grass or dirt on this side of the property line since Linc's fence line backed up against an alley.

A figure dressed in black pounded the pavement in his haste to flee from Mason. Heading toward Azalea Street, he chased the guy, cutting between two homes, and darting toward the intersection where the peeper had probably parked for a quick escape. What did he hope to see at midnight? The only light on in the house was a lamp in the living room on its low light setting.

The runner banged into a trashcan and sent the neighborhood dogs into a barking frenzy. Mason's lips curved when he spotted the figure heading exactly where he thought the guy would go.

Putting on a burst of speed, he veered to the left and slid in right behind the runner. Mason tackled him and took him to the ground. Felt good using those football skills from his high school and college days. The man fought to turn over, but Mason controlled him with a knee on his back, arm twisted behind him.

"Get off," the man snarled. "I didn't do anything wrong."

"Trespassing on private property and peeking into a window in the middle of the night isn't behavior to write home about." He hauled the runner to his feet, easily quelled another escape attempt, and propelled him back toward Linc's. "Let's go."

When Linc opened the door to admit them, satisfaction filled his gaze. "You nabbed our rabbit."

The stranger scowled. "Let me go, and I won't call the cops on you."

"Already done. They'll be here soon. Escort him to the kitchen, Mase."

"Where are the women?" Mason asked. He wouldn't take this man near Nicole.

"Security room." He sent Mason a wry look. "It was all I could do to prevent your woman from following you. She's not happy that I refused to let her go or assist you."

The dark-haired man with brown eyes glared at Linc and Mason in turn. "Let me go. I didn't do anything wrong."

"Tell that to the cops." Linc inclined his head toward the kitchen. "Once he's secure, go to your lady, Mase."

"Nicole?" The stranger called out, twisting to free himself from Mason's hold. "Come on, baby. Tell these thugs who I am, will you? You know I'm not here to hurt you, right?"

Baby? Mason wrenched the man's arm higher up his back, causing him to curse. Who was this guy? Did he know Nicole or had he created a relationship that didn't exist?

Nicole rushed into the living room. Shock was soon replaced by outrage on her face. "Why are you here, Ivan?"

Mason scowled as understanding slammed into him. "You must be Ivan Dannon."

"Tell this Neanderthal to let me go," Ivan groused.

"You didn't answer my question." Nicole moved closer, hands fisting on her hips. "Why are you here?"

A smug smile curved his mouth. "You know why."

"I don't." Mason tightened his grip, his tone curt. "Spell it out for me."

"To get her back, of course." Ivan looked at Mason as though he were dense. "We're in love. We just had a little misunderstanding." He looked at Nicole again. "You'll give me another chance, right?"

Linc snorted. "You're an idiot if you think she'll take you back." He took over Mason's hold on Ivan and steered him toward the kitchen. "Let in the cops when they arrive, Mase. I'll keep our friend company."

Wonder if that was a euphemism for persuading him to confess everything, including Riva's murder? Mason tilted Nicole's face up to his. "Are you okay?"

"I will be. He scared the daylights out of me," she muttered. "What would make him think he could waltz in here and convince me to pick up where we left off? That wouldn't happen if he was the last man on earth."

"Did you know he was in town?"

When she hesitated, Mason stilled. "Nicole?"

"I thought I saw him a few days ago, but I thought I imagined him when I didn't seem him again. I haven't talked to Ivan since I dumped him two years ago."

He considered what she said and what she omitted. "Has he contacted you recently?"

Another scowl. "He left phone messages and sent emails, all of which I deleted without responding."

"Why didn't you tell me?"

"Because he doesn't matter. Ivan is part of my distant past, one I have no intention of revisiting under any circumstances. I didn't think he'd come to Otter Creek, especially since he received no contact or encouragement from me."

"When did you think you saw him?"

"About the time Riva was killed." She glanced toward the kitchen. "He couldn't have killed her. Ivan didn't have a motive."

Mason could think of one good motive. To send him back to prison and get him out of Nicole's life, leaving the field clear for Ivan. He brushed his thumb gently over her bottom lip. "If I wasn't in the picture, would you take him back?"

"Never. I learned my lesson the hard way."

Mason's eyes narrowed. "What does that mean?"

"Nothing. I'll go sit with Dawn. She's watching the security screens."

When she tried to free herself, Mason stilled her movement with an arm around her waist. "He hurt you?"

The stubborn woman remained silent, a mutinous glare coming from her beautiful eyes.

"I can find out the truth." Favors he could call in at Fortress. "I'd rather hear it from you."

"I don't want you to overreact."

Whatever happened wouldn't be good if she worried he'd lash out. "Tell me."

"He pressured me to give him money since he was strapped for cash, and I refused. I had plans even then to start my own business, and I'd set money aside for that purpose. Ivan accused me of being a controlling and selfish witch for refusing to help him over a rough patch." She fell silent again, cheeks turning pink.

"Go on," he prompted.

Nicole scowled. "The argument became heated and he...."

"What did he do?" Although he could guess.

"He hit me." She grabbed his arms and held on. "An open-handed slap. That was the one and only time. I broke up with him the next day, and that was the end of it."

"Did you file charges against him?"

She shook her head. "I didn't want to press charges for assault since I punched his nose in retaliation. If I filed assault charges, so would he."

That gave him a small measure of satisfaction. "Let me go, sweetheart," Mason said evenly. He looked toward the kitchen. "I want two minutes with your ex."

"No." Nicole tightened her grip. "The police are up the street. You can't touch him, baby. You'll be the one who pays the price, not him."

"He hurt you."

"Two years ago. Mason, please don't do this. He's not worth the grief you'll get from Ethan. I'm asking you to let it go for me."

"Josh is here," Dawn called from the security room.

Mason placed a gentle kiss on her mouth. "Go answer the door."

"Mason..."

He laid his finger against her lips. "Trust me."

She growled. "I better not have to bail you out of jail. I'd be tempted to leave you behind bars for not listening to your future wife."

He grinned at her bad-tempered response. "I hear you." Mason nudged her toward the door. "Go. Keep Josh busy for a minute before you let him inside."

With that request, he stalked toward the kitchen. Linc's arms were folded, his attention focused on Ivan whose hands were restrained behind his back. "Give me a minute," he murmured to the operative.

"No bruises." Linc left without a backward glance.

Ivan glared at him.

Aware of the time constraint, Mason said, "Nicole and I are getting married soon. Congratulate her, and get out of town once the police are through with you."

Belligerence gleamed in his eyes. "Why should I? You afraid I'm going to steal Nicole away from your sorry hide? You should be, man. She's mine."

Mason walked behind him and exerted pressure on Ivan's shoulder exactly as Nate and Alex had taught him. Nicole's ex gasped, blood draining from his face.

He leaned close to the man's ear. "Listen carefully, Ivan. I'm only going to say this once. Nicole is mine to love and protect. I know what you did to her."

"What are you talking about? I didn't do anything she didn't want me to."

"You hit her." When he tightened his grip, Ivan moaned. "Nicole deserves to be treated with respect and gentleness. No man worthy of the name would hurt a woman. If you ever touch Nicole again, I will take you apart. Are you hearing me, Dannon?"

He nodded.

Linc walked in. "Time's up, Mase."

Mason released Ivan and moved away from him a second before Josh strode in.

Suspicion in his eyes, Josh's gaze swept over Ivan. "What's going on, Mason?"

"Ivan Dannon trespassed onto Linc's property and looked in windows. He scared Nicole."

Eyebrows rose. "You know this guy?"

"We've been getting acquainted. He's Nicole's former boyfriend."

He glanced at Linc. "You pressing charges?"

"Depends."

"Cut him loose, then you and Mason follow me to the cruiser. We'll talk."

When Mason followed Josh and Ivan into the living room and outside, Nicole was nowhere in sight. One less thing to worry about. He didn't want her anywhere near Ivan. The less this guy saw of her, the better.

Once Josh placed the man in the back of his cruiser, he turned to Mason and Linc. "What's really going on here?"

"Exactly what I told you."

"And?"

"He's been in town since the day Riva was murdered."

"Interesting timing," Linc said.

"He says he's in Otter Creek to win Nicole back."

"You believe him?" Josh asked.

"He's convincing."

"What do you want me to do with him?"

"Introduce him to Ethan or Rod. The timing of his appearance in town might be a coincidence, but with Nicole's safety at stake, I don't want to take a chance."

"If he's clear, will you press charges, Linc?"

"No point. Trespassing is a minor offense. As long as he leaves Nicole alone, I won't press charges."

"I'll pass the word along." Josh looked at Mason. "Do I need to worry about unexplained injuries?"

He shrugged. "I tackled him when he rabbited. Ivan might have a couple of bruises."

Durango's leader rolled his eyes. "Let me guess. You had a few private lessons from Nate or Alex on interrogation techniques."

Mason folded his arms without confirming or denying the assertion. He wouldn't rat out either man and get them in trouble with their team leader.

"Never mind. I don't want to know. What I don't know, I can't testify to." He slid a look at Linc. "I suppose you didn't see anything."

"I was with you."

"Yeah, asking about my wife and daughters. If I didn't know better, Creed, I'd say you were distracting me."

"I have no idea what you're talking about, boss."

A snort. "Sell that to Ethan. I'm not buying it. Anything else I should know before I take him in?"

"The reason why Nicole dumped him two years ago is because he slapped her during an argument," Mason said.

Linc and Josh scowled. "Did she report it?" Josh asked.

"No. Nicole punched him in response. She figured if she pressed charges, so would he. When she broke up with him, she considered the matter finished."

"Good for her," Linc said.

"Did she know he was in town?"

Mason relayed his conversation with Nicole on the subject, ending with, "Ivan thinks he has a chance with her. Although I don't understand how anyone in Otter Creek would know about him, find out if he had an anonymous email."

"Explain that."

He told Josh about the encounter with Todd and Gage Fitzgerald earlier in the evening. "Gage received an email from an anonymous source. I asked Zane to trace it."

Josh rubbed his jaw. "A smear campaign. Someone wants you out of the way."

He'd arrived at the same conclusion. The question was, did they want him out of the way bad enough to kill him?

CHAPTER TWENTY-THREE

Nicole fumed as she stared at the computer screen and watched the three men talking beside the police cruiser containing her former boyfriend. What gave Ivan the idea that she would take him back? She made herself clear the day she broke up with him. Ivan Dannon was the biggest mistake of her life, and she didn't repeat bad decisions.

"What's going on, Nic?" Dawn asked. "Do you know this man?"

"He's a former boyfriend from a time when my taste in men was deplorable. Ivan Dannon is a selfish jerk who I thought I loved for a nanosecond. I wised up."

"Why did you part ways?"

"He was more interested in my bank account than me." She glared at the image of Ivan on the screen. "Ivan became angry during an argument about money and hit me."

Dawn gasped. "What did you do?"

"Gave him a black eye and dumped him."

Her friend grinned. "You're my hero."

"I just corrected a dumb move on my part."

"You stood up for yourself. I admire that."

"I'm lucky Ivan doesn't have a spine. Otherwise, he would have mopped the floor with me. I'm going to correct that, though."

"How?"

"The wives of Durango and Bravo train with the teams on self-defense skills. If they practice at a time when I'm free, I'd like to join them."

Dawn's mouth gaped. "You're serious?"

"Oh, yeah. I don't want to be caught unprepared again. Besides that, Mason is Rio's cousin. Durango's job isn't safe at the best of times. If trouble follows them home, Mason and I could become targets, too."

The other woman stared at her a few seconds, then sighed. "Sign me up."

"Because you're with me during the workday?"

"That's one reason."

A slow smile spread across Nicole's face. "I knew it. You and Linc?"

"Maybe."

She laughed, delighted at the blush spreading across her friend's cheeks. "Definitely. You're perfect for each other."

"We're still in the getting-to-know-you phase, Nic. This relationship might not work out."

"And it might be exactly like I said. Perfect."

Dawn shook her head. "You're a hopeless romantic."

"Only since I met Mason." That brought her gaze back to the computer screen. What were the men talking about so intently? "He's everything I've ever wanted in a mate. I can't believe I'm marrying him in two months and two days."

"I can't wait to see Mason's face when he sees your dress."

"I hope he'll be blown away." The dress had been super expensive. But, hey, a girl only married the love of her life once.

When Josh broke away from Linc and Mason to climb behind the wheel of the cruiser, Nicole pushed back from the table and headed for the living room with Dawn close on her heels.

"Is Ivan under arrest?" Nicole eyed each man in turn.

"Not at the moment." Mason captured her hand and kissed her knuckles. "Ethan and Rod will determine if Ivan has anything to do with Riva's murder or the attempts on our lives. If he's clear, he'll be encouraged to leave town for his own safety."

Dawn's eyes widened. "You threatened him?"

"I explained the facts to him. The truth is being around me or Nicole isn't safe." His eyes twinkled. "I might have encouraged Josh to share that point with his brothers-in-law."

He squeezed Nicole's hand. "Go to bed. If anything happens overnight, I'll let you know."

"Same goes for you," Linc said to Dawn. "You ladies have an early start to your workday."

That was the truth. Their first four-legged baby would arrive at the shop at 7:00 a.m. Nicole glanced at the clock on the wall and winced. Great. That meant the alarm would go off in four hours. Two gallons of coffee, and she'd be able to function at peak efficiency. Maybe.

Dawn groaned. "Our first customer is Titan."

Linc looked from her to Nicole and back. "Who's Titan?"

"He's a gorgeous American Husky. Titan has the sweetest personality but takes forever to groom."

"Why?"

"He has beautiful, thick fur. No matter how many times we brush him, we collect a pile of fur, and he takes a long time to dry. He's not a fan of the dryer, either. We'll be wrestling him for an hour or longer."

"He's one half of a bonded pair," Nicole added.

"Another Husky?" Mason asked.

"A gray cat named Elmo. He and Titan always come in together."

"Why is that a problem?"

"Elmo hates both of us. We'll be sporting scratches inside of fifteen minutes."

Linc grinned. "Wish you had a camera in the workroom. I'd love to watch the show."

"You wouldn't say that if you were within striking distance of Elmo's claws." Dawn sighed. "Come on, Nic. If we don't get some sleep, we won't be able to outwit that stubborn feline."

Mason chuckled. "I'll have hot coffee waiting for you both."

"I better get a good morning kiss, too," Nicole groused.

"Deal." He nudged her toward the hallway.

Nicole followed her friend to the end of the hall where the guest rooms were located. Five minutes later, she slid under the covers again and willed herself to return to sleep. Following a restless hour of fruitless tossing and turning, Nicole gave up. She trudged to the security room.

Mason spun around for the second time that night and stood. "Problem?"

"Can't sleep. I'm too wound up, and I keep wondering what's happening with Ivan."

"Go make your favorite tea. I'll text Josh to see what he knows."

Nicole beamed at him. "Thanks." She found chamomile mint tea in the pantry. After nuking water and dumping a tea bag into the steaming liquid, she carried the mug into the security room and curled up on the love seat at the side of the room. "Did Josh respond?"

"Ethan and Rod are questioning Ivan now. Ethan said he'd contact us later today."

The ball of ice in her stomach began to melt. Good. At least Ivan wouldn't cause more trouble tonight. She had a feeling that the two policemen would keep him busy for hours.

Once she finished her drink, Mason tucked a quilt around her and brushed strands of her hair away from her cheek. "Rest. I'll be right here."

Nicole snuggled under the blanket and soon drifted off to sleep. She woke later to the sound of two men speaking in low tones. She peeked at the window. Still dark. Linc must be getting ready to leave for PSI. She hoped he functioned a lot better than she would today with the interrupted night of rest.

Soon, the front door opened, then closed again, and Mason returned to the security room with a mug of coffee clutched in his hand.

"Hi," she murmured.

"It's four o'clock. You have another two hours to sleep."

"Linc is doing PT with the trainees today?"

"Josh insists that the trainers keep in shape and work out with the trainees at least three days a week. Durango or Bravo go up against them in PT every day."

"Ugh. That's not what I want to do before the sun rises."

Mason smiled as he returned to his seat in front of the monitor.

"I've been thinking."

"Uh oh."

She frowned. "Ha ha. I'm not that dangerous."

He chuckled. "What's on your mind, Nicole?"

"I hear you're training with Bravo and Durango."

"I wanted to be able to protect you. Why?"

"Did you know the teams train their wives in self-defense, too?"

He nodded.

"Do you think they'd allow me and Dawn to join the women?" She smiled. "Dawn admitted she and Linc are dating."

"I'll ask Rio about you two attending the next training session. Why the sudden interest?"

"I want the ability to take care of myself and protect our children." She sat up. "Plus, Rio's job is dangerous. The danger might follow him to Otter Creek."

"I can train with you."

"Are you kidding? After training with Special Forces guys, you'll wipe the floor with me."

He chuckled. "I'll be gentle."

"After we're married, we'll make good use of the gym in your house. In the meantime, I'll join the women if they don't mind."

"I'm sure it's fine." He tugged Nicole to her feet. "I'm brewing another pot of coffee which should be finished by the time you change clothes. If you want, I'll toast a bagel for you, too."

Nicole gave him a quick kiss. "You spoil me."

"Then I'm doing things right." He cupped her cheek. "You deserve to be spoiled."

Was it any wonder that she was head-over-heels in love with Mason Kincaid? He treated her like a princess. "I won't be long."

Nicole hurried to her room, grabbed fresh clothes, and showered. Twenty minutes later, she sat beside Mason at the security console, sipping her coffee and eating her bagel. By the time Dawn emerged from her room, Nicole had finished her breakfast and was reviewing the day's schedule on her phone.

She smiled at her friend. "Good morning."

"Don't talk to me until I've had at least two cups of coffee." She eyed Nicole. "You look chipper for a woman who had a broken night of sleep."

"That's what happens when I get a head start on the coffee consumption. I'm two up on you."

"Nice. No excitement overnight?"

Mason shook his head. "Linc left at 4:00 a.m. He'll be at the salon by 2:00 this afternoon." He glanced over his shoulder with a smile. "Congratulations, by the way."

She smiled. "Thanks. Now, please tell me there's more coffee."

"A full pot."

Dawn made a beeline for the kitchen.

At 6:30, Nicole booted up the salon's computer and waved her brother-in-law to a stool behind the counter. "If the phone rings, grab it."

"I'm not your receptionist, Nic."

"You are today. Ryan has classes until noon, and we have back-to-back appointments today."

"I already have a job. Babysitting you."

She grinned. "Today, you're demonstrating the time-honored skill of multitasking."

"Brat."

After a few quick instructions on how to work the software program to book appointments, Nicole placed a noisy kiss on Trent's cheek. "You're the best, T."

"Uh huh. A kiss won't pay off the debt."

"Look at it this way. You're earning serious brownie points with my sister by helping out." She nudged him with her elbow. "And if you play nice with my customers, I might stop at the clothing boutique across the square and purchase a very slinky nightgown for Grace."

His eyes lost focus for a moment before he growled. "That nightgown better be extraordinary."

With a laugh, Nicole patted his cheek and hurried into the workroom to help Dawn set up for Titan and Elmo. By the time the dynamic duo left the shop clad in spiffy new neckerchiefs, Nicole and Dawn had two scratches each from Elmo's claws, and they'd combed enough fur from

Titan to practically make another dog. Considering the number of scratches they'd had in the past from Elmo, the women considered today's appointment a success.

A few minutes before noon, Trent poked his head in the door to the workroom. "Nic, Rod's here. He says he needs to talk to you."

She shook her head. "I'm elbow deep in suds here. He'll have to wait."

"I already told him you were booked solid until closing. The detective wasn't impressed."

Nicole rolled her eyes. "Fantastic. Tell him if he wants to talk, he can come back here. I don't have time to stop working. We have two Great Danes arriving in twenty minutes. The big babies are 150-pound chickens who are afraid of everything, including water."

Soon, Rod Kelter strode into the workroom with a grim expression. "I have questions, Nicole."

Nicole hoped she had answers to satisfy him.

CHAPTER TWENTY-FOUR

Nicole eyed the red-haired detective. "As you can see, I'm a little busy at the moment." She currently had her hands in the suds-filled fur of a Wheaton Terrier. "If you want to ask questions, you'll have to do it while I work. Otherwise, I'll draft you to help with the Great Danes due soon for a bath and nail trim."

She inclined her head toward the stool to her right. "Pull up a stool and make yourself comfortable, Detective."

Rod set the stool where he could see Nicole's face. She turned back to Pierre and lathered more shampoo into his fur.

"Are you always so busy?" he asked.

"Most of the time. We're the only pet groomers in town, and most pet owners don't want to drive to the Cherry Hill pet store to use their groomers. Pet Palace does a brisk business every day. If you think this is bad, you should come in during the holiday season. Last year, Dawn and I worked 16-hour days for six weeks running from the middle of November until the first of the year."

He looked puzzled. "Why? Aren't people too busy shopping and cooking for holiday meals to schedule pet grooming?"

Nicole grinned at him. "Pet owners want to show off their fur babies during the holidays when friends and relatives visit. I guess you and Megan don't have a pet."

"Does a gold fish count?"

"Nope."

"Our schedules are too crazy for anything except fish." He waited until she'd rinsed off Pierre and rubbed him with a towel to start the drying process before he slid a notebook and pen from his pocket.

"I'll take Pierre to the back room," Dawn said. "He loves the dryer."

"Thanks." As Dawn led the Terrier from the room, Nicole glanced at the white board to see who was next. "Can you wait for one minute while I get Princess?"

He frowned. "Make it quick, Copeland."

"You could roll up your sleeves and lend a hand. You can work and question a suspect at the same time, right?"

"If it will get my questions answered before next week, you're on." Rod slid from the stool and shoved the notebook and pen back in his pocket. "Okay with you if I use a digital recorder while we talk?"

"Be my guest. I'll be right back." Nicole went to the holding area to retrieve Princess, a Blue Heeler. "Come on, sweet thing. Let's get you all cleaned up for Mama." She led the dog to the workroom and the tub.

"What do you want me to do?" Rod eyed the dog while Princess looked him over.

"Keep your hand on her back. Otherwise, we'll both be getting baths, too." She grasped the nozzle and aimed the warm spray on Princess's back. "What do you want to know?"

"Tell me what happened last night at Linc's. Don't leave anything out."

"Have you already talked to Mason and Linc?"

"They're next after I speak with Dawn." He made a face. "If I can get her attention for five minutes."

"We'll work it out." Somehow.

"Details from last night, Copeland. Let's hear them."

She relayed the events, starting with dinner at Tennessee Steakhouse and ending with Josh driving off in his cruiser with Ivan in the backseat.

"Why did Dannon come to Otter Creek?"

"He said he wanted to win me back."

"You don't believe him?"

"I haven't heard from him in two years, Rod. I'm in love with Mason, and we're getting married in two months and two days. I don't care what Ivan thought. I would never take him back. I don't know why he thought he had a chance."

"He says you invited him to come."

Nicole stared at the detective. "That's crazy. I didn't. Why would he lie?"

"You tell me."

"No clue." She lathered Princess's fur. "Ivan and I didn't part on good terms."

"Explain."

She did. To her surprise, Rod grinned. "Good job, Copeland. I'm impressed."

"Don't be. He's spineless. Otherwise, he would have retaliated. He made me angry, though. Slapping me was way out of line."

"Yeah, it was. So maybe you contacted Dannon and encouraged him to come so Mason would retaliate against your abuser."

Outrage shot through her. "You're out of your mind, Detective. I wouldn't put Mason in that position, knowing he could end up in jail. Self-defense is one thing. Deliberately putting him in harm's way is out of the question."

"The evidence says otherwise."

"Either the evidence is wrong or your interpretation is. I'm not responsible for Ivan being here. I'd prefer he disappeared as quickly as he appeared."

"You're going to stick with that story?"

She scowled. "It's not a story. I'm sorry you don't recognize the truth when you hear it."

"Do you have an explanation for the attacks and close calls happening to you and Mason?"

"No."

He waited a beat, then said, "That's it?"

"You do understand what the word no means, right?"

He laughed. "You remind me of my wife. Do I have your permission to search your computer at home and here at the shop?"

"Have at it. I don't have anything to hide."

"You're not going to fight me on this?"

"Why should I? I'll lose the fight. Forcing you to obtain a search warrant makes me look guilty and ticks you off because of the delay."

"Also true. I'll start here in the shop if you don't mind."

"As long as Trent or Ryan can access the reservations software, go ahead."

She rinsed Princess with the sprayer, then grabbed a towel to rub her fur before she turned Rod loose to troll through her computer. Nicole led the dog into the back room where she stood the Blue Heeler under the second dryer beside Pierre.

"Is Rod gone?" Dawn asked.

"He's checking our computer."

"Why?"

"Ivan said that I invited him to Otter Creek."

"Why would you do that?"

"That's the question of the day, isn't it? This is starting to feel like a conspiracy."

"Rod won't find anything. I use the shop computer as much as you do, and I'm in the emails all the time. There's nothing in there to incriminate you."

"The detective plans to check my home computer as well."

She shrugged. "Let him. He won't find anything there, either."

"I hope you're still okay with all the intrigue and drama when it's your turn to talk to Rod."

"My turn?" She stared at Nicole. "I don't have any information."

"He'll want to confirm that for himself."

Trent walked in. "Roscoe and Rascal have arrived. You weren't kidding about the size of the dogs. Those boys are enormous."

Dawn stood. "I'll take them to the holding cage after I put Pierre in his crate."

"I'll be there as soon as Princess is dry." She grinned at Trent. "Get ready, buddy. We might need help wrestling those two into the tub."

"Oh, joy." His tone said he felt anything but that. Trent returned to the reception area.

With a laugh, Nicole finished drying Princess and escorted the dog to her holding crate. Dawn waited for her beside the cage with the two Great Danes inside, shaking like leaves in a stiff breeze.

The next hour was spent bathing the two dogs who had to be coaxed and bribed with doggy treats through every step of the process. By the time the boys were dry and resting in their holding cage from all the trauma, Dawn and Nicole were as exhausted as the dogs.

Nicole shoved her hair away from her hot face. "Who's next?"

"Pixie."

Thankful the next dog was a Chihuahua, she headed for the reception area. "I'll bring her back while you catch your breath."

Trent and Rod turned when she opened the door of the workroom. "Are the boys still alive?" Trent asked.

"Of course they are."

"The way they howled and carried on, we thought you were torturing the poor things."

"Yeah, water torture is part of the grooming service. Didn't you know that?"

Rod chuckled. "They weren't happy."

A woman walked into the shop with a black Chihuahua in her arms. "Hello, Nicole. Thanks for working Pixie into the schedule. We're going out of town to see my husband's parents tonight, and my mother-in-law doesn't like dogs. We need Pixie to look her absolute best."

Nicole loved on Pixie for a moment before she took the trembling dog from her owner's arms. "We'll let you know when she's ready, Dora."

"You're the best, Nicole." After kissing Pixie on the top of her head, the woman left.

Trent stared at the small dog. "Looks like a black rat."

She rolled her eyes and returned to the workroom where Dawn was bathing a Corgi. "Here's our girl."

"Pixie!" Dawn's eyes lit up at seeing the small dog. "How's my favorite sweetheart?"

The Chihuahua yipped in excitement, making both women laugh. Since Pixie was terrified of the dryer, Nicole dried her with towels and set her in the crate, much to her displeasure. The little dog joined in the unhappy chorus of dogs barking and whining in the holding room.

When she returned to the reception area for the next pet, Rod pushed away from the computer. "Any chance I can talk to Dawn without the canine chorus putting in their two cents?"

Nicole checked the schedule. "She's due for a break. I'm sure she'd appreciate a cup of coffee at Perk."

"Are you sure you can handle the howling horde while she's with me?"

"I'll survive for thirty minutes." She grinned. "If I have to, I'll draft help from Trent."

"Hey," her brother-in-law protested. "I have two jobs already. I can't answer the phones and provide security if I'm elbows deep in suds."

"Lucky for you, Ryan is due in a few minutes. If I can't handle the deluge of dogs alone, you're elected."

Trent scowled. "Just because I'm married to your sister doesn't mean you can order me around."

"Are you forgetting about the nightgown for Grace?"

Rod held up his hand. "Whoa. I don't want to know about that. Send Dawn out here so I can get out of your way."

"Chicken," Nicole teased.

"Yes, ma'am."

That made her laugh as she met the next pet owner at the door of the salon. Nicole confirmed the details of what the German Shepherd's owner wanted, then escorted the beautiful white dog into the workroom. "Dawn, Rod's ready to talk to you. Take a break."

"We're too busy, Nic."

"He won't take no for an answer. Go on. He's taking you to Perk for coffee."

Dawn finished sweeping up the dog hair from the latest grooming and turned toward Nicole. "Do you want anything? I'll be happy to bring back something for you."

"Coffee, please. Get lunch while you're out. You might not have a chance to eat otherwise."

"I'll pick up lunch for both of us. We'll squeeze in lunch somehow."

"You're the best."

"Yeah, yeah. Just remember that when it's time to review my salary." With a wave, Dawn left.

Nicole grinned and glanced down at the German Shepherd. "All right, Patty. Time for your beauty treatment." The dog barked.

While she brushed the dog and shampooed her, Nicole thought about Rod's statements and questions, and wondered if she would face a lot more questions in an interrogation room.

CHAPTER TWENTY-FIVE

Mason used his screw gun to secure the outlet cover. When finished, he wiped sweat from his brow with his forearm and stood. He set the screw gun aside and glanced at his partner. "How's it going?"

Dean got to his feet and stretched. "Finished. What's next?"

Before he could answer, Mason's phone signaled an incoming call. He glanced at the screen. "I need to take this. Next on the list is installing closet doors in each of the units."

"I'll get started in here."

"I won't be long," Mason promised as he strode toward the door and swiped his screen. "Kincaid."

"It's Zane. Can you talk?"

He answered when he stood outside Building 6. "Go ahead."

"I traced the emails sent to Gage Fitzgerald and Ivan Dannon."

"What did you find out?"

"It appears that Nicole sent them."

Mason froze. "No chance."

"I don't think so either, but law enforcement might be inclined to think she's guilty."

"She wouldn't do that." Knowing his history with the Fitzgeralds, Nicole wouldn't contact them for any reason, especially to confirm Mason's location. Based on her last experience with Ivan, he was the last person she would want to exchange emails with. "What's the proof?"

"I tracked the IP address to the Otter Creek public library. While the emails weren't signed, I tracked the account through several layers to the original owner who claimed to be Nicole Copeland."

Mason sat on the step in front of unit 3 and dragged a hand down his face. This was crazy. Who would try to throw Nicole under the bus and why? He was the major threat, not her. "It's not Nicole. Someone is doing his best to muddy the waters and send the police on a rabbit chase."

"Any idea why?"

"Not yet, but I will find out."

"Watch your back, Mason."

"Always." He'd learned to do that in prison to survive.

"Think about who stands to gain the most if you're out of the way and no longer have Nicole's full support."

He scanned the area to be sure he was still alone. "Look into a couple of men on Elliott's crew. Gene Patton and Ed Fisher. For some reason, I'm getting a ton of animosity from them. Could be they just hate my guts or don't trust me because of my prison record."

"Anyone else?"

"Nicole's former boyfriend, Ivan Dannon." He explained about the last argument between the couple. "I want to know if he's harboring plans for revenge against her. With his ego, he wouldn't be able to tolerate Nicole getting the best of him. He fought with her over money. With her inheritance, she doesn't have money issues now. He might think if he wins her back, he'll have access to her bank accounts."

"I'll check them out and get back to you." Zane ended the call.

Mason returned to unit 3 and helped Dean install closet doors.

When they finished the first set, Dean said, "Everything okay?"

"Not really."

His friend frowned. "Want to talk about it or should I shut up and mind my own business?"

"Nicole's former boyfriend is in town. He showed up at Linc's at midnight and scared Nicole."

"What does he want?"

"What do you think? Nicole."

Dean stared a moment, then shook his head. "Incredible. How did she handle it?"

"Told him she'd never take him back." He scowled at the memory of her confession. "During their last encounter two years ago, Dannon hit her."

"Is he still alive?" Dean's tone was wry.

"For the moment. I told him that if he ever touched her again, I'd take him apart."

"Think he believed you?"

Mason's lips curved. "He got my message. The problem is Dannon received an email that he assumed was from Nicole. The email implied that she missed him and would welcome him back into her life."

"Fat chance of that happening. She's crazy in love with you. Since Nicole didn't send the email, then who did?"

"Zane looked into it. He said the trail ends with someone who claims to be Nicole and sent the message from the Otter Creek library."

"The library might have security cameras. If Zane can tell you what time the email was sent and the computers are under camera surveillance, you should be able to see who was using the computers at the time." He shrugged. "At least it would narrow your search to less than the population of Otter Creek."

"That's a great idea. I should have thought of that myself."

"You would have if you'd slept more than five hours over the past few days."

Yeah, probably. "If the library has security footage, I'll have to figure out how to obtain a copy of the recording."

"That's easy. Leah is good friends with the head librarian, and the lady is a customer of Nicole's. I don't think Leah will have a problem getting what you need."

A surge of hope swept through Mason. If he could get the recording, he could prove Nicole wasn't the one who sent the emails. The police would eventually get the footage, but Zane could obtain information without warrants. If Mason found the evidence he needed, he'd have Z pass it along to the police anonymously. The Fortress tech wizard had ways to erase his electronic tracks so the police wouldn't be able to trace the information to him.

He sent a text to Zane, asking for the times the emails were sent. "I'd appreciate Leah's help, but only if she agrees. I don't want her to help if it makes her uncomfortable."

Dean waved that aside. "I'm sure it won't be a problem."

Later, as he and Dean sat under a tree to eat lunch, they talked about the work in Building 6 and discussed ways to streamline their process to save time.

Patton and Fisher walked up. Mason eyed them as he finished the last of his tea.

"Where's your thug friend?" Patton said.

"If you're talking about Linc, he's working."

"You sent him after us," Fisher accused. "All we did was stick around to see if you needed help, but you turned on us."

"Linc was protecting his girlfriend from someone watching us in the darkness."

"Oh, come on. That's not a crime."

"He's responsible for Dawn's safety and takes that job seriously since she ran into Riva's killer. If your woman's life was in danger, you'd check a potential threat to her, too."

He snorted. "Please. That little dog groomer don't have a thing to be scared about. Not like your woman."

Mason stiffened. "What does that mean?"

"Don't play dumb, Kincaid. Your lady got up close and personal with a killer. Dawn just happened to be in the wrong place at the wrong time and ended up on her very fine backside."

"Wouldn't be wise to let Linc hear you talk about Dawn that way."

"Maybe your woman poked her nose in where it doesn't belong." Patton folded his arms.

Mason leveled a stare at the belligerent construction worker. "The only thing Nicole is guilty of is doing a favor for a friend."

"You sure about that?" Glee gleamed in Fisher's eyes.

"If you have a point, get to it. My lunch break is over."

"Rumor has it your woman is ready to dump you and date someone better, a real man."

The Otter Creek grapevine was working overtime these days. Mason stood and picked up his lunch box. "Don't believe everything you hear."

He and Dean left the other men, locked their lunch boxes in their trucks, and returned to Building 6.

"Patton and Fisher wanted to get a rise out of you."

"They were blatant about it, too. The question is, why?" Mason picked up the checklist from Brian. "After we hang the closet doors in unit 12, the next task is installing the pantry shelves."

"Let's get to it. I'd like to get home before 8:00 tonight. Leah is complaining about us working so much overtime." Dean glanced at Mason as they opened another box containing closet doors. "Have you given more thought to Brian's offer?"

He nodded. "I'm still not sure I want to take that on."

"Why not? You're perfect for that position, Mase."

"Customers might refuse to hire Elliott Construction because I'm the project manager and in charge of the home rehab division."

"Some customers might refuse to hire us but not all of them. They can search for another contractor. Too bad for them Elliott Construction is the best in the area. They either take us with you at the helm or they settle for second best."

Mason smiled. "There's a long wait list for contractors."

Dean clapped him on the shoulder. "Take the promotion. You deserve it and will love the work."

They returned to the work at hand, using the tactics they'd worked out during lunch. The plan to cut the time required for various tasks worked so well, Mason and Dean had nearly completed the entire checklist by the time Brian walked in an hour before the end of the workday.

"How's it going?" their boss asked.

"Nearly finished with the list." Mason turned to face his boss. "Do you need anything?"

"An answer."

He stilled. "To what question?"

"Will you accept the promotion I'm offering?"

"I thought I had until the end of the week to make my decision."

"You did. I have to move up the decision deadline." Brian's eyes sparkled with excitement.

A slow smile formed on Mason's mouth. "We got the project?"

"It's ours."

"Congratulations, Brian." Dean grinned at his employer. "When do we start?"

"I'm meeting with the architect tonight. The client has the construction loan already secured. If they're satisfied with the architect's recommendations, I'll start applying for permits by the end of the week. Provided we don't have any delays and the town council agrees to the plan, we start construction in a month. I need your answer, Mason."

"Come on, Mase," Dean murmured.

He drew in a deep breath. Dean was right. Mason loved the home renovation and repair work. While they'd been working side-by-side for the past few hours, he had considered and discarded several options. In the end, there was only one answer. If the clientele refused to work with him at the helm, he trusted Brian to let him know. He could rejoin the regular construction crew. "Yes."

Brian grinned and slapped Mason on the back. "Great news! You won't regret it, buddy."

"I'll take it on one condition."

"Name it."

"Dean comes with me. I want him permanently assigned to me."

"I don't have a problem with that. You two are a great team." Brian rubbed his hands together. "This is perfect timing. Our company cookout is tomorrow evening. I was going to announce the new project. Now, I'll be able to announce the establishment of the home rehab division of Elliott Construction and your promotion to division head and project manager."

Mason held out his hand. "Thank you for trusting me, sir."

"You earned it several times over, Mason. Hiring you was one of the best decisions I ever made. Finish your list and get out of here. I'm sure you want to celebrate with Nicole."

Brian shook Dean's hand. "Congratulations, Dean."

"Sir?"

"Your new job in the home rehab division comes with a promotion as well."

After a few more instructions on the remaining work in Building 6, Brian left.

"I can't wait to tell Leah about this. She'll be thrilled."

"Nicole, too." Mason glanced at his friend. "We'll be scrambling to keep up with the work."

"Can't wait. Home rehab is a challenge."

"The best kind." The work involved taking something old and restoring it to usefulness or replacing it with something better. Sure, there were roadblocks along the way, problems to work around, but in the end, the result was beautiful, functional, and rewarding.

Home rehab reminded Mason of his own life. Once broken, Nicole had helped him heal.

His jaw clenched. Now someone was determined to destroy his life a second time. No matter what the cost, he wouldn't let that happen. This time, he had too much to lose.

CHAPTER TWENTY-SIX

Nicole straightened with a groan and dumped the last of the dog clippings into the waste bin. "Finished. Finally."

"Same here," Dawn sighed. "I think we set a new salon record. Thirty dogs in twelve hours."

"And that included the Great Danes with a water phobia." She smiled. "We deserve a pat on the back."

"I'll settle for a hot shower, dinner, and Band-Aids to cover the scratches from Elmo."

"Same. Would Linc mind stopping at the grocery store?"

"Not if we tell him we're cooking dinner tonight."

"I'm craving Mexican food, and I'm not in the mood to put up with people staring at us while we eat."

"I'm in as long as I shower before we cook. I smell like dog shampoo."

"Talk to Linc about the grocery store stop while I make sure everything is secure."

With a nod, Dawn headed for the reception area.

After collecting trash from the bins, Nicole walked through the salon, checking windows and doors in each room. Reaching the store room, she headed for the exit.

In the alley, Nicole set the bags of trash on the ground and attempted to lift the Dumpster lid. She failed, needing a couple more inches in height. She'd use the door on the side and pray the bin wasn't stuffed full.

"Let me give you a hand with that." The gruff voice at her back startled her.

Nicole whipped around to face one of the two men she'd seen at the steakhouse the night before. Was this Patton or Fisher?

The man with sandy hair and piercing green eyes crowded closer to her and easily lifted the Dumpster lid as Nicole eased away from him. Something about this guy made her skin crawl.

"There you go." He picked up the bags of trash and tossed them into the container before turning back to her. "Need help with anything else?"

She edged toward the door. "No, thanks. I appreciate the assist."

He moved closer, and Nicole retreated until her back hit the wall. Oh, man. She should have side-stepped. Now, her escape route was cut off. "Back up."

The man gave a low laugh. "Or what?" His smile sent shivers up her spine. "Your man isn't here." He lifted his hand and trailed his fingers down her cheek to her neck. "You deserve better than Kincaid."

She pushed against his chest. He seemed as immovable as a boulder. If she engaged him in conversation long enough, Dawn or Linc would come looking for her. "You know Mason?"

"I don't want to talk about him." He leaned closer, breathed deep, and groaned. "Oh, baby. You smell good."

If you liked the scent of dog shampoo. "Move." She shoved harder.

"Don't be like that, sweet thing. I won't hurt you." Another slow, suggestive smile. "Unless you ask me to."

Nicole opened her mouth to scream for help. Before she uttered a sound, the man was gone, his body sprawled on the ground with Linc standing in front of her.

"The lady asked you to back off," Linc said. "Get lost, Fisher."

"I'm just trying to be neighborly."

"By pawing her?"

"I did her a favor."

"You test my patience. Unless you want my fist in your face, leave."

Fisher stood. "Threatening me isn't smart, Creed."

"I'm shaking in my shoes."

Fisher's gaze shifted to Nicole. "See you later."

Nicole sagged against the wall as the man sauntered out of the alley.

Linc turned. "Did he hurt you?"

"Thanks to you, no. Why is Fisher hanging out in the alley behind the salon?"

"I don't know, but you need to tell Mason about this. I guarantee Fisher will brag to Mason."

She shook her head. "I don't want to add to the pressure he's under."

"He'd rather hear the news from you than be blindsided by a man looking for reasons to goad Mason into reacting. Did Fisher say anything to you?"

"Aside from telling me I smelled good, no." She glanced away. "I really need a shower now. I feel dirty."

Linc wrapped his big hand around her upper arm and urged her toward the salon door. "Let's go. I understand we have another stop to make."

Right. Important things first. Food. "I'm craving Mexican, and I don't want to eat out."

"Sounds great. Everything secure?"

She nodded. "The trash was the last thing on the list."

"For the record, that's the last time you take trash to the Dumpster. You don't have any security cameras or lights back here."

Nicole frowned. "I have a business to run. I can't stop doing my job because someone scared me."

"Until Mason learns what's going on and the police arrest Riva's killer, have Ryan dispose of the trash."

Wise words from an experienced bodyguard. "All right. You sure you don't mind stopping at the grocery store, Linc?"

"Are you kidding? I benefit from the detour. I also ran two extra miles today as part of PT. Trust me, I'm more than ready for dinner, especially one that's homecooked."

She smiled. After locking the back door behind them, she strode through the salon to the reception area where Dawn waited. Nicole grabbed her purse from the drawer beside the computer. "I hear tacos, nachos, and burritos calling my name."

Linc moaned. "Please say dinner won't take long. The menu is causing my mouth to water already."

"An hour, tops."

"Thank goodness."

In the grocery store, Dawn pushed the cart along the aisles while Nicole selected the ingredients for the meal and Linc eyed everyone who neared them with suspicion.

Once they purchased the food and left the parking lot, Linc frequently checked the mirrors as he drove home.

"Is someone following us?" Dawn asked.

"I haven't seen anyone, but I won't take your safety for granted." He wrapped his hand around hers.

Nicole turned her face to the window to hide her smile, happy for them. The couple might not realize it, but their emotions were already involved.

When her thoughts turned back to the incident in the alley, her stomach knotted. Nicole dreaded the moment when she told Mason about Fisher. He'd looked ready to kill Ivan when he learned her former boyfriend had slapped her. Mason wouldn't be happy that his coworker had been at Pet Palace.

Why did Fisher get into her face? Even if she broke up with Mason, Nicole wouldn't look twice at Fisher. Something about him gave her the willies.

Linc parked in the driveway near the door. "Wait here." He exited the SUV and scanned the area. When he was satisfied, he unlocked the front door and returned to the vehicle for Dawn and Nicole. "Go inside. I'll bring in the food."

Dawn laid a hand on his arm. "We can help carry the bags."

"Not this time." Linc nudged her toward the house.

Nicole tugged her friend toward the door. "Come on. The sooner we clean up, the quicker we start dinner. Linc, store the cold stuff in the refrigerator while we change clothes."

"Yes, ma'am."

She and Dawn walked into the house and to their rooms. Minutes later, refreshed and dressed in clean clothes, Nicole returned to the kitchen to see Linc and Dawn breaking a lip lock at her entrance. "Oops. Sorry."

Dawn's face flushed. "What's first?"

"Dice the onions and brown the hamburger."

"Need me to help?" Linc asked.

Nicole shook her head. "We've got this."

"I'll be in the security room." Linc saluted them.

Dawn and Nicole worked fast to gather ingredients, and dice onions and garlic. "Open the cans, Dawn, and we'll start cooking. Mason should be here in a few minutes."

"Wow. He must have worked like a demon today. I overheard him talking to Linc about the inspections scheduled every day this week."

"He has something to tell me."

Dawn slid her a glance. "I hope it's good news. I've had enough bad news to last a lifetime."

Within fifteen minutes, their burritos baked in the oven. They set up the taco and nacho bar on the kitchen counter, then laid out plates, utensils, and glasses.

Linc walked into the kitchen. "Mason's here. You need to talk to him, Nic."

"I'm not hitting him with this as soon as he walks in the door." She lifted her chin, daring Linc to challenge her decision. Mason needed time to clean up and relax a little first.

"What did I miss?" Dawn looked from Linc to Nicole.

"Something happened in the alley behind the salon." Nicole nailed Linc with a glare. "I'll tell Mason. We don't keep secrets from each other, but I'm not starting his evening with this."

The man held up one hand. "Fair warning. If you don't tell him tonight, I will."

"I wish someone would tell me," Dawn muttered.

"I'll give you details later." Linc dropped a quick kiss to her pouting mouth. "I'd love iced tea to go with dinner. You and I can make that while Nicole lets Mason inside."

Guess that was clear enough. Nicole sighed. Maybe she should talk to Mason sooner rather than later. She went to the living room and unlocked the door. She smiled and brushed her lips over his. "Hi."

"Hello, sweetheart." Mason closed and locked the door. "How's my best girl?"

Her heart turned to mush. "I'd better be your only girl, Kincaid."

"No one holds a candle to you, Copeland. There's only you for me."

"Sweet talker."

"Nope. Just honest." He drew her in close for a longer, deeper kiss. A long time later he eased back. "Mmm. That's much better. How was your day?"

"Crazy busy. We took care of 30 dogs today along with a handful of cats, a new salon record."

"Wow. Did you have time for lunch?"

"We managed. Dawn and I took turns."

He breathed deep and turned toward the kitchen. "What smells so good?"

"Tacos, nachos, and burritos. Dinner will be ready in 30 minutes if you want to clean up first."

Mason cupped her cheek. "Something happened today."

How did he do that? "A couple of things. They'll wait while you unwind."

He studied her face, then kissed her with a gentleness that stole her breath. "I'll return soon."

Relieved that he agreed to wait, she retraced her steps to the kitchen.

Linc scowled. "You chickened out?"

"Delayed. I'll talk to him after dinner."

True to his word, Mason returned soon, and they sat around the table to eat. Halfway through dinner, Nicole said, "You haven't told us how your day went, Mason. How did the inspection come out?"

"Building 7 passed with flying colors. Dean and I worked on Building 6 today."

"Is scheduling so many inspections back-to-back normal?" Linc asked.

Mason shook his head. "Brian accelerated the pace for good reason. We landed a new development and, if everything goes according to plan, we start building soon. We need the Oakdale site complete before then."

"That's great," Nicole said. "Brian must be ecstatic."

"He is. No one else knows, though. He plans to announce the deal tomorrow evening at the company picnic."

She'd forgotten about the picnic. Nicole glanced at Dawn who already had her phone out. "Are you checking our schedule?"

"Yep." A moment later, she said, "Thank goodness. We have a slow day tomorrow. Only 15 dogs, four cats, and a rabbit. As long as we don't have a run on drop-in appointments, we should be finished by 4:00 tomorrow."

"That's perfect." Mason squeezed Nicole's hand. "The picnic starts at 5:00."

"Do we need to bring anything?"

"I'll take care of it. Brian promised to turn us loose tomorrow at 3:00." He looked at Linc and Dawn. "You're welcome to come."

"Sounds like fun." Linc glanced at Dawn. "You game?"

"Sure. We'll stop by the store for chips and a dessert. Thanks for asking us to come, Mason."

After dinner, Linc and Dawn volunteered to clean up. With Linc's pointed look at her, Nicole knew she couldn't delay talking to Mason any longer. "Want to sit outside for a few minutes?"

"More stargazing?"

"Just to talk."

He wrapped his fingers around hers and led her to the swing on the deck. With her tucked against his side, he asked in a quiet voice, "You ready to tell me what's troubling you?"

"Before I do, you said you had good news. Did you mean the new development?"

"The new development prompted Brian to ask me again about the home rehab position."

She straightened. "What did you tell him?"

"I agreed to take it as long as Dean was assigned to me permanently. Brian agreed. You're looking at the head of the home rehab division of Elliott Construction."

Nicole hugged Mason. "Congratulations! You worked hard and deserved that promotion."

"We'll see if the rest of the crew agrees with you. They'll find out tomorrow at the picnic when Brian announces the news about the development." He eased back from her. "Now, tell me what's going on, Nicole."

She first told him about Rod's visit to Pet Palace.

"Zane traced the emails to the Otter Creek library. Leah, Dean's wife, might be able to help us with that. I'll find out tomorrow if she was successful. What else happened?"

"You know me too well, Mason. One of your coworkers stopped by the salon today."

He stilled. "Who?"

"Ed Fisher."

That brought a frown. "What did he want?"

"I'm not sure." She summarized the incident in the alley, ending with, "He didn't hurt me, Mason."

"Because Linc stopped him."

"I'm fine. I don't want you to do anything to Fisher."

"I can't let this pass without addressing it."

"You won't have to do anything. Fisher will brag about his assistance. I don't understand why he was in the alley behind the salon."

Mason rubbed the back of his neck. "I'll owe Zane a boatload of favors before this is finished."

"Why?"

"He's our best resource to find out if security cameras are nearby at the right angle. Surveillance footage might show what he was up to."

"If we're lucky." Nicole sighed. "I guess I need to talk to Fortress about a security upgrade for the salon."

"Excellent idea."

"First thing Monday morning," she promised. "You'll let Fisher come to you?"

"I'll think about it."

"He's pushing you, hoping you come after him. I guarantee he'll press charges for assault if you give him what he wants. Don't let him goad you into reacting with anger. I don't want to marry you in a prison chapel."

He flashed her a quick grin. "Neither do I. I've already bought plane tickets to our honeymoon destination."

She moved close until her lips brushed his with every word she spoke. "So, where are you taking me for our honeymoon?"

Mason chuckled. "It's a surprise, one I think you'll love."

"I don't care where we go as long as I'm with you and we shut off our phones for a week. All I want is to have you to myself."

"A few more weeks, and you'll be my wife."

She could hardly wait. With trouble swirling around them, though, Nicole prayed they lived long enough to enjoy their honeymoon.

CHAPTER TWENTY-SEVEN

Mason stood outside Nicole's bedroom door, reluctant to leave her. He'd hidden his reaction to her news of the incident in the alley. In truth, he worried about her safety. Fisher had an attitude like a schoolyard bully, throwing his weight around to get what he wanted. Did he want Nicole or was he taunting her to get a rise out of Mason?

Why go after her in the first place? Another thought made Mason's blood run cold. Was Patton or Fisher the construction worker Riva was dating? No matter what the grapevine thought, Riva's secret man wasn't Mason.

"Mase?" Linc's low voice drew his attention. "Everything okay?"

With one last glance at the closed door, Mason retraced his steps down the hall. "Not really."

"Nicole talked to you?"

He nodded. "Thanks for protecting her in the alley."

"No thanks needed, buddy. I'm glad I was there."

"Did you know Rod Kelter came to the salon today?"

Linc's eyes narrowed. "Dawn told me. What did he want with Nicole?"

Mason summarized what she'd relayed to him. "I talked to Z today. He traced the emails sent to Gage and Ivan back to an account established by someone claiming to be Nicole. They were sent from the town library. I have a friend checking to see if security cameras are in place to watch the computers."

"If there are, we'll be able to narrow our search for the sender." He flicked his gaze toward Nicole's door. "Nic told me she was fine. Is she?"

"I'm not convinced." Mason walked into the security room. "Rod asked her if she set up the confrontation with Dannon so I would retaliate against him for his behavior two years ago."

Linc laughed. "She did fine on her own. Two years after the incident, Nicole isn't interested in revenge. The only thing your lady wants is to marry you."

Good to know Linc saw things the way Mason did. The trick would be to find enough proof to convince Rod of Nicole's innocence and his own. He hadn't forgotten that he was the prime suspect in Riva's murder. "What did Dawn think about Rod's visit?"

The smile on Linc's face faded. "One of the other PSI instructors saw her while she had coffee with Rod at Perk. He said Dawn looked upset."

"Was she?"

"She's outraged that Rod thinks Nic is setting things up in Otter Creek to get you out of her life or to pay back Dannon. No one who knows you two would consider that to be true."

"Seems like the standard operating procedure for Rod is to irritate the people he interviews."

"As long as he gets the right man behind bars, I don't care how irritating he is." Linc clapped Mason on the shoulder. "Get some rest, Mase. We won't solve this with the information we have at the moment. I have the first watch. Nate is taking the second shift since his wife is on duty overnight."

Mason returned to his room and sprawled on the bed fully dressed, a quilt draped over his body. If trouble developed overnight, he'd be ready to respond.

He woke briefly when Nate arrived for his shift, then settled back into sleep. When his alarm woke him at 4:00, Mason rolled out of bed and stumbled to the shower.

Walking into the kitchen minutes later, he was surprised to see Nate at the stove. "I thought you were on shift."

The EOD man glanced over his shoulder. "You look more rested than the last time I saw you. And, yes, I am on shift. Linc agreed to watch the security screens while I whipped up breakfast for everyone."

"Don't you have to cook for the trainees this morning?"

"Not on weekends. We have two trainees in this class with cooking experience. They cover the weekend meals to give me a break." He inclined his head toward the coffee pot. "Coffee's fresh. Help yourself."

"When is Stella's shift over?"

"Hopefully in four hours. If she catches a case, it might be later."

Mason poured coffee into a mug. "Thanks for the coffee and food, Nate."

"No problem. Any new developments?" The chef slid a plate with an omelet and home fries across the breakfast bar along with utensils.

While he ate, Mason updated the operative.

"Have Rio contact Fortress about the upgraded security system for Pet Palace. The boss will cut Nicole a good break because she's family or will be soon."

Nicole opened her bedroom door shortly before Mason left for work. She snuggled into his embrace with a sigh of contentment. "Good morning, handsome."

"Good morning, beautiful." He bent his head and indulged in a leisurely kiss. "Two months and one day," he murmured when he ended the kiss.

"Can't come soon enough for me." Nicole studied his face. "You look rested. No excitement overnight?"

He shook his head. "Linc will drive you to work. Alex and Josh will split guard duty at Pet Palace today. Let one of them take out the trash for you, okay?"

"I learned my lesson. Be careful today."

"Always. I love you, Nicole."

She crushed her lips to his in a hard, fast kiss. "I love you, too. I'll see you this afternoon."

Thankfully, Mason's day passed in a blur of activity. He and Dean tackled Brian's list for Building 4, redoing tasks they knew had been finished properly. After consulting with the boss, Mason made another trip to the hardware supplier for more locks.

Knowing they were under a time crunch, he and Dean skipped lunch to keep working. By the time 3:00 came, they had finished their list.

"Whew." Dean glanced at Mason. "I didn't think we'd make it."

"We almost didn't. Did you notice we're fixing the same problems we repaired in the other buildings?"

"Yep. I don't suppose Brian talked to Josh about having the PSI trainees provide security at night?"

"Not sure, but I'll ask him at the picnic. The sabotage has to be in-house."

"What's the point? We're still on schedule to finish the buildings by the deadline."

"The sabotage is the same as the sloppy work we pointed out to Brian."

"Patton and Fisher." Dean sounded disgusted. "I should have known. They're targeting our work now."

"Looks like it."

"They're looking for an excuse to cause you trouble, aren't they?"

"More than you know. Fisher showed up at Pet Palace last night."

Dean straightened. "What happened?"

"He cornered Nicole in the alley when she took out the trash. Although she says she's fine, Fisher upset her."

"What did he want?"

"Honestly, I think he wanted to tell me that he could get to her any time he pleased. Believe me, I got the message."

"Watch your back, Mase. Once Brian announces his choice for the head of the home rehab division, things will become more antagonistic around here."

He picked up the last of his tools and stored them in his tool box. "Let them come. I'll handle them." He'd survived more dangerous men than Patton and Fisher in prison. "Come on. Time to go."

"Leah planned to talk to the head librarian today. I might have information for you at the picnic."

"I can stand some good news. At the moment, I have nothing but questions." And a ton of fear for the safety of his bride-to-be.

After reporting the completion of their tasks to Brian, Mason left the Oakdale site and returned to his home to shower and grab more clothes. He'd owe Linc a big favor when this was over. Not only had the PSI instructor opened his home to three extra people, he also pulled more than his fair share of night watch to keep them safe.

He thought about the various things that needed to be repaired or remodeled around Linc's place. Perhaps he could repay the favor by volunteering his services when Linc was ready to make changes in the kitchen and bathrooms. His friend mentioned gutting the kitchen more than once. Mason had the skill and connections to make the job easier and cheaper.

After packing his bag with more clothes, Mason set off for the bakery to pick up the order he'd called in to Zoe during lunch.

Parking in front of the store, he walked into the bakery and smiled at the woman behind the counter. "Hi, Zoe."

"Good to see you, Mason. How are the wedding plans going?"

"According to Nicole, everything is on track and under control. Is my order ready?"

Zoe grabbed a box from the work counter. "I packed all Nicole's favorites. I also set aside several in a smaller box for you to take to Linc's. They're good for a light breakfast."

"I should pay you extra for helping me score major points with the lady."

She waved the offer aside. "No need. I'm happy to accommodate her. She brags about my fruit tarts all over town. Word-of-mouth advertising like that is priceless."

Mason paid for the croissants and fruit tarts, including a generous tip for the baker. A group of several women entered the bakery as he left. A couple of them shied away from him, their gazes shifting from his. Guess they believed he was guilty of murder. Mason mentally shrugged off their reaction and carried his baked goods to the truck.

Minutes later, he parked in Linc's driveway, then took the food and his bag into the house. Mason sat at the breakfast bar with a glass of iced tea. He'd downed half the contents when his cell phone rang.

He glanced at the screen and punched the speaker button. "What do you have for me, Z?"

"Information on the three men you wanted me to investigate. Your buddy, Gene Patton, has a spotted past going back to his teenage years. He's a real sweetheart, Mason. Petty theft, robbery, assault, attempted rape, just to name a few charges. He has a rap sheet as long as my arm."

His hand clenched around the phone. "Prison time?"

"Did seven years on the robbery charge. The rest of the charges were dropped. I don't understand why Brian would hire this one, but your boss has a soft spot for guys with prison records."

"I know. Brian's the reason I have a job." No one else around town had been inclined to offer him work.

"You were a good bet, Mase. Patton wasn't."

"What about Fisher?"

"He's also been a guest of the state. Assault and battery, DUI, embezzlement, grand theft. He's associated with a biker gang."

Mason frowned. "I don't know of a biker gang around Otter Creek."

"They're based in Cherry Hill where Fisher lives. He and Patton met in prison. They were cell mates."

He stilled. Time in confined quarters helped some cell mates form close friendships. "Anything else on them?"

"From everything I've been able to dig up, Fisher is the alpha of the pair. Patton goes along with whatever his buddy wants. Neither of them is shy about violence."

"Understood. What did you learn about Ivan Dannon?"

"He's a loser."

He snorted. "Tell me something I don't know."

"He's still broke and has had a steady stream of women since Nicole dumped him. No surprise, he's gotten in over his head with a loan shark and is hunting for a quick fix to his problem."

"Why is he blowing through money?"

"He likes to play the ponies."

"Since he's in trouble with a loan shark, I'm guessing he doesn't have a good system to pick winners. Police record?"

"Assaults and DUIs. No time served. He usually hooks up with a woman, ingratiates himself into her life, and romances her hard. As the relationship progresses, he hits her up for money to cover his bills because he's a little short this month. The next months, he gives a different reason for needing cash. You get the picture."

Yeah, he did. It was the same pattern he'd used on Nicole. At least she'd wised up fast enough to get rid of him before he emptied her bank accounts. "You said he has a history of violence?"

"Assaults similar to Nicole's. None of the women filed charges against him. Each one agreed to let it go if he left them alone from that point forward. He did, and that was the end of it."

"Any chance he was in Otter Creek sooner than he claims?"

"His bank accounts don't bear that out. He had several charges on his credit card in Destin, Florida around noon on the day your friend died. I checked the airlines and didn't see his name on the passenger lists."

"He could have presented false ID."

"It's possible. Do you want me to look for security footage of the airline passengers?"

Mason considered the offer and rejected it. Zane had already carved out more time than he could probably spare for the background investigation. "Let's hold off on that. I might have another angle to explore."

"If nothing pans out, contact me. I'll troll through security feed."

"Thanks for the help, Zane. If you need anything repaired or remodeled around your house, call me. I'll be glad to make a trip to Nashville to repay you for your time."

"I might take you up on that offer as long as you bring Nicole. If Rio and Darcy are available, bring them along."

"Deal." He ended the call as the front door opened and he heard the voice of the love of his life.

"Mason?"

"In the kitchen." He stood and hugged her. "Did you have a good day?"

"It was great. The dogs, cats, and rabbit behaved themselves."

Dawn walked in with Linc and headed for the bakery box. "What did you pick up? I don't want to purchase the same desserts." She lifted the lid and moaned. "Fruit tarts and croissants. Too bad dinner isn't for another two hours. I'm hungry already."

"The smaller box on the counter contains more fruit tarts. Those are for us to keep here."

"Yes! You don't have to tell me twice." Dawn opened the small box and picked out a fruit tart. "Anyone else want one?"

Nicole eased away from Mason. "I do. Mason? Linc?"

Both men declined the offer. Once the women left to shower and change into fresh clothes, Linc sat beside Mason at the breakfast bar. "Any news?"

He summarized his conversation with Zane.

"The three men are real princes." Linc eyed him. "You think one of them is responsible for Riva's death?"

"I'm beginning to wonder if Patton or Fisher is to blame. As much as I'd like to name Ivan as the guilty party, I can't see what he would gain from killing the real estate agent. Also, the town grapevine says that Riva was dating a construction worker in secret. That lets out Ivan, and it definitely wasn't me."

"That leaves Patton and Fisher. Your gut lead you to either man?"

"Maybe Fisher. Truthfully, I don't like or trust either of them. Both men will be at the cookout this evening. Perhaps they'll say or do something to clear things up." Turmoil swirled inside Mason, his gut knotting at the thought of Nicole near either man. He was running out of time to figure out who wanted to set him up for a hard fall.

His greatest fear was Nicole would be caught in the crossfire.

CHAPTER TWENTY-EIGHT

Nicole filled a small plate with desserts and glanced at Dawn. "Can you believe this spread?"

"I'll have to run extra miles to burn the calories." She slid a fruit tart onto her plate. "This place is packed."

Nicole scanned the large grassy area behind Elliott Construction's headquarters. Tables were set up along one edge of the yard, all loaded with food. Other tables were arranged for people to sit and eat while visiting with friends and coworkers, the air filled with the sound of conversation.

She filled a second plate for Mason while Dawn chose desserts for Linc. "Your relationship with Linc looks promising."

"I can't believe he's interested in me."

"He's a smart man."

"Get a move on, sweet cheeks," a low voice said from behind Dawn. "You're holding up the line."

Nicole stared at Gene Patton. "Walk to the other side of the table."

"I prefer the view on this side." His gaze skimmed over Dawn. "The most mouth-watering item isn't on the table."

Linc walked up and eased Dawn behind him. "Is there a problem here, Patton?"

The man smirked. "Just admiring the view."

"The view is better at another table."

"I'm just paying a sincere compliment." With a low laugh, Patton sauntered away.

Linc cupped the side of Dawn's neck. "I'm sorry. I should have stayed at your side."

"You were talking to a potential trainee. Public relations is part of your job. The man made a few suggestive comments, but he didn't hurt me."

"What did he say?"

"Nothing important." Dawn handed Linc one of the plates she held. "Since I wasn't sure what you liked, I chose a variety of desserts."

"I'll eat anything that doesn't eat me first."

Nicole wrinkled her nose. "Really?"

"Can't afford to be picky when your rations run out, and you're behind enemy lines."

"I guess not. Where's Mason?"

"Talking to Brian about Monday's work schedule and the security situation on site."

She froze. "Security situation?" Nicole didn't like the sound of that. "Have vandals targeted the Oakdale apartment complex?"

"You could say that."

Nicole and Dawn exchanged glances. "You know more than you're saying," Nicole said.

"Maybe. If you want to know more, wait until we're home to ask Mason." Linc steered Dawn and Nicole toward their table.

As Mason headed their direction, different members of the construction crew stopped him to talk, impeding his progress. Finally, he slid into the seat beside Nicole.

"Everything okay?" she asked.

He nodded, frowning when he noticed Linc watching Patton and Fisher. "Something I should know, Linc?"

"Patton made some remarks to Dawn while I spoke with Campbell."

"What did he say?"

"I'll tell you at home." Nicole wrapped her hand around his fist. "Don't let those men spoil a pleasant evening." The last thing she wanted was to allow the men to goad Mason into a public response. They were up to something, and she didn't want Mason to fall into their trap.

Brian moved to a microphone set up for him to address the crowd. Nicole tuned out the greetings to the employees and families, and scanned the crowd. All but Patton and Fisher paid attention to Brian's speech. They talked to each other in hushed tones.

Her attention returned to Brian when he said, "I have two announcements and thought our company cookout was the perfect time to give you good news. First, we signed a contract with Richland Development Group to build their new housing development. That means Elliott Construction will be busy for the next 18 months or more. There's a possibility that Richland will be buying more land in our area. If they do, Elliott Construction will be their first choice of builders."

He waited for the applause and whistles to die down. "My second announcement has been in the works for a while. As you know, Elliott Construction is the largest contracting firm in Otter Creek and Dunlap County. Because of our reputation for excellence in jobs of all sizes, we're the first choice for homeowners who need repairs or remodeling projects completed. That side of our business has exploded in the past two years."

Brian glanced around the crowd until he spotted Mason. "Mason, join me, please."

Whispers and low-voiced murmurs erupted as he walked to stand beside his boss.

"As you know, Mason Kincaid joined Elliott Construction two years ago and has been a huge asset to this firm. He and his team of workers are largely responsible for the explosion in home remodels and repairs. Because of the Richland development contract, I felt the time was right to create a new division in the company geared toward the home repairs and remodeling market. I'm pleased to announce that Mason will lead the home rehab division. Dean Connor will be his assistant. Join me in congratulating Mason and Dean on their promotion."

Brian held up a hand after a moment to still the applause. "If you want to work in the home rehab division, see Mason or Dean to throw your name in for consideration," he continued. "Exciting days are ahead for Elliott Construction. Thank you for your hard work and loyalty. There's plenty of food left. Help me out by eating more. If you don't, my wife will have me eating hamburgers and hot dogs for months."

Amid laughter, Brian moved from the microphone and clapped Mason on the shoulder.

"Looks like everyone is pleased about Mason's promotion," Dawn said.

"Not Patton and Fisher." Linc inclined his head their direction.

The men glowered at Mason and Brian for a moment, then rose and stalked around the side of the building. A ball of ice formed in Nicole's stomach. Those men were trouble.

Mason started toward their table, but workers and friends stopped him to shake his hand and share a word with him. Nicole smiled. At this rate, he might make it to their table in time to leave for home.

When Brian's wife, Emily, began to clean minutes later, Mason was still working his way through the crowd of well-wishers.

Nicole leaned close to Dawn. "I'm going to help Emily. No one seems to be helping her box up food."

"I'll help, too."

When they rose, Linc started to stand. Dawn shook her head. "We're going to help Emily put away food. You'll be able to see us from here."

He looked as though he'd argue with her when a coworker of Linc's sat next to him to talk. Linc nodded at his friend in greeting, then said to Dawn. "Stay close."

She smiled, then joined Nicole at Emily's side.

"Need help?" Nicole asked the other woman.

Emily hugged her. "I'd love the help. You must be proud of Mason and his accomplishments."

"I am. We owe Brian for giving him the chance to prove himself." She introduced Dawn to Brian's wife.

"Did I see you with that handsome PSI teacher?"

Dawn smiled. "His name is Linc Creed."

They worked fast to box leftover hamburgers, hot dogs, and buns.

"What's next?" Nicole asked.

"We store the food in the company refrigerator. If no one takes the food tonight, Brian and I will transport it to the fire station and the police station to share the bounty."

"That's a great idea." Dawn picked up a large container of hamburgers and followed Emily toward the building.

Nicole searched the crowd for Mason or Linc. Both men were in deep conversation with other people. The trip to the kitchen would only take a moment. She grabbed a large container of hot dogs and trailed after Emily and Dawn.

Once they stored the food in the refrigerator, she and Dawn retraced their steps to the food tables to pick up another load. When they filled their hands with food containers for the fourth trip, Dawn said, "This is the last of the meat and buns."

They carried the boxes to the kitchen and wrangled the containers into the full refrigerator. "Do you need help with anything else?" Nicole asked Emily.

Brian's wife turned from the sink, shaking her head. "I have a few more utensils to load into the dishwasher, then I'll be finished myself. You two go enjoy yourselves."

Nicole and Dawn headed back to the festivities. "I don't know about you, but I'm ready to go home," Dawn said. "These short nights and early mornings are about to get me."

"Same. I don't understand how Linc and Mason still function at peak efficiency."

"I don't know Mason's secret, but Linc's military training helps him handle the strain."

The lights went out in the hallway, and a hard hand clamped over Nicole's mouth.

CHAPTER TWENTY-NINE

Nicole fought against the strong hands restraining her but failed to break free. An elbow to the man's gut resulted in muttered curses and promises of retaliation.

She recognized the voice. Fisher. Fury overwhelmed the fear swamping her. What did this idiot think he was doing?

Fisher wrapped an arm around her waist and yanked her against his body. "Keep fighting, wildcat. I love it when women fight me," he whispered.

Dawn, a few feet ahead of Nicole, started to turn when Patton clamped a hand over her mouth and brandished a knife in front of her face. The blade glittered in the low illumination of an exit sign. She froze. "Very good, sweet cheeks," he murmured. "You're going to come with us, nice and quiet. If you don't, you and your mouthy friend are going to pay hard. Sure would be a shame to cut such beautiful skin. Understand?"

Her gaze sought Nicole's, eyes wide with fear.

This was crazy. Patton and Fisher couldn't possibly think they'd get away with this.

Patton jerked her head back and pressed the knife to her throat. "I asked you a question. You better answer unless you want the next few hours to be unpleasant. Do you understand what I'm telling you?"

Dawn gave a small nod.

"Let's go," Fisher said. "If you fight us, you'll regret it. Scream, and we'll gut Dawn first, then you." With that, he propelled Nicole toward the side exit away from the crowded yard.

Nicole's heart sank. No one was in sight. She'd hoped someone would be near, see the abduction, and go for help. Looked like she and Dawn were on their own for a while.

Mason would find her. Hurting Mason was the point of taking her in the first place. They didn't need Dawn. Maybe she could convince Fisher to let her friend go.

The men forced them toward the trees to the left of the property. Her breath caught in her lungs. Were they planning to kill them in the woods and leave their bodies for Mason and Linc to find?

No. Resolve hardened inside Nicole. She had a wedding in two months and one day. She was marrying Mason no matter what these thugs planned.

Nicole and Dawn stumbled in the darkness as the men dragged them deeper into the trees. "Where are you taking us?" Nicole asked.

Fisher shoved her back against a tree and slapped her. Her head whipped to the side as the crack of sound broke the silence in the woods. "Keep your mouth shut," he hissed.

Tears stung her eyes, but Nicole refused to let them fall and give this jerk the satisfaction of knowing he'd hurt her. Her cheek felt like it was on fire from the blow.

Satisfaction bloomed in his eyes when she remained silent. "Move," he ordered and jerked her into a fast walk at his side.

As they progressed through the woods, Nicole's cheek began to swell. She prayed Mason kept his head when he saw her. The group emerged from the woods onto a little used side road where a large black truck was parked in the shadow of the trees.

Nicole and Dawn exchanged glances. This wasn't good. While grateful they were still alive, if the men took them from the area, she and Dawn would be harder to locate. "Please, let Dawn go. I'm the one you want."

Fisher unlocked his truck with a remote and shoved her toward the cab. "Get in and keep your trap shut or I'll gag you. Don't get any bright ideas about trying to escape. Patton has a gun on him, too. He loves that gun. Give him an excuse, and he'll demonstrate his skill."

Without other options available, Nicole climbed into the backseat. Dawn followed her inside. Patton shoved her over, hopped in beside Dawn, and aimed his gun at Nicole. "If either of you moves, I'll shoot the other one. At this range, I can't miss."

Fisher cranked the powerful engine and sped away from the woods.

Although Nicole attempted to keep track of the turns, she was soon hopelessly lost. The roads didn't have signs and the countryside looked the same to her. Too bad she didn't have breadcrumbs to drop.

She still had her phone. Hopefully, Fisher would stash them in a room by themselves and she could call for help then.

"Get their phones," Fisher ordered his partner in crime.

Patton waved his gun. "You heard the man. Hand them over." An evil smile curved his lips. "Unless you want me to take them from you by force."

Since the idea of either of these men putting their hands on her made Nicole want to barf, she handed him her phone and nodded at Dawn to do the same. He gave them to Fisher who turned them off while he drove and tossed them on the floor.

When they emerged onto a highway, Nicole saw what she needed to orient herself. Fisher had taken them by the back roads to Highway 18. Soon, he took the Cherry Hill exit and raced toward a destination known only to him and Patton.

He drove through town and several miles into the countryside before turning onto a dirt road. Fisher pressed the accelerator to the floor.

When they emerged from the heavy tree cover into a clearing, she saw an old campground with multiple cabins scattered throughout the area.

As she glanced around, she noticed the motorcycles parked in front of the cabins and a main lodge. Fisher had driven them into the middle of a camp occupied by a motorcycle gang?

Fear for Mason's safety exploded inside her. He might be trained by the military's best, but he couldn't use weapons and he was outnumbered. Even Linc wouldn't be able to even the odds.

Fisher parked in front of the lodge and yanked open Nicole's door. "Out." He wrapped his fingers around her wrist and jerk her from the truck.

"What you got there, Fish?" A man with a gravelly voice sauntered from the lodge and gawked at Nicole.

"Bait."

Gravel chuckled. "Pretty bait. You pulled off the plan after all, huh?"

"Told you it would work."

He inclined his head toward Dawn who now stood beside Nicole. "And this one?"

"Got a score to settle with her man."

"What if he don't want her?" Gravel's gaze trailed over Dawn in evident appreciation. "I wouldn't mind a piece of that."

"She's mine," Patton snapped, voice a growl.
"Settle down." He held up his hand. "Didn't know you had a prior claim. If you get tired of her, though, I want first dibs."

Dawn flinched.

"Shut it, Patton." Fisher glared at his partner. He dragged Nicole toward the lodge entrance.

Nicole stumbled over the threshold and barely caught a glimpse of a comfortably furnished living room and reception area before Fisher forced her upstairs and down a hallway to a bedroom.

He shoved Nicole face down on the bed and zip tied her wrists together. "Scream all you want. No one will help you. These boys are family and friends."

Patton pushed Dawn into the room and used the plastic ties to bind her wrists behind her back. "You ain't going to escape. If you try, you'll tick me off. You won't like me when I'm angry."

"I don't like you now," she muttered.

He hit her with the back of his hand. "First lesson. Don't sass me. Next time, the response will be worse. Your man might coddle you. I won't."

Dawn scowled, her cheeks flushing.

Recognizing the signs of an impending explosion of temper, Nicole nudged Dawn's ankle with her foot and shook her head. They couldn't antagonize the cretins. She and Dawn had to remain injury free to run if they had the chance.

"A guard's at the door," Fisher warned. "Cooperate, and you'll see Kincaid one more time."

Patton stared at Dawn, his hand skimming down her cheek and her shoulder.

"Not now," his buddy snapped. "Later, G."

He flicked Fisher a glance, then refocused on his prey. "Get on the bed." When she didn't move, he narrowed his eyes.

"Dawn," Nicole murmured. At the moment, she and her friend were bruised, but healthy enough to run. If they challenged Patton and Fisher, she and Dawn would come out the losers in the skirmish.

Dawn glared at Patton but sat beside Nicole. Triumph filled his eyes before he turned and left the room.

"Why are you doing this, Fisher?" Nicole asked.

He paused in the doorway. "Kincaid stole my woman and interfered with my plans. No one gets away with that." He walked out, closing the door behind him.

Nicole turned to Dawn. "Are you all right?"

She nodded. "I bet Fisher killed Riva."

"And set up Mason to take the blame."

"He works with Mase every day. He has easy access to Mason's tools."

"He'd also have had ample opportunity to dose his drink with ketamine." Was Fisher responsible for the drive-by shooting, too?

She refocused on the problem at hand. Escape. "We have to escape." Nicole twisted her wrists, hissing when the bonds refused to give and dug into her skin. Sliding her wrists from the plastic loop was impossible. "My zip tie is too tight to slip free. You?"

Dawn wiggled and strained for a moment, then shook her head. "No good. I have something that will work, though."

"What?"

"A knife strapped to my calf."

Nicole stared. "Are you normally armed with a deadly weapon?"

"Linc was worried about my safety. Since I don't know self-defense or how to fire a gun, a knife was the best option. I need help retrieving it."

"Which leg?"

"Outside of the right calf." Dawn rolled until her back pressed against Nicole's. "The knife will slide easily from the sheath."

"I hope I don't cut you."

"If you do, I'll heal. Hurry, Nic. One of the men will check on us soon."

She tugged on Dawn's jeans-covered leg until the material cleared the sheath. Working by touch alone, Nicole wrapped her hand around the hilt and inched her way up the bed until the knife slid free. "Got it."

"Turn the knife around so the blade is pointing toward our heads, and I'll take it from there."

Nicole rolled onto her right side. Working by touch, she turned the knife, stopping each time the rumble of male voices neared the door.

A few more minutes, and they'd be free. Then came the hard part, escaping this room.

CHAPTER THIRTY

Mason finally freed himself from the knot of well-wishers offering congratulations on the new promotion. Under normal circumstances, he'd appreciate the sentiments from friends and coworkers. Now, however, he wanted to return to Nicole's side.

Every moment he spent away from her stoked his worry. Didn't make sense to be anxious since she and Dawn were in the middle of a crowded yard. Of all people, though, Mason understood things changed in the blink of an eye. He couldn't escape the feeling danger stalked his bride-to-be tonight.

After another coworker shook his hand and asked to be considered for the new crew, Mason eased around groups of people chatting and headed for his table.

Mason stopped when he noticed the table was empty and scanned the area. Although he didn't see Nicole and Dawn, Linc was conversing with one of the construction crew.

Linc looked up, saw Mason, and mouthed the word, "Kitchen."

The knot in his stomach eased. Nicole and Dawn must be helping Emily. He turned as another friend called his name.

"Congratulations, Mase. That promotion is well deserved." Henry slapped him on the back, his gray hair gleaming in the outside lights.

"Thanks. Would you be interested in working with the home rehab division?" Henry was the best Mason had ever seen with an electrical grid. Some of the old houses had tricky electrical problems. He and Dean had called on Henry more than once for his expertise in the field.

A slow grin from the older man. "If I'm working with the right crew."

"Throw in with me, and I'll make sure you're with a good team."

"Sounds like a plan. Thanks for taking on an old man like me." He shook Mason's hand. "Brian made a wise choice when he hired you, my friend." Easing closer, he dropped his voice, and said, "Some folks aren't as pleased with this change in leadership as I am, though. Watch your back, Mason."

"I'm not surprised. What have you heard?"

"I sat close enough to Patton and Fisher to hear their reaction when to Brian's announcement. They were hot under the collar, and that's stating it mildly."

"Did they say anything in particular or were they mouthing off?"

"I didn't hear specifics, but they used the word payback." Henry laid his hand on Mason's shoulder. "I recognized the tone, though. Those boys believe you wronged them, and they intend to cause trouble."

What was that about? As far as he knew, he'd never wronged either of them. "I appreciate the warning."

"Fisher has dangerous connections."

"I'll be careful."

With a nod, Henry moved off to speak to someone else.

Gut churning, Mason scanned the crowd for Nicole again and still didn't see her. Also absent were Fisher and Patton. Hopefully, those two left and took their lousy attitude elsewhere. He didn't want either man near Nicole.

He headed for the rear of the building, stopping several times to accept handshakes and congratulations. After exchanging a few words with each person, he continued across the yard until he entered the building. Once inside, he picked up his pace as he walked to the company kitchen.

He rounded a corner and pushed open the kitchen door. Scanning the interior, Mason frowned. Empty. Where were Nicole and Dawn? Had he missed them in the press of the crowd?

Retracing his steps, he emerged from the building and strode toward Linc. The PSI instructor took one look at his face and broke away from the man he was speaking with. "What's wrong?"

"Nicole and Dawn aren't in the kitchen. Have you seen them?"

Linc's jaw hardened as he searched the crowded yard. "The last time I saw them was ten minutes ago. I should have checked on them, but Simmons asked about the bodyguard training program. Take the right side of the yard. I'll take the left. If you see Emily Elliott, ask her if she's seen them."

As Mason searched, he grabbed his cell phone and called Nicole. His call was dumped into voicemail immediately. "Nicole, where are you? Call me, baby."

Growing more afraid for Nicole's safety as each minute passed, he moved faster through the crowd until he spotted Emily with a group of women. He reached her a moment later and gently separated her from the group.

"Congratulations, Mason. I'm so happy for you." Brian's wife hugged him. "Brian is a lucky man to have you working for him."

"Thanks. Have you seen Nicole?"

Emily released her hold on him and stepped back with a frown. "Not for a few minutes. She and Dawn left the building before I did, maybe ten minutes ago. Since the only thing I had left to do was load the dishwasher, I sent them back out here. A lot of people are milling around, Mason. Did you call her phone?"

"She's not answering."

"That's strange."

Linc hurried to Mason's side. "Anything?"

He shook his head. "When I called Nicole's cell, I got her voicemail."

A grim expression settled on the instructor's face. "Same response from Dawn. She wouldn't turn off her phone. I asked her to keep her phone with her at all times."

"I asked Nicole to do the same. Something's wrong."

"Is there anything I can do?" Emily asked Mason.

"Keep looking for Nicole and Dawn. If you spot them, have them call me."

"Sure. Let me know when you find them, all right?"

"Yes, ma'am." He and Linc moved away from the group of women. "Suggestions?" he asked Linc.

"Let's scout around the front of the building first. If we don't find them there, we call Fortress."

"What good will it do if their cell phones are off?"

"The tech will be able to tell us the last known area before the cells were turned off. It's not great, but it's a start. Right now, we don't know where to begin our search."

They had almost reached the side of the building when Dean caught up with them. "Got a minute?" he asked. "I have the camera feed from inside the library."

"Send it to my email."

His coworker frowned. "I thought you'd be excited about the footage. What's wrong?"

"We can't find Nicole and Dawn, and they aren't answering their phones."

Dean tapped his screen a few times, then said, "I sent you the footage. I'll help you look for the women."

When they rounded the corner to the front of the building, Mason's heart sank. "They're not here." Where was Nicole?

"Mase, you and Dean start at the center of the yard and go toward the left. I'll take the right. I'll call Fortress and have one of the techs pinpoint the last area their phones pinged a tower."

Mason and Dean moved until they were a few feet apart and began to walk, looking for anything out of the ordinary. They found nothing until they reached the edge of the tree line with sparse grass and plentiful patches of dirt.

He crouched in front of a large area of dirt littered with footprints. Mason glanced over his shoulder. "Linc."

The instructor jogged over. "What do you have?"

"The boot prints look like the ones at Riva's place. It's a common boot tread, though."

"The impression is fresh." Linc pointed at two sets of smaller shoe prints. "Those are the size of women's running shoes."

Shoes like Nicole and Dawn wore. "What did the Fortress tech say?"

"Like we thought, the phones have been turned off. However, the tech said the last known location was in this area."

Frustration gnawed at Mason. He had to find Nicole, but they didn't have a starting point.

"Fortress can't narrow the area down?" Dean asked.

"Not unless the phones are on. I don't see a security camera so that avenue is out."

Mason stood. "We need to call Ethan." He grabbed his cell phone and called the police chief.

"Blackhawk."

"It's Mason. Nicole and Dawn Metcalf are missing."

"Where are you?"

"Elliott Construction. We were attending a company cookout."

"Ten minutes." Ethan ended the call.

Mason slid his phone into his pocket and looked at Dean. "Find Brian. Tell him we'll have a police presence on the grounds soon."

With a nod, his friend hurried off.

"While we're waiting, send the library security footage to my email." Linc unlocked his vehicle. From a secured compartment, he pulled out a laptop.

After connecting to his hotspot, he downloaded the footage from his email. "What time were the emails sent?" When Mason told him the times, he fast-forwarded the footage until he reached the appropriate time for the first email. Linc froze the frame. "See anyone you recognize?"

Five people sat at the computers, three of them grandmothers. One was a teenage girl. The final person was a burly guy. Mason frowned. He didn't recognize him, but something about the man looked familiar. Maybe he'd seen him around town. "Save that screen shot to compare to the next one."

With a couple taps on the keyboard, Linc said, "Done. Let's see who was present when Gage received his email." He changed to the second security footage, fast-forwarded to the right time, and froze the frame.

Mason stared at the burly man who was once again at a library computer. Who was he? "Would Fortress run his face through their databases?"

Linc chose the best picture, attached it to an email, and sent it to Fortress. He grabbed his phone. "Yeah, it's Linc Creed. I need you to run the photo I sent through facial recognition." A pause. "As fast as you can. My principal is missing and the man in the photo may be connected to her disappearance." He ended the call a moment later.

Mason eyed him a moment, pondering his friend's choice of words. "Do you consider Dawn only a principal for you to protect?"

"If you're asking whether I'm emotionally invested in our relationship, the answer is a resounding yes. Although I'm crazy about her, I don't want my personal life batted about the Fortress grapevine. Referring to her as my principal protects her privacy and mine."

"She's a friend. I don't want to see her hurt."

"I don't play games, Mase. I'm with her because I want to be, not because she's a job."

Three police vehicles roared up the driveway and parked in front of Elliot Construction's headquarters. Ethan headed toward Mason and Linc. Rod hurried to catch up with his boss. Josh Cahill stayed by the third SUV.

"Talk to me," Ethan said to Mason.

He updated the policemen and showed them the shoe prints.

The police chief crouched and studied the prints. "They were moving fast. The men were in a hurry, the women stumbling here and here." He pointed as he spoke. "Work boots on the men, like the ones I've seen you wear."

"Nicole and Dawn are wearing running shoes."

Ethan stood. "Anything else I need to know before I start tracking?"

"Dean's wife, Leah, obtained security footage from the library computer area. Linc froze the frames at the time the emails were supposedly sent by Nicole. You need to see them."

"Show me."

Linc showed the side-by-side photos on his computer screen. The police chief and detective studied the screen.

"The gray-haired brigade isn't behind the emails," Rod said. "I know those women, and they each have dogs that are customers of Nicole's. I've heard them bragging about how Nicole and Dawn spoil their pets."

"The girl is doing research for a botany paper," Ethan said, pointing to the computer screen in front of the teen. "That leaves the man. Do you recognize him, Rod?"

The detective studied the screen a moment, then shook his head. "I feel like I should, though."

"You and Josh canvass the cookout attendees still here. I want a timeline and names of those who last saw the women, including the people who left before we arrived."

"Patton and Fisher left," Linc said. "Talk to Emily Elliott, Rod. Dawn and Nicole were helping her right before they disappeared."

"You sure you don't need me, Ethan?" Rod asked.

"If I run into our perps, Linc and Mason will give me a hand. Go." Ethan motioned for Mason and Linc to follow him. "Walk where I walk."

"Yes, sir." Mason fell in behind Ethan with Linc bringing up the rear.

Although he mentally urged the police chief to hurry, he didn't want Ethan to miss a clue. As far as Mason could tell, the trail was nonexistent.

Ethan stopped at one point and held up his fist. Mason and Linc froze as Ethan shifted to the left and bent to examine prints near a tree. Whatever he saw caused a thunderous expression.

"What is it?" Mason asked.

"From the prints, one of the men shoved a woman against this tree."

Linc growled.

Mason's blood sizzled, his hands clenching. He had a pretty good idea who the woman was. Nicole had probably tried to reason with the men or asked them to leave Dawn behind. If they hurt Nicole, the men would regret it.

Ethan stood. "She walked from here, propelled by the man. But she was mobile."

Although he appreciated Ethan's information, the news was small comfort. The knowledge that Nicole was hurt and Mason was unable to protect her made his gut clench. "Hurry, Ethan."

The police chief set off again. He didn't stop until they emerged from tree cover at the side of a dirt road. Ethan signaled for Mason and Linc to wait, and continued forward, gaze focused on the dirt. A few minutes later, he returned. "They're in a heavy-duty truck based on the tire tracks." He inclined his head toward the right. "They drove that direction."

"Where does this road lead?" Linc asked.

"This area is filled with back roads. They could have gone in any direction from here. I can follow the tracks to the next crossroads, but most of the crossroads are paved. I won't be able to tell which direction they drove once the truck hit asphalt."

"We have to find Nicole and Dawn." Mason shoved a shaking hand through his hair.

"We're doing everything we can at the moment." He looked at Linc. "Did you send the photos to Fortress?"

A nod.

"Let me know if they get a match. We should return to the others. Perhaps Rod and Josh came up with something while we've been following the trail."

They fell into step behind Ethan, maintaining their silence until Linc's cell phone rang. The operative glanced at the screen and answered the call on speaker. "It's Linc. You're on speaker with Ethan and Mason. What do you have for me?"

"Got an ID on the guy in the photo. He has a record a mile long and some interesting associates," came the response from Zane Murphy. "Name's Zeke Fisher. Ring a bell for you?"

Mason frowned. "Is he related to Ed Fisher, the construction worker I asked you to look into?"

Ethan's eyebrow rose at that question. Tough. Mason wouldn't apologize for working around the law, not when his bride's life was at stake. If Mason got into trouble for it, he'd gladly pay the fine.

"Zeke is Ed's cousin and a member of the Road Devils, the motorcycle gang we talked about. He also has computer skills."

"We need to talk to him, Zane," Ethan said. "Do you know where he or the MC went to ground?"

"Somewhere around Cherry Hill."

"Number of members?"

"At last count, 35. This MC is into weapons. If you take on these guys, activate your SWAT teams. Your cops will be outnumbered and outgunned from the start."

And Nicole and Dawn were in the middle of this dangerous gang. How would Mason and Linc free them against such odds?

"Thanks for the information." Linc ended the call and looked at Ethan. "What now?"

"I have some phone calls to make. You want in on this?"

"Try to keep me away."

"Figured as much." His gaze shifted to Mason. "I know you won't stay behind when we locate their encampment. I don't blame you, but you can't carry a gun. However, I'll permit you to have a knife. Self-defense only and last resort."

"With or without a weapon, you won't stop me from coming. My future wife could be in the hands of these men."

A nod. "Move out. We have work to do."

CHAPTER THIRTY-ONE

Nicole sat up and turned to check Dawn's progress with the zip tie. Some, but not enough. "You're getting there."

"This is hard work one handed. Freeing you will be faster."

"I'm going to look out the windows and see if we can escape that way."

"We're on the second floor."

"We can't make plans until we have the facts."

"I'd rather deal with heights than fight the men in this camp. Be careful, Nic. Don't let anyone see you looking out."

"Don't worry." The last thing she wanted was one of the men barging into the room to see Dawn with a knife.

She walked to the window at the side of the room and peered out. Nothing to aid an escape. The view revealed a sheer drop from the window to the ground with an occupied cabin ten feet from the lodge. If she and Dawn used this window, the men in the cabin would see or hear them hit the ground. That didn't count the possibility that she and Dawn might sprain an ankle or break a bone in the fall.

"Anything?" Dawn asked, voice soft.

"Not on this side. I'll try the bathroom window."

She crossed the room, freezing when a board squeaked. Her head whipped toward the bedroom door, praying the man on the other side of the door hadn't heard.

When no one appeared to investigate, she breathed easier and continued toward the bathroom. Nicole eased the curtain aside and looked out.

Her breath caught. A tree grew near the back of the lodge. Close enough to jump and catch hold of a limb?

"Nic, I hear one of the men who grabbed us," Dawn said, voice low.

Nicole hurried back to the bed and scooted across the surface. She'd just stretched out on her side and pressed her back against Dawn to hide the knife when the door opened and Patton came in, gaze locking on Dawn.

He smiled. "Miss me?"

"Like a bad rash."

The smile faded. He crouched in front of her and wrapped his meaty hand around the back of Dawn's neck. Patton drew her forward until her lips were a fraction of an inch from his.

"Leave her alone," Nicole snapped.

"Shut up."

"And if I don't?"

An ugly smile curved his mouth. "All I have to do is tell Fisher you backtalked me. He'll do the rest. You won't be sassing anyone after he's finished with you. No wonder you chose a wuss like Kincaid. You can run roughshod over him."

Patton's gaze shifted to Dawn. "Your boyfriend is no match for me." His gaze dropped to her mouth. "I want a taste."

Dawn jerked against his hold. Patton grinned at her ineffectual retreat and ground his mouth against hers.

"Leave her alone," Nicole shouted.

"What's going on up there?" Fisher yelled up the stairs. "Patton, get down here. We have work to do."

Patton broke away from Dawn, licked his lips, and strode from the room. The door slammed behind him.

"Are you okay?" Nicole asked.

"I will be after a shower and a strong antiseptic mouthwash. Move away so I can work more on the zip tie. I almost have it."

Nicole edged to the bottom of the bed and sat up again. She glanced at Dawn's hands and winced. "You're closer, but you cut yourself."

"Believe me, I know. What if Linc and Mase can't find us?"

"They will."

"Come on, Nic. Be realistic. No one noticed Patton and Fisher take us, and we drove back roads until we were close to Cherry Hill."

"We'll find a way to escape, with or without Mason and Linc."

"What good will that do? We're in the middle of nowhere without our cell phones. Aside from the small problem of an army of motorcycle riders who look as though they eat nails for breakfast, we don't know which direction to go for help. Add to that, it's dark outside."

"Wow. You're not pessimistic or anything, are you?"

"Realistic," she corrected. "The odds are stacked against us. I don't see how we can escape these men."

"We'll figure it out one step at a time."

"Better be fast steps," her friend muttered. "I don't think Fisher will be able to rein in Patton much longer." She drew in a shuddering breath. "Thanks for what you did."

"I didn't know what else to do except attract Fisher's attention."

"Your tactic worked." She glanced at Nicole. "What did you see outside the bathroom window?"

"A big, sturdy tree that looks close enough to jump to from the bathroom."

"Listen at the door in case Fisher or one of the others decides to pop in. They don't trust us."

"With good reason. I have a wedding in two months and one day. I'm not letting Fisher murder Mason." She left the bed and went to the door. Occasionally, she heard movement from the hall. The guard must be restless and bored.

Men's voices rumbled in the distance, growing louder, angry tones and sharp words that Nicole couldn't make out. She backed away from the door. "Hurry," she whispered. "Someone's coming."

At that moment, Dawn gasped and her wrists separated. "Got it. Now you."

Heavy footsteps moved closer.

Nicole shook her head. "Go into the bathroom, fast. Get out if you can and run. I'll stall them."

"I'm not leaving you."

"This might be our only chance to get help. They won't hurt me. Fisher wants me as bait for Mason. Take the knife in case you need it for protection."

"Nic..."

"We're running out of time. Go," she hissed.

With a determined expression, Dawn whispered, "I'll be back with help." She hurried into the bathroom and closed the door.

A second later, Nicole heard the soft scrubbing of wood, then silence. She prayed her friend escaped this nightmare. The way Patton had touched Dawn made Nicole fear for her safety.

Fisher would draw Mason to this campground, but her groom-to-be wouldn't come alone. At least, he'd have Linc and perhaps one of the teams stationed at PSI as backup. Since they weren't in Otter Creek, Ethan wouldn't have jurisdiction here. Knowing him, though, Ethan would find a way to be part of the action.

The doorknob rattled and turned. Fisher came into the room with Patton on his heels.

Nicole's stomach pitched and rolled, afraid she wouldn't be able to give her friend a large head start. Patton would go after Dawn. If she delayed them long enough, her friend could at least find a place to hide.

Patton scowled. "Where is my woman?"

"She's not yours."

Fisher strode to the bed, grabbed Nicole by the hair, and twisted hard. "Where's your friend?"

"The bathroom," she snapped through clenched teeth. "Where do you think she'd be? A guard's outside the door."

Patton pounded on the bathroom door. "Hurry up."

No response.

Nicole's heart slammed against her ribcage. Had Dawn escaped?

More pounding by Patton. "You got one minute. If you make me come after you, you'll regret it."

"Oh, come on," Nicole said. "It's hard to use the facilities when your hands are tied. Give her longer than a minute." She looked at Fisher. "When will you let us go?"

Mason's coworker laughed. "You know better than that. I'm going to take care of business, then you'll disappear along with your friend."

Her blood ran cold. He planned to kill them. "What business? What's your plan?"

"I'm going to kill your boyfriend and Linc Creed."

"I'm done waiting." Patton turned the knob and scowled. "She locked the door." He moved back a few steps and kicked the door. The wood held. Muttering curses under his breath, he reared back and slammed his foot against the door. This time, the door gave way and smacked against the bathroom wall with a loud thud.

Patton's face reddened in fury. "She's gone." He rounded on Nicole. "Where is she?"

"I don't know."

He reached for Nicole but Fisher stepped between them.

"Make sure our other guest has arrived, then go after Dawn. Drag her back here kicking and screaming if you have to, but I want you back before the fun starts."

Patton stalked from the room, cursing.

Fisher turned to Nicole and balled his fist.

CHAPTER THIRTY-TWO

Mason paced Ethan's office as he spoke on the phone with the Brighton County sheriff. Linc leaned one shoulder against the wall. His casual appearance didn't fool Mason. His friend's jaw was clenched, gaze fixed on the Ethan as he listened to every word the police chief uttered.

"Two women from Otter Creek have been kidnapped, and I have reason to believe men associated with the motorcycle gang in your county are holding them hostage."

Ethan's scowl deepened as he listened to the sheriff's response. Finally, he said, "We checked the residences of the men we suspect. They aren't at their homes or answering their cell phones. I also have a witness who saw them speeding out of town an hour ago with the missing women in their vehicle. If you're finished playing power games, I need everything you have on the Road Devils and their whereabouts." He was silent for a long time, listening. "You sure about the location?" Another pause. "All right. Here's what I need."

Minutes later, Mason rounded on the chief when the call ended. "Well?"

"He'll go along with the plan. He and his men will set up a perimeter. Tate will contact the Cherry Hill police chief. The last known location of the Devils is a campground. The area is remote and covers close to 200 acres. Even with the county and Cherry Hill law enforcement added to OCPD forces, the chance of someone slipping through the perimeter is too high."

"They're willing to work with you?" Linc asked.

"Once I explained the situation, Tate was willing to let me take the lead as long as he receives credit for the bust."

The PSI instructor's eyes glittered. "Dawn and Nicole's lives are on the line, and Tate is angling for headlines?"

"He might be a glory hound, but Tate will cooperate."

"With arm-twisting from you."

"I don't care who receives the credit, Linc. The only thing that matters is freeing the women and capturing their kidnappers."

"You and the other cops won't be able to handle the Devils alone." Mason dragged a hand through his hair.

"I'm aware." The police chief shifted his gaze to Josh Cahill who stood near the door, arms folded. "You in?"

"Yes, sir. Durango and Bravo are already on standby."

"We need intel on this camp."

"Fortress will provide what we need."

A nod, his gaze locked on his brother-in-law. "You're on leave as of this moment."

"Understood, sir."

"War room?"

"PSI conference room. One hour."

"I'll be there." Ethan looked at Mason. "Patton or Fisher will contact you soon. Agree to the demands, but you will not meet them until we're in place and ready."

"Yes, sir."

"They want you dead, Mason."

"I know."

"I'll be ticked off if they succeed."

Although he longed to race for the campground to rescue his bride, Mason's lips curved. "I won't be happy about that, either, sir. I have plans." Ones involving a certain beautiful blond with a heart she'd entrusted to him. He refused to let her down.

"As dangerous as this operation is likely to be, I can't let you go into that camp armed except for the knife."

"Fisher and Patton aren't stupid," Linc said. "They'll check him for weapons and confiscate whatever they find."

"Then it's better they find one I can explain to the authorities." Ethan squeezed Mason's shoulder. "We'll free Nicole and Dawn, but the price might be high."

Fisher and Patton had made the choice to kidnap two innocent women in a bid for revenge against Mason for an unknown offense. "As long as Nicole and Dawn are safe, I'll deal with the fallout."

Josh opened the door. "I'll meet you at PSI." With that, he left the office.

Linc straightened from the wall. "Time for us to go, Mase. Need anything else for the moment, Ethan?"

"I have a few things to do here. Don't start the planning session without me."

With a nod to acknowledge the order, Linc led the way from the police station. "You might not be able to carry weapons, but you should have protection. I have a couple of things in mind. We have what you need in the weapons vaults at PSI."

Mason paused in the act of fastening his seatbelt. "PSI has vaults?"

Although worry filled his eyes, Linc smiled. "Rio hasn't shown you our toys? You're in for a treat."

Despite his interest in seeing the vaults, Mason wanted to insist Linc find the campground and mount an assault to rescue the women. He longed to hold Nicole in his arms again. If anything happened to her, Mason's life was over. She was everything to him.

Linc drove up to the gate at PSI and swiped his card across the reader. The iron gates slowly swung open. He parked in the employee lot behind the main building. After passing through another two security measures, they entered the building.

"This way." Linc led Mason along a long, dimly-lit hallway to an alcove tucked into a dead-end corridor, then pressed a series of places on a blank wall.

To Mason's surprise, the wall slid away to reveal a large vault. After entering a security code, Linc opened the heavy steel door.

"Behold the toy box," Linc murmured. "Forget you saw this."

He walked inside and scanned the huge room lined with weapons and body armor as well as cabinets and drawers. "Wow. Do I want to know how many weapons are stored here?"

"No."

He wandered from one wall to the next. Frowning, he considered how many students filled the dorms and the weaponry routinely used by Fortress operatives on missions. The weapons in this room weren't enough to supply the needs of Durango and Bravo. "This isn't the only vault on campus, is it?"

Linc smiled.

"That's what I thought. With the Fortress teams in residence plus more than one hundred bodyguard trainees in each cohort, this weapons supply wouldn't be enough." He glanced at Linc. "How often do you go on missions?"

"When Maddox needs me. Most of the time, I'm needed here more than in the field."

"Dawn knows you could deploy?"

"She knows."

"She's okay with it?"

"Not your business, Mase."

He held up his hand. "Fair point, but I don't want to see her hurt. What equipment did you have in mind for me?"

Linc moved to the right side of the room and selected a vest. "Put this on over your shirt."

Surprised at the weight of the vest, he slipped it on over his chest. "It's heavier than I thought it would be."

"I don't notice it anymore." Linc helped him with the straps and tossed a black t-shirt and black camouflage pants to him. "Put those on. Your white shirt will stand out like a beacon."

Once he changed clothes, Linc glanced at Mason's running shoes and found a pair of black tactical boots in the right size. "Use these. You'll be at a disadvantage if Fisher and Patton are still wearing work boots."

After switching to the boots, Mason stood. "Anything else?"

Linc opened a drawer and pulled out a small device. "Put this in your ear. When it's time to activate the comm system, tap it and you'll be connected to the teams. You'll hear their orders and they'll hear every word you say. No sharing secrets, buddy, or everyone will know. Remember that when you rescue Nicole."

He slipped the small device into his ear and practiced turning it on and off. When he was sure he could operate the equipment, Mason glanced at the wall of knives. "I need two knives, one for Fisher and Patton to find and a second one to keep hidden."

Linc handed Mason a sheath to strap onto his calf as well as a knife with a five-inch blade. "This is the one you surrender." The instructor handed him a second knife with a four-inch blade. "A sheath is built into the inside ankle of the boots. Knives are close-quarters weapons. What's the first rule of combat with a knife?"

Mason's lips curved. "You're going to get cut."

"Be prepared. The second rule is that a gun trumps a knife every time. If your opponent has a gun, you'll have to disarm him. We taught how to do that, Mase. Trust your training." Linc gathered the weapons he needed from the vault and motioned for Mason to follow him.

Two minutes later, they entered a large conference room. With the exception of Nate, the members of Durango and Bravo were already studying a map of a campground.

Josh glanced up, noted Mason's attire, and gave a nod of approval.

Mason moved closer to the screen. "Is that the campground where the Road Devils are staying?"

Josh nodded. "According to Tate Abrams, the Devils have been there for several weeks. The owner of the campground rented the grounds to them for six months. As long as they don't damage the buildings, he won't evict them unless we prove Nicole and Dawn are being held captive there."

"Too late to do any good when we do," Linc growled.

Durango's leader inclined his head in agreement. "You still want in on this op?"

"Try to keep me out."

Quinn smirked at the PSI instructor. "Have something to tell us, Creed?"

"No."

Trent shook his head, his lips curving. "Don't torture our weapons master. He'll be an excellent addition to this op." He turned to Josh. "When is Ethan due?"

"Any minute. He's bringing a few officers with him."

Mason's gut knotted. He knew several of the officers on the force. Most of them weren't experienced enough to survive what was to come without serious injury.

Nate walked into the room followed by Ethan, his brothers-in-law Nick Santana and Rod Kelter, and Stella, Nate's wife. All of them were dressed similar to the

Fortress operatives, including body armor and several weapons each.

"Sit rep," Ethan said.

Josh updated him on what Fortress discovered about the campground. "The owner is more interested in the money than in kicking the Road Devils off his property. Zane found blueprints for the campground buildings and will monitor the grounds via satellite."

"Have any good news to share with the class?"

"PSI trainees will assist law enforcement in guarding the perimeter. They'll wear jackets clearly marked so the LEOs don't mistake them for gang members. They also have body armor. We selected trainees with previous law enforcement experience for this mission to minimize the risk."

"Excellent." Ethan studied the map. "Zane's sure this is accurate?"

"Yes, sir."

The police chief turned and faced the room's occupants. "Here's what we're going to do."

CHAPTER THIRTY-THREE

Mason rode shotgun in Linc's SUV, tension building with each passing mile. Was Nicole still alive? "I should have heard from Fisher by now."

"He'll call. The delay gives our side time to get into position. We want to capture every man involved in the kidnapping."

He glared at his friend. "How can you be so calm?"

Linc snorted. "I'm far from calm. Sticking with the plan will take every ounce of control I possess when what I want to do is kill each man in the campground for taking the women. You're not the only one who wants his hands on Patton and Fisher. The way I feel at the moment, they'll be lucky to make it into custody. In fact, I'd prefer they didn't."

At that moment, Mason's cell phone rang. He glanced at the screen, his heart rate soaring. "It's Fisher."

"Remember the plan. We need another hour."

Although everything in him rebelled at leaving Nicole in the hands of Patton and Fisher one more minute, he didn't want to be responsible for injuries to his teammates by going in too early.

Mason drew in a deep breath, swiped the pad of his thumb across the screen, and put the call on speaker. "Kincaid."

"Mason?"

His eyes widened at the sound of Nicole's voice. "Are you all right, baby?"

"I can't answer that."

Oh, man. Her answer told him two things. She was hurt and unable to talk freely.

A slap sounded over the speaker. Seconds later, she said, "There's an old campground outside Cherry Hill. Be here in 30 minutes or they'll hurt me."

Linc scowled and shook his head.

"Let me talk to Fisher or Patton."

"No talk, Kincaid," Fisher snapped. "You be here in 30 minutes."

"I can't. I'm on the far side of Dunlap County," he lied. "Driving to Cherry Hill will take me at least an hour, and I don't know where this campground is."

Silence, then, "One hour. If you're one minute late, your woman will pay. Bring Creed or his woman receives the same treatment. No cops or the women die."

"Don't, Mason," Nicole shouted. "It's a trap." Her outburst was followed by glass breaking and her ragged groan.

"Fisher!" Mason's grip tightened around the phone. "Don't hurt her."

The call ended.

Face white, Linc contacted Ethan. "Fisher called. Our deadline is in one hour. Based on what we heard, he's been working Nicole over, probably Dawn, too."

"Copy that. Stay with the plan. We'll get them out."

Linc ended the call without acknowledging the police chief's order. "We can't fail, Mase. If Fisher and Patton escape with Dawn and Nicole, we'll never see them again."

His gut churned. Taking unwilling hostages wouldn't be worth the trouble. Killing Nicole and Dawn, then running would be an easier option.

Mason willed Linc to go faster. The plan, however, couldn't be altered. Too many moving pieces must be in place for the plan to work. While Ethan wanted to free the women, he also wanted to scoop up the gang members complicit in the kidnapping. Like rats deserting a sinking ship, they would scatter as soon as they realized Mason and Linc brought reinforcements.

At the designated rendezvous point, Linc pulled off the road to wait for the rest of their team. Within minutes, Ethan and Nick pulled in behind Linc followed quickly by the members of Durango and Bravo.

They gathered at the front of Ethan's SUV and went over the plan once more, this time with an accelerated timeline. When he finished, Ethan said, "Questions?"

"Do we have confirmation of life?" Alex asked.

Mason's hands clenched. "As of 30 minutes ago, Nicole was alive but hurt. Fisher didn't give me the opportunity to talk to Dawn."

"She better be alive," Linc said. "If she isn't, Fisher and Patton will regret the day they were born."

Ethan eyed him. "If you can't keep it together, step back."

"No one will stop me, Ethan. Not even you."

"This is not a time for vigilante justice. I want them to pay as much as you do. Those women are under my protection as are the other citizens of Otter Creek. We're doing this my way so I don't have to slap handcuffs on the wrong perps. Unless you want her to visit you in prison, you'll follow my rules."

He turned to Mason. "This is your last chance to back out, Mason. Are you sure you want to do this?"

"They want me and Linc. We have to give them what they want to have a chance to free the women." A slim chance. Fisher and Patton wouldn't let the women go without a fight even though their main goal was to kill Mason and Linc.

"If the men open fire, you better hope they hit the vest," Trent said. "Plenty of unprotected places on your body are vulnerable."

"Understood."

He pointed at Mason. "No injuries, understand? I don't want Grace upset with me if anything happens to you."

"Same goes," Rio chimed in. "I don't want to call your dad and explain why you're in the hospital or the morgue."

"Time to move," Josh murmured. "Linc, you and Mase turn on the comm system as soon as we leave. Keep it on. We'll get eyes on the camp, and convey the setup."

"Yes, sir."

Except for Rio, the operatives melted into the shadows of the trees. He came to stand in front of Mason. "We have your back, Mase."

"Nicole and Dawn are your priority. I don't care what happens to me. Protect them."

Rio squeezed his shoulder. "We'll protect all of you. Be safe, cousin." He followed his teammates.

Ethan signaled Nick. Within seconds, the two policemen disappeared from sight.

"Now comes the hard part," Linc said. "We wait."

Five minutes before he and Linc left for the campground, Alex's voice sounded over the comm system. "Mason."

"I'm here."

"I have eyes on the camp and Nicole. Prepare yourself."

Mason's blood ran cold. "Tell me."

"Someone beat her."

He staggered back against the SUV, grief stricken. "How bad?"

"Enough. You can't let her appearance rattle you or you give the enemy more leverage to use against you. She's mobile and will heal."

"Stay with the plan, or you're dead and so is Nicole," Ethan whispered.

"Yes, sir." The plan didn't prevent him from beating Fisher to within an inch of his life when he got his hands on the jerk. Mason knew that Fisher caused Nicole's injuries.

"Dawn?" Linc asked, voice tight.

"Nothing so far. Still looking. Liam?"

Liam McCoy, Bravo's sniper, whispered, "No sighting."

The PSI instructor's eyes closed, his expression one a mix of anger and pain.

"Check in," Ethan ordered. One by one, the operatives acknowledged that they were in position as did Rod and Stella. "Mase, Linc, go."

"Copy that," Linc said.

The two men climbed into the vehicle. "Let's do this," Linc said.

"Dawn's smart and tough."

Linc drove toward the campground, jaw clenched. With two minutes to spare, he parked in front of the largest building in the compound.

"Slow and easy," Alex murmured.

Easy for him to say. His woman wasn't in the hands of abusers. Mason exited of the vehicle and rounded to the front of the hood where Linc joined him.

The front door of the lodge opened and Nicole stumbled out, arms restrained behind her back, head down. Fisher's hand gripped her upper arm as he propelled her across the porch and down the steps.

Several burly men moved from the shadows with their guns aimed at Linc and Mason.

"Twenty bogies," Linc murmured.

"Four or five in the lodge," Liam whispered.

"Five confirmed," Ethan said. "Two more in the cabin to the west of the lodge."

"Right on time," Fisher said. "Too bad. I hoped you'd be late, Kincaid." He jerked Nicole to a halt. "Want to see my handiwork?" He grinned. "Show him, Nicole."

She shook her head.

"Steady, Mase," Rio whispered in his ear. "He'll pay."

Fisher scowled, wrapped her hair around his free hand, and yanked her head up.

Fury ripped through Mason with the force of a tornado. Fisher's handiwork had left Nicole bruised and battered. One eye was swollen, the other bruised. The careful way she moved indicated she'd received body blows as well. He took an involuntary step toward Nicole, desperate to free her from Fisher's clutches.

Linc threw out his arm to block his forward progress, then shifted away from Mason to give them room to maneuver. "Where's Dawn?"

"Spending quality time with Patton."

"If he hurts Dawn, he's a dead man."

Nicole stared at Linc until the operative looked at her. She looked to her left, back at him, then to her left again.

Linc gave an almost imperceptible nod.

Nicole might be injured, but she wasn't broken. She still fought to give them information while acting the part of a defeated woman.

Fisher snorted. "Big talk for a man outnumbered and outgunned. You're no threat to him."

Mason dragged his gaze from Nicole to Fisher whose eyes glittered. "You wanted us here. We came. Let Nicole and Dawn go, and we'll do whatever you want."

"Toss your weapons on the ground." He pressed the barrel of a gun to Nicole's temple. "Two of my friends will frisk you when you're done. If they find weapons on you, Nicole will receive another beating with you as witnesses. You first, Creed."

"Move closer to Nicole, Mase," Josh murmured.

As Mason closed more of the gap between himself and Nicole, Linc shifted further to the left and removed weapons, laying them on the ground near his feet. By the time he finished, a nice pile had formed.

Fisher's buddies stared at the weapons stash, then exchanged glances with each other. One of them whistled.

"Now you, Kincaid."

Mason slowly reached for the knife at the back of his waist. He shifted closer to Nicole and laid the knife on the ground.

Fisher's eyes narrowed. "That's it? One lousy knife?"

"I have a prison record. I can't carry a gun."

He sneered. "See, Nicole? Look at how pathetic your boyfriend is. A real man would have stolen a gun or bought one off the street to protect you. Instead, he brought a pitiful knife to the party." Fisher leaned down and nipped her ear, making Nicole flinch. "You deserve a real man, sweet cheeks, not a loser like Kincaid."

"Hold, Mase," Trent ordered.

"After I take care of him," Fisher bragged, "I'll use his knife to carve my name across your stomach."

"What do you want, Fisher?" Mason inched closer. "Whatever it is, you can have it if you release Nicole and Dawn. They're innocents in your game."

"What do I want? You, dead. Creed, too."

One slow step at a time, he walked closer. "Why? What did we do to you?" A few more feet was all he needed.

"That's far enough," his opponent snapped, taking the muzzle of the gun from Nicole's head and pointing it at Mason.

He moved two steps closer and stopped. "Why do you want to kill Linc? He didn't do anything to you."

"He interfered with my plan. I had everything worked out until Creed stuck his nose in where it didn't belong."

"What plan?" Linc asked. "I protected the women. Protection is my job, Fisher."

"The women saw too much."

"When?" Mason asked.

"At Riva's."

And there it was. The hint that Fisher was responsible for Riva's death. "You killed her, didn't you?"

A sly smile curved his mouth. "Your wrench was the murder weapon. The cops think you killed Riva."

"Why would I? I had no reason to kill her."

The smile faded. "You were sleeping with her. No one takes what's mine."

Mason shook his head. "I love Nicole. I would never betray her with another woman."

"Don't lie to me, Kincaid. She mouthed off all over town about how wonderful you are, how considerate and gentle. She tried to end things with me to be with you."

"You killed Riva, and when Nicole and Dawn drove to the house to drop off Cosmo, you panicked and fled, hurting Nicole in the process. You were afraid they'd eventually recognize you."

Linc shook his head, his expression one of disgust. "They didn't know anything. You're an idiot, Fisher."

"Shut up." Fury flashed in his eyes. "Every word of disrespect from you will lead to more pain and suffering for your girlfriend."

"Let her go, and I'll submit to whatever punishment you want to dish out."

"What about you, Kincaid? You willing to suffer for your woman?"

He nodded.

"Would you take a bullet for her?"

"In a heartbeat. Let her go. You've already hurt her. The women are no threat to you."

"That's where you're wrong. They definitely know too much now. This has never been about the women, you know. The target was you from the start."

Mason froze. "Why?"

"You waltzed into town fresh from prison and immediately, Riva noticed you. Made plays for you, too, but you were too stupid to notice. Then, you got the promotion that should have been mine. Two years you worked for Elliott and because you kissed up to the boss, he gave you the promotion. I worked with him almost from the start of his business. But did he reward my loyalty? No. He was all about you."

"You went after Todd, too, didn't you?"

"Taking him out was pathetically easy. He thought I was you. If everything had gone the way I planned, I would have the promotion and Riva. I'd be Elliott's right-hand man, not you."

Mason dragged a hand down his face. "This whole thing has been an elaborate smokescreen, hasn't it? You killed Riva and attacked Todd, then tried to lay the blame on me to send me back to prison."

"Would have worked if the cops weren't so stupid. Doesn't matter now. It's too late for all of you." Fisher flicked a glance at one of the men holding a gun aimed at Mason. "Bring our other guest out here."

Linc remained motionless although his eyes followed the progress of the man into the lodge. A moment later, his face lost all expression.

Mason turned and stared at the hostage struggling to break free of his captive's grip. Gage Fitzgerald stumbled and fell to the ground at Mason's feet.

CHAPTER THIRTY-FOUR

Mason crouched beside Gage Fitzgerald. The man looked as though he'd gotten up close and personal with more than one pair of fists. His lip was split, one of his eyes fast turning black. He also sported a large bruise on the left side of his jaw. "Is Todd with you?" he murmured.

Gage shook his head. "He's probably back at the B & B. A couple of these bruisers jumped me in the parking lot and stuffed me in the back of a van. What's going on?"

"Get up," Fisher ordered him. "I'm going to offer you the chance of a lifetime."

Mason already knew where this was going. The only question was, would Gage take Fisher up on his offer? He assisted the other man to his feet.

"What are you up to?" Linc asked.

"Giving Fitzgerald the chance to avenge his wife and daughter's death."

Gage backed up a step. "I don't understand."

"Simple. I'm offering you the privilege of killing Kincaid."

"You're crazy. I'm not killing him or anyone else."

Fisher shrugged. "By the time I'm finished tonight, the cops will believe you shot and killed him. His good friend, Creed, will die trying to protect him."

Linc rolled his eyes. "The cops won't buy that drivel."

"Why not?"

"Even if Fitzgerald managed to kill Mason, I wouldn't miss my shot. I'm one of the weapons trainers at PSI. With my military background and constant practice with weapons, Blackhawk won't buy that story."

Fisher scowled. "Fine. If Fitzgerald won't do the job, I'm tempted to beat the daylights out of both of you. Dead is dead, whether from a bullet or my fists."

"Try it," Linc taunted. "You'll lose."

The construction worker slowly shook his head. "I don't think so. I prefer to shoot you and save my energy for more pleasurable pursuits with Nicole."

Nicole stared at Mason, determination gleaming in her eyes.

He gave a slight head shake. Mason didn't know what she had in mind, but it could interfere with Ethan's plan. Of course, Fitzgerald's presence was a wild card no one had counted on.

Mason's bride-to-be narrowed her eyes. A second later, she lowered her head. He drew in a slow breath, preparing himself for anything.

Fisher glanced at one of his friends. "Search them for weapons."

"Wait for my signal," Ethan whispered over the comm system.

A linebacker-size man lumbered over to Linc. "Hands locked behind your neck and legs spread, Cowboy. You move, you die a long, slow death."

The PSI instructor complied with Linebacker's order, his gaze locked on the man as he patted Linc down.

After a thorough search, the man stepped back. "Nothing, Fish."

"Now Kincaid."

Mason kept his attention on Nicole. From her body language, she was gearing up for something, but what?

Linebacker patted him down and turned to Fisher. "He's clean, too."

"Last chance, Fitzgerald. Otherwise, I'll take care of business myself."

"I'm not a murderer."

A lazy shrug. "You made your choice. You'll have to deal with the consequences."

"I'm not killing Kincaid."

"You can die with him and his buddy." Fisher raised his gun.

"Now," Ethan snapped.

At that moment, Nicole slammed the back of her head into Fisher's nose. He howled, cursing and releasing her to clutch his face. She ran toward Mason, but stumbled and fell to her knees.

As the closest person to Gage, Mason shoved him to the ground as gunfire peppered the night. He dove for Nicole and covered her body with his. He wrapped his arms around her head and prayed bullets that hit him didn't pass through his body into the woman he loved with his every breath.

A bullet slammed into his back, punching with the force of an actual blow. He jerked at the impact, then again when another bullet hit.

"Mason," Nicole cried. "No!"

"I'm okay, baby. Stay still."

"You've been hit."

"Trust me."

A roar of fury sounded near Mason. Seconds later, Fisher plowed into him, shoving him off Nicole. "I'm going to kill you. My cousin's dead because of you." Fisher landed an uppercut to Mason's jaw.

The next roundhouse punch, Mason blocked. He headbutted the construction worker again and flipped the man over his head. In a flash, Mason was on his feet in a low crouch, shifting away from Nicole to prevent further injury to her.

Fisher rushed him. Mason sidestepped enough to throw the other man off balance, followed through with a blow to the back of the neck. His opponent rolled to his feet, shook his head as though trying to clear it, and came after Mason again.

He took Mason to the ground, pounded a fist into his face, stunning him for the few seconds it took for Fisher to wrap his meaty hands around his throat and begin to squeeze.

Glee filled Fisher's eyes despite the chaos, shouts, and gunfire around them. "Die knowing that your woman is going to be warming my bed, Kincaid."

No way. Fisher would never touch Nicole again. He intended to marry the woman he adored and live a long life, filling their home with as many children as she wanted.

Mason fisted his hands, brought them between Fisher's arms, and hit his inner elbows to break the stiff-armed hold. He cupped Fisher's left elbow as though he was doing a chin up and forced Fisher to loosen his grip on Mason's neck. Wrapping his arm around the other man's neck, Mason hooked Fisher's cheek with a forefinger, and yanked the head around, forcing his opponent to roll onto his back. Mason slammed his fist into Fisher's face three times in quick succession and followed with an elbow to the temple.

Fisher's head whipped to the right. He lay motionless.

Durango, Bravo, and the Otter Creek police converged on the clearing. "Get down on the ground," Ethan ordered. "Now. I've got Fisher, Mase. Go to Nicole."

He scrambled off Fisher and raced to his girl. He grasped the hilt of the boot knife, slid the blade between her wrists, and sliced the zip tie. Nicole hissed as her wrists separated. Figuring she'd been trussed up like that since shortly after she'd been kidnapped, Mason massaged her shoulder joints to bring circulation into the area.

When her breathing eased, he wrapped his arms around her and drew her against his chest.

"How bad are you hit?" Nicole's hands roamed over his back and sides, pausing when they discovered the holes in the fabric. "Wait. Are you wearing a vest?"

"Linc insisted."

"Thank God. Take me home, Mason."

"After a trip to the hospital."

"I hate hospitals." She lifted her head from his chest. "If I have to be checked by a doctor, so do you."

"Deal." Whatever it took to persuade Nicole to let a doctor look her over. Mason worried she had internal injuries in addition to bruises.

Alex spoke over the comm system. "Linc, go. West side. Dawn's on the run with Patton on her heels."

The PSI instructor was up and sprinting for the trees before Alex had finished his sentence. In the woods, a woman screamed.

CHAPTER THIRTY-FIVE

Linc raced into the trees. "Direction?" he demanded of Alex.

"Six hundred yards ahead. Move it, Linc."

Another scream ripped through the night.

Linc put on another burst of speed, thankful the moon was bright and full.

"Movement to your left on an intercept course."

"Copy," he whispered, slowing his speed a fraction, using techniques he'd learned in Delta Force to mask his approach. The guy heading his direction wasn't a Fortress operative. He sounded like an elephant rampaging through the woods. No Special Forces operative would approach a quarry like that unless he had a death wish.

A branch snapped to his left. He shifted into deep shadow and waited. A minute later, one of the gang members hurried closer to Linc on his way toward the sounds of a struggle up ahead.

A loud crack sounded in the night, followed by Dawn's cry of pain.

Linc's target pivoted that direction and started forward to either assist Patton or watch. Either option was the wrong choice for the sake of his health.

Linc slipped out of cover and, with soundless steps, caught up with the thug. He wrapped an arm around the man's neck and squeezed. Although he struggled, the gang member was unconscious in seconds from the sleeper hold.

Lowering him to the ground, Linc took a few seconds to bind his hands. He didn't want this guy to blindside him while Linc tangled with Patton.

"No," Dawn screamed. "Stop."

Another loud crack. "You heard those gunshots. That's my buddies drilling holes in your boyfriend. He's dead. No one's going to save you now."

Linc ran in the direction of the voices. "Sit rep," he whispered to Alex.

"Only Patton and Dawn. You're clear."

"Copy." One hundred yards later, he crested a ridge.

Patton straddled Dawn whose shirt was ripped in half. Her captor fumbled with the zipper of her jeans. Dawn reached for a nearby rock, but couldn't stretch far enough to grip it.

Linc sprinted across the clearing and launched himself at Patton, forcing him off her. The construction worker cursed and threw punch after punch while they rolled on the ground, each determined to gain the upper hand. Linc blocked and countered with his own roundhouse punches.

Patton shoved him aside and scrambled to his feet. He circled just out of reach, motioning for Linc to come and get him.

Linc waited, his attention focused on the other man despite a driving need to check on Dawn. Patton wasn't patient and would soon make his move.

The construction worker swung a roundhouse punch at Linc who shifted enough to throw Patton off balance and leave his side open to attack. Linc kicked him in the ribs.

More curses poured from Patton's mouth. He threw another punch. Linc blocked and landed another strike, this time to the temple. Dawn's attacker dropped to the ground and lay still.

Not willing to chance the other man regaining his senses and threatening them, Linc restrained Patton's hands behind his back. He stripped a knife and Sig from him and tossed them under a bush before he turned to Dawn. She'd scrambled away from the fight and located a sturdy stick that she held in her hands like a baseball bat.

His breath caught. Though bruised and battered, she personified a courage that wouldn't quit. Linc had never admired anyone more than Dawn Metcalf, and acknowledged to himself that he was falling in love with her.

He slowly approached her, unsure of his welcome after her rough treatment at Patton's hands. "It's over, Dawn. You're safe now."

She blinked. Tears streamed down her cheeks, breaking his heart. Dawn dropped the stick and threw herself into his arms.

Linc held her while she cried. "I've got you, sweetheart," he murmured. "No one will hurt you again."

When her tears subsided, she whispered, "I couldn't stop him."

He stilled, praying she didn't mean those words the way they sounded. Patton and Fisher had held her and Nicole hostage for hours. Had they raped the women? "I know Patton beat you. For the sake of your health, tell me the truth, Dawn. Did Patton or Fisher rape you?"

She shook her head. "Patton kissed me, but Nicole prevented him from going any further. I don't think he would have stopped if she hadn't. Although He said he just wanted a taste, Patton got caught up." She shuddered and buried her face against Linc's neck. "He would have raped me with Nicole in the room."

Linc closed his eyes, thankful that she'd been spared and for Nicole's quick thinking. He owed her, big.

"Is she okay? I didn't want to leave her, but Patton and Fisher were coming, and I didn't have time to cut her loose. If I'd tried, they would have caught me and confiscated the knife you gave me. Nicole told me to run." More tears slipped down her cheeks. "I had to hide from gang members roaming the woods at first. When Patton found me, I ran. Please tell me Nic's okay."

He cupped her bruised face. "She will be."

Dawn gripped his biceps. "What did Fisher do to her?"

"He beat her." Whether Fisher did more than that was a question Mason would have to broach with his girl. "I don't know how bad her injuries are. When I came after you, Mason was holding her in his arms. She was awake and alert."

"I should have stayed with her. Fisher hurt her because I ran away, didn't he?"

"Those men were a good 80 pounds heavier than either of you and more than half a foot taller. By splitting up, you forced them to separate. Together, Patton and Fisher encouraged each other to greater atrocities. Your actions kept Patton busy hunting for you instead of allowing their agenda to unfold as planned." He trailed the back of his hand over her cheek, careful to avoid a bruise caused by Patton's blows. "You did the right thing, Dawn. The plan was a solid one."

"But I failed."

"You frustrated both men and threw a monkey wrench into their plan." He lifted one of her hands to his mouth and pressed a soft kiss to her knuckles. "I'm proud of you. Even though Patton had you on the ground, you were still fighting."

"I want self-defense training. I never want to be that helpless again. My father taught me some things, but I need more if…"

"If what?" he prompted.

"If I'm dating you."

"You definitely are." If their relationship continued to progress at the current pace, she'd be wearing an engagement ring in the near future. "I'll be glad to train you to defend yourself."

Although he didn't want to let her go, they had to return to the compound. "Come on. Let's get out of here." Linc stripped off the black shirt covering his vest and helped her into it.

"What about Patton?"

"He's not going anywhere." He nodded toward Rod and Stella who approached Patton. "Time to take you to the hospital."

"I'm fine."

"For my peace of mind, I want a doctor to confirm that." She might as well get used to it. Her health and safety would be his priority from now on.

Linc lifted Dawn into his arms and carried her away from the clearing.

CHAPTER THIRTY-SIX

Pain dragged Nicole from a fitful sleep. She blinked, staring at the bland walls with a television mounted in the corner. Where was she? The antiseptic smell brought back the memory of Dr. Anderson insisting she stay overnight in the hospital.

She had to admit that Fisher had done a number on her. At least, he hadn't raped her.

Her experience with Patton and Fisher had solidified her desire to pursue self-defense training. Never again would she be that vulnerable. First on the agenda was learning how to free herself from zip ties.

Nicole became aware of warmth pressed against her side. She turned and her heart melted. Mason. He hadn't left her side, even insisting on riding in the ambulance with her.

His eyes opened. A slow smile curved his mouth. "Hello, beautiful."

"Hello, handsome."

"How do you feel?"

"Like I've gone ten rounds with the heavy-weight champion."

"You did, and you won."

That made her smile. "How are the ribs?"

"With you in my arms, I don't feel a thing."

"Without me in your arms?"

"The ribs are sore enough that I can't breathe deep. Work Monday will be an exercise in torture."

"Tell me about it." She smiled. "I guess we aren't going to make it to church today."

"I'm afraid not. Next week." He kissed her, the touch light and easy. "Two months until our wedding."

"If not for the sake of the wedding pictures, I'd beg you to marry me today. Life is too short to waste. I want to spend every minute with you."

"I'd take you up on the offer except Durango deployed two hours ago, and Rio would kill me if I married you without him at my side. Besides, I need to set up the home rehab division and make sure everything is running smooth before our honeymoon. I don't want anything to take my attention away from you while we're gone."

"I like the sound of that."

A knock on the door brought Mason to his feet, his body between her and the visitor. When the door opened, Ethan walked inside.

"How are you, Nicole?" he asked.

"Sore and happy to be getting married in two months."

He chuckled, dropping into a chair at the foot of her bed. "What did the doc say about you?"

"Two cracked ribs from Fisher kicking me. The other injuries are bruises that will heal soon."

The police chief shifted his attention to Mason. "You good?"

"Yes, sir. Deep bruises where bullets smacked into the vest. A few minor ones from the skirmish with Fisher."

"You did well out there, Mason. Training with the teams at PSI paid off."

Mason settled beside Nicole and tucked her against his side. "Thanks."

"Patton and Fisher confessed to everything. As you know, Riva was interested in you, and Fisher killed her for it. He did his best to frame you for her murder and Todd's injuries."

"What about the drive-by shooting?" Nicole asked.

"The intent was to kill Mason. If that failed, they hoped the shooting would pass as a random event, and the frame job would send Mason back to prison. Fisher was also responsible for poisoning you with ketamine."

Mason frowned. "If the goal was to get rid of me, why did Fisher accost Nicole in the alley behind Pet Palace?"

"He wanted to push you into attacking him. His planned to press charges or kill you and claim self-defense."

"How did they hook up with the motorcycle gang?" Nicole leaned her head against Mason's shoulder.

"Fisher's cousin was in the gang as had been his father and uncles before them. Fisher and Patton rode with them some, but they weren't interested in full-time membership. In the Devils, they'd have been low down on the chain of command. Neither of them wanted that. Fisher's cousin was the group's leader which is why Fisher and Patton recruited the Devils to kidnap Gage Fitzgerald and stash the three hostages on the campground."

"What would the Devils get out of it?"

"Relatively safe places to do weapons deals. Fisher believed he'd get the promotion at Elliott Construction with Mason out of the way. With multiple job sites around the county and supplies being delivered all the time to those sites, no one would have noticed an extra vehicle or box. Safe places to complete weapons deals was the price of aid from the Devils."

Ethan stood. "I'm going home to sleep for a few hours, but wanted you to know you won't have to worry about

Patton or Fisher again until their gray-haired old men. You'll have to testify against them in court unless I convince them to save the taxpayers some money. Those men are out of your life for good. Also, Ivan left town an hour ago. He says he won't be back."

"Thanks, Ethan." Mason got to his feet and shook the police chief's hand.

"Both of you get some rest. I'll see you Friday, Mason." Ethan left.

An hour later, another knock sounded on the door. Nicole's eyes widened when Todd and Gage Fitzgerald entered the room.

Mason stood, wariness in his gaze. "Todd, Gage."

"We wanted to check on Nicole before we left town," Gage said.

Stunned, she stared at the two men. "Aside from bruises and cracked ribs, I'm fine."

"I'm glad." He shifted his attention to Mason. "Thank you, Mason. I'm embarrassed to admit that I froze when the gunfire erupted in that compound. If you hadn't shoved me to the ground, I might be in the morgue instead of on the way home to hug my family."

"You were a pawn in a bid for revenge."

"You could have left me to fend for myself. You risked your life to save mine. I won't forget that." He studied Mason a moment, then said, "You aren't the man I believed you to be for the past 15 years."

"I haven't been that same stupid kid since the moment I walked into prison," Mason said.

A slow nod. "I can see that. I'll tell my family what happened last night, the risk you took for me."

"That's not necessary."

"It is if I'm to have any hope of convincing them to drop their vendetta against you. We'll never be friends. The loss my family suffered is too deep. However, I'll do my best to smooth the way for you to visit your father without fear for your safety or that of your family."

"Thank you."

Todd held out his hand which Mason accepted. "Truce. No more pictures." After nodding goodbye to Nicole, the two men left.

When Mason sat beside her again, Nicole kissed him, her touch gentle. "You can go home now."

He shook his head. "Not home. You're home to me. I'll never be comfortable in Liberty, but it's good to know I'll be able to help my father move without fear of reprisals."

The door opened an hour later, and Grace walked in with Trent who carried a small duffel bag with a change for clothes for her and Mason. She hugged Nicole, her embrace gentle. "You look colorful, Nic."

Nicole wrinkled her nose. "Thanks a lot. Where's Dr. Anderson?"

"He just started his rounds on this floor. He should be here in a few minutes." Grace laid her hand on Mason's shoulder and kissed his cheek. "Thank you, Mason."

"For what?"

"Protecting my sister. You put your life on the line for her. I won't forget that."

"Good job, Mase." Trent clapped him on the shoulder. "I think you would make a great operative."

"No." Nicole glared at her brother-in-law. "You can't have him."

He flashed her a grin. "Figured you'd say that. No worries, Nic. I've already had the same conversation with Grace."

"I'm happy in construction," Mason said. "Besides, I want to be here in case Grace needs something when you're deployed."

A slow smile curved Trent's mouth. "She's going to need a lot of help in a few months." Happiness gleamed in his gaze.

Nicole gasped. She gripped Grace's hand. "Grace? Does that mean what I think it means?"

Her sister beamed as she nodded. "I planned to tell you at dinner tomorrow night. Our baby is due in seven months."

"Congratulations!" Nicole hugged Grace. "I get first dibs on babysitting. Trent's teammates can get in line behind me."

Mason shook Trent's hand and kissed Grace's cheek. "I'm happy for both of you. You'll be great parents."

Dr. Anderson tapped on the door and stepped inside. He smiled. "Well, looks like we're having a celebration."

"We will be as soon as you sign my release papers," Nicole said. "I have a wedding to prepare for." And a baby shower for her sister to plan.

"Let's take a look and send you on your way, my dear. Everyone except the guest of honor needs to wait in the hall, please."

Mason leaned down and kissed Nicole. "I'll be right outside the door."

As soon as the room cleared out, Nicole leveled a stare at Otter Creek's favorite doctor. "I want out of here, Doc. I have plans with that handsome man out in the hall."

"Unless you developed an unforeseen problem overnight, you'll be free to leave in time to buy breakfast at Delaney's."

"With my face like this? I don't think so."

Anderson laid his hand on her shoulder. "Those bruises are a testament to your courage and strength, Nicole. You survived a harrowing experience and walked away with a few injuries. The shame belongs to Ed Fisher and Gene Patton. The only person whose opinion of your appearance really matters is Mason. Based on what I saw when I walked in, that young man sees the woman he loves, not the bruises."

She blinked against the sting of tears. "Thanks, Doc." Her voice came out husky.

After another shoulder pat, the doctor checked her injuries and vitals, and declared her fit enough to leave the hospital. "I'll send Grace in to help you dress. A nurse will bring your discharge papers soon. I'd like to see you in the office in a week. Otherwise, call if you need me."

In less than an hour, Nicole met Dawn and Linc in the lobby. Dawn flinched when she saw Nicole's face. "Oh, Nic."

Yeah, guess she looked pretty bad.

Linc frowned, then flicked a glance at Mason. "We should have drawn out the fight with Patton and Fisher a few more minutes for more payback."

"Let's get out of here," Mason said. "I'm hungry."

"Delaney's or my house?"

"Delaney's," Nicole said. "The whole town will be talking about us anyway. Might as well give the grapevine something to talk about."

"If the attention is too much or you become tired, we'll leave." Mason threaded his fingers through hers.

She settled into the backseat of Linc's SUV, her head pillowed on Mason's shoulder. Minutes later, they sat in a booth at Delaney's. Soon, diner patrons began stopping by the table to express their shock and outrage at their injuries, and wish her and Dawn a speedy recovery.

By the end of the meal, Nicole figured the grapevine had enough fodder for the next week. What gave her the most satisfaction was the admiration and respect shown to Mason and Linc.

They returned to Linc's home to pack their bags. When Mason tucked her into the passenger seat of his truck, Nicole noted that Linc had wrapped his arms around Dawn.

She smiled, hoping they were able to form the kind of relationship that she and Mason were building.

Throughout the drive to his home, Mason retained his hold on her hand as though afraid to let go of her. She understood. It would be a long time before she was ready to be away from him. She'd almost lost him. As soon as they were inside his home with the door closed, Nicole wrapped her arms around Mason's waist, her hold tight.

"I was terrified I'd be too late," he whispered. "That I wouldn't find you in time. I've never been more afraid in my life than when I realized you were missing."

"I knew you would come. I was afraid that Fisher would kill you, and I'd have to live the rest of my life alone."

"You're the strongest woman I've ever known. If the worst had happened, you would have been all right."

She shook her head. "My heart would have broken into a million pieces. I love you, Mason. Now and forever."

"I am the most blessed man on the planet. You couldn't give me a greater gift than your heart. Eternity won't be long enough to show you how much I love you, Nicole."

Nicole kissed Mason with the consuming passion welling up inside her. Although bruised and battered, she and Mason had prevailed against men with hearts of evil. Now that Mason wasn't under suspicion, they had a bright future ahead, one full of love, laughter, and family.

ABOUT THE AUTHOR

Rebecca Deel is a preacher's kid with a black belt in karate. She teaches business classes at a private four-year college outside Nashville, Tennessee. She plays the piano at church, writes freelance articles, and runs interference for the family dogs. She's been married to her amazing husband for more than 25 years and is the proud mom of two grown sons. She delivers occasional devotions to the women's group at her church and conducts seminars on personal safety, money management, and writing. Her articles have been published in *ONE Magazine*, *Contact*, and *Co-Laborer*, and she was profiled in the June 2010 Williamson edition of *Nashville Christian Family* magazine. Rebecca completed her Doctor of Arts degree in Economics and wears her favorite Dallas Cowboys sweatshirt when life turns ugly.

For more information on Rebecca...

Signup for Rebecca's newsletter: http://eepurl.com/_B6w9

Visit Rebecca's website: www.rebeccadeelbooks.com

Printed in Great Britain
by Amazon